Thirty Four Minutes DEAD

a macabre journey into the mind

*****

By Steve Hammond Kaye

GW00391694

STANDARDCUTMEDIA

Copyright Notice

Published in 2012 in the UK by:

STANDARDCUTMEDIA
International House
39 Great Windmill Street
LONDON
W1D 7LX
www.standardcut.co.uk
publishing@standardcut.co.uk

A catalogue record of this book is available from the British Library.

ISBN 13: 978-0-9574795-0-0
ISBN 10: 0957479506

TABLE OF CONTENTS

PROLOGUE   1
CHAPTER ONE   9
CHAPTER TWO   20
CHAPTER THREE   31
CHAPTER FOUR   42
CHAPTER FIVE   52
CHAPTER SIX   76
CHAPTER SEVEN   96
CHAPTER EIGHT   104
CHAPTER NINE   119
CHAPTER TEN   132
CHAPTER ELEVEN   167
CHAPTER TWELVE   179
CHAPTER THIRTEEN   202
CHAPTER FOURTEEN   216
CHAPTER FIFTEEN   237
CHAPTER SIXTEEN   251
CHAPTER SEVENTEEN   266
CHAPTER EIGHTEEN   276
CHAPTER NINETEEN   283
EPILOGUE   285
ABOUT THE AUTHOR   286
ACKNOWLEDGEMENTS   288
THE SCREAM OF FEYER   289
(SEQUEL)

PROLOGUE

Julia Venison, one name, one number, but she felt immortal on this particular summer evening. A magenta shred refused to die in the fading sky and the retreating light cast a final glint amongst her careless golden hair. Life was being kind to Julia, giving her a new superior Account Planning job and a rural home she had only ever dreamed of before.

Tonight her quest was The Burleigh, a clichéd country public house on the outskirts of Godalming, in Surrey that had not changed a great deal in the last three centuries. Here Julia found her own private niche, a place where she could savour the rural atmosphere and withdraw into the privacy of her own imagination. The Burleigh had a clientele who didn't ask why a woman should sit alone on a bar stool, a Landlord who didn't look for the male presence that all women are supposed to have in a pub and an ambience that carried the mind to far away days.

Julia hadn't always been the solitary figure in the corner. At 33 she would laugh inwardly at the number of serious affairs that had catalogued her life since her early modelling days at the age of sixteen. She was totally content in her current isolation, more concerned with her new Advertising responsibilities and the safe haven of the inner peace she had found.

Upon entering The Burleigh, Julia nodded to a few of the familiar faces and laughed at the Landlord's poor attempt to change her standard bar order.

1

He failed.

"Three glasses of red wine, no more no less? I can read your order like a book Julia, two to stand one to begin".

"That's right Harry, the fusty air in your old pub really brings out the body in your over priced red!"

With a wry smile Harry poured the consignment of three and then began a jovial dialogue with Julia asking how she was progressing in her new promotion. Julia was inwardly glad when the customers rallied Harry into service. She liked the 60-year-old Landlord but in a similar fashion to her wine sips – small brief encounters.

As The Burleigh began to fill Julia envisaged herself in her favourite holiday destination - the Harz Mountains in Germany. She was so absorbed with her own thoughts that she didn't notice the voice immediately.

"Excuse me return dreamer, is this yours?"

Standing next to her was a tall well-attired gentleman. He had shoulder length black hair, which was cut to Italian precision, a well-chiselled face and cultured features that signified breeding and natural good looks. His eyes were dark and they burned with an inquiring intensity as he made the request to Julia. After being initially taken aback by this Armani clad stranger, Julia blurted out a response.

"My necklace, why yes, thank you. It must have a broken clasp yet again!"

Reclaiming the necklace, the man fastened it around Julia's neck and carefully positioned the offending link back into position.

"Thanks, it was rather precious to me, the last gift my sister gave me before she left for Canada".

After Julia had recovered from the disruption of her dream world the two strangers became less isolated, with Canada providing common ground for both of them. The gentleman expressed curiosity at Julia's bar order and for a quarter of an hour a conversation ensued, which extolled the virtues of The Burleigh as a location to find escapism.

Upon his departure the well-spoken gentleman handed Julia his card and uttered a curious grandiose comment.

"Well now you are a Godalming Lady and we have The Burleigh as our communal hideaway you must have one of these".

After thanking her for her company the gentleman took his leave. Julia studied the card meticulously. 'Royston Sandford-Everett' - Merchant Seavillia Exports read the card in ornate gold embossed lettering. Her eyes widened, realising that the tall stranger was the junior partner of the famous MSE Global Shipping chain. She remained puzzled by the Godalming Lady reference because she had always resided in that locale and wasn't titled either.

After second thoughts however, she felt sure that she hadn't actually stated where she resided during their brief dialogue. She just dismissed the comment as a curious turn of phrase.

After the Everett departure, Julia enjoyed some cosy moments alone and was then pounced upon by a stream of 'acquaintances' that complemented her upon her vocational success whilst complimenting themselves at the same time in louder voices.

Julia did not really wish to join in with the mutual admiration society that was forming around her, and so when The Burleigh clock chimed half past ten she made her departure with an excuse relating to the heavy additional workload that she had now accrued.

The warm night air smelt sweet and Julia was filled with a sense of triumph after escaping what was becoming an increasingly boring conversation.

A few spots of rain started to drift through the streetlight, and at first Julia welcomed the cool droplets upon her face. Julia's new house was situated about twenty-five minutes walking distance from The Burleigh and she only got a Taxi home when the weather really turned for the worst. She was a considerate individual who didn't like the environmentally damaging factors associated with short car journeys. Subsequently the 911 stayed at home and the casual flat shoes went out when she ventured into Godalming.

As the droplets turned into a steady flow of rain Julia quickened her pace. She was approaching the outskirts of Godalming and the junction traffic lights a hundred yards ahead of her marked the halfway point of her journey. Julia suddenly became aware that a dark car was stationary at the green light that she was approaching. A minor rush of adrenaline started to course through Julia, and with this new heightened awareness she started to scrutinise her immediate surroundings intently. The car now thirty yards ahead was almost certainly black. It was a top of the range Jaguar and the streetlight just enabled her to discern the number plate - RSE 2. There were no other cars in the vicinity, no other people walking the pavements and no other pedestrian-friendly alternative routes.

The sound of the front seat passenger door froze Julia. She had expected the sound but when it came she hadn't anticipated the muscle seizure that barred her movement.

"I say, it is you Godalming Lady isn't it", said Everett, leaning out of the passenger side door.

If Julia had felt uncomfortable by this title before, it now represented security, and to a level, safety. The woman raced the remaining yards to Everett's car at a speed that broke a trot and beckoned a canter.

Everett, recognising that Julia was quite distraught, added to his initial sentence.

"Look, can I run you home? Rain and darkness don't make an attractive combination for a female pedestrian in this day and age". Julia hesitated for a moment before accepting Everett's offer.

"Right, direct the reins then, and this beast will take you to your door".

"Thanks, it's merely five minutes driving time - if that!

"Two lefts from here and then down Stirleone Drive - number seven please".

Everett helped Julia with her seat belt and then sped off following her directions.

As the car approached Stirleone Drive, Everett gradually slowed before speeding up to a pace that they had not previously experienced on their journey. Stirleone Drive came and went.

"It was that turning there, that left," said Julia indignant that such an easy instruction could be misinterpreted.

The electric doors locked and the face turned.

"Don't feel special, you're nothing, you were just there. At times some women get above their station, hearing the word equal and making a false equation. Don't get me wrong, the meat's tender but promise me, don't feel special. You..."

Julia cut in.

"Just drop me now. Just..."

The fist cut her short a powerful fist that bloodied her mouth and left it's sting.

"Look, let's get things straight, put our cards on the table. Your best outcome involves lungs that still expel air, eyes that still see and lips that can still feel the trickle of blood upon them. Your worst outcome - well you know that don't you?

"Now enjoy the journey but do, oh please do remember you're not special, you're nothing - a non-event".

The car journeyed on and Everett put a Tamala-Motown Greatest Hits CD in the Car stereo. Occasionally the volume was lowered so that Everett's verbal rape could continue. Julia said nothing. Advertising, The Burleigh and three glasses of red were now worthless - she just had hope, the hope that brought tomorrows. The car had been cruising through well laid 'Greenbelt' roads and Julia suddenly felt the hairs on the back of her neck rise as Everett slowed to a halt at the bottom of a side track which had left the main highway.

Everett got out of the car and roughly pulled Julia out with him.

"This copse seems right, don't you think so Julia? It's funny you know, how quiet the bubbly Julia has become. I wonder why - it's beyond me. Can you smell the pine? It's one of my favourite aromas, so invigorating and natural, don't you think?"

Julia was forced away from the crude dirt based car park. As the pair approached the fringes of the fir copse the woman was dealt a powerful downward blow to the back of her head. She hit the ground hard, cutting her temple on a protruding pine branch. She became aware that Royston Sandford-Everett was kneeling above her. She could just discern his powerful muscular shape in the moonlight, but the silence that had taken over her routemaster was the factor that forced the sweat to moisten on her brow. After a couple of minutes Everett broke the quiet.

"Take this lighter. Light it and illuminate my noble face. The lesson is nearly read my Godalming Lady, but one needs a spotlight to celebrate the closure doesn't one?

"I congratulate you on your attentive nature, it means I could share the occasion to its fullest level".

Julia did as she was told and the powerful lighter cast an eerie light upon Everett's wild-eyed visage.

"You have a choice now bitch - shattered, tattered or battered?"

Julia saw the face twinge, as if Everett was reconsidering. She saw hope for a fleeting second, but then her hope faded as she saw the glint of steel in the previously inactive right hand. She saw the fist descend once again, Everett's one act of mercy, before the knife pierced her heart and delivered the darkness.

ONE

"We've got one, Vain".

"How long gone?" responded Gregory Vain, not fully believing that D-Day had actually arrived.

"About two and a half hours. Caucasian, female with ID putting her at 33".

"Cause of death?"

"One direct stab wound through the heart. She would have died anyway. Looks like a haemorrhage was just starting".

"Will it effect the demonstration?"

"I doubt it, but the perfect corpse can't be direct mailed you know!"

"Point taken. Any signs of rape, Mason?"

"No, none. Evidence of blows to mouth region and the back of the cranium. The latter probably offset the haemorrhage".

"Have you sent the Volks for the triad pick up?"

"No. You're all going separate. M.O.D overruled by the C.I.A on this one. Your driver will give the usual signal. Look for a black battered Scirocco, registration CV3N 79S. They've been waiting nearly two weeks for the right corpse. Let's hope it doesn't disappoint them. Pick up is in about ten minutes. Good luck Vain".

"Cheers, Mason. Let's hope she captured a full HV range. Passing out, base off".

Gregory Vain nullified his Comm-Lynx signal and hurriedly collected the small suitcase that he had in readiness in the hallway for this moment. Vain's wife Tanya observed his movements.

"Still can't tell me Greg?"

As the couple travelled upstairs Vain returned a familiar response.

"No, sorry Tan. You know the score - want for nothing, know nothing!"

"Well take care, love. I bet you must laugh at me if your job isn't dangerous but it must be. I mean the Comm-Lynx, night visits and swift departures all point to it darling, don't they?"

"No comment Tan. You know that, don't apply the stranglehold".

Tanya Vain proceeded to apply a mock stranglehold upon her husband's neck and Vain sparred back with a playful tickle directed to her midriff. The couple ended up in a heap on their replica four-poster bed and whilst entwined enjoyed a deep kiss that added a spice to their play.

The hiss of their electronic gate intercom interrupted their shenanigans. Greg quickly went to the receiver and encoded his part of the applicable signal.

"Save it for tomorrow. Let's save it. Save it".

The desired reply came back.

"Tonight burns brightest. Let's make it. Make it".

Vain opened the gates and waited alone in the porch for the car to proceed up the long gravel drive. Once he recognised that the type of car and plate number were correct, he called a farewell to Tanya.

"See you Tan. Keep it warm, spend our money. I love ya".

Tanya responded in a similar humorous fashion commenting that the milkman would be gentle with her! She finished by returning the 'I love ya' and proceeded to watch the pick up car snake it's way down the drive.

The battered Scirocco confused her even more. Greg's employers, whoever they were, paid all the bills and cash seemed to be present in large quantities. Tanya hadn't been a big fan of the private school education both their children were 'advised' into by Greg's employers but nine year old Rachel and seven year old Gary seemed to be progressing well none the less. The burly gentlemen who collected the kids each morning and returned them each evening were the most uncomfortable factor for Tanya to cope with. The kids loved the pair and they were very polite to all the family but without firmer explanation, they just added to the greyness surrounding Greg's employment.

On occasions Tanya was sure she had been 'shadowed' when she shopped in Epping, in Essex. She even changed her shopping locale to neighbouring Theydon Bois but street corner gentlemen appeared there too. She mentioned the shadow factor to Greg but instead of showing the concern she expected, he displayed a binary reaction seeming pleased by her revelation. She assumed that this was another work-related factor and so put up with the intrusion.

Privacy didn't always come easy, but Tanya contented herself that for a slim youthful looking thirty-two year old she was experiencing life to its fullest. The kids were settled, Greg and her had the spice of lovers despite their traditional marriage relationship, and their standard of living achieved grade A proportions. Tanya had more questions concerning Greg's employment but they could wait.

* * * * *

"Did Mason fill you in Gregory?"

The speaker was known as Mr Voight, no more no less. Voight was quite a senior with regard to Vain and his teams work.

"He gave me two desired demographics concerning gender and age. I'm short of a name, career base and death location".

"Julia Venison, just appointed as an Account Planner for BMP DDB advertising agency. Found dead in full view, propped upon a style adjacent to a dirt road car park eleven miles out of Godalming".

"The home of Ad Planning. She was doing well for herself. Where's the venue tonight; Desig D or E?"

"We've reverted back to B. The R.A.S decomposition factors are radically reduced by this venue. Venison's body is there now, as are Tavini and Ko-Chai. In a nutshell we went for the most local site. Site B keeps the subject fresh in comparison".

Vain laughed to himself about the Reticular Activating System reference. One of his salient research points devalued the durability of the RAS in favour of the MC Vault he had discovered in the Cerebral Hemisphere. Voight remained locked in the body mechanics of yesterday, but he liked the pompous superior and was pleased that the demonstration arena had been re-sited to Desig B which was the closest venue to his Epping base. Vain looked taut with contemplation. He was a different man from the one who had play wrestled with Tanya some thirty minutes previous. Five years research was on show tonight, and the sceptical audience who were largely clothed in ignorance would be unconvinced to a person if Julia Venison's Memory-Camera fired blanks in the demonstration arena.

The car proceeded down the driveway of designation B. Upon arrival Voight and his two bodyguards ushered Vain out of the Scirocco and through the main entrance of the Neo-Gothic Manor House that represented Designation B.

Once inside, the four were greeted by an attractive woman in her mid forties dressed in a grey suit.

Her greeting was flawless in its tone and precision.

"Mr Voight, Mr Vain good evening. The assembly await your presence in the Lower Chamber. Mr Denison has requested that security staff remain on the Ground Floor in Drawing Room number three.

"Miss Ellis will escort them there. Now, Mr Voight and Mr Vain if you will kindly follow me, I will escort you to the Lower Chamber".

Upon entering the Lower Chamber, both gentlemen were initially dazzled by the powerful spotlighting that illuminated the demonstration area. The Lower Chamber was a very spacious room that easily accommodated the forty-six people who had been invited to the demonstration. The chairs were arranged in a semi-circle that was split down the middle to enable access to the main spotlit area. Mr Voight sat in a seat in the front of the semi-circle, whilst Vain continued walking to take his place in the spotlit area. He nodded to his Research Team - David Tavini and Mishimo Ko-Chai who were standing in front of the assembly. In front of all three was Leif Denison of the CIA. This powerfully built man was the Project Leader, and as he shook Vain's hand in greeting Gregory was aware of the trim physical condition this fifty-five year old had kept himself in. It was Denison who first addressed the assembly.

"Fellow professionals, thank you for coming here tonight. Thank you for being in immediate readiness for thirteen days. None of you know the full extent of our Memory-Camera research. You have been weaned upon a diet of rumour, speculation and truth.

"Tonight, our demonstration will show you how far we have come and will hopefully reveal the identity of a criminal who perpetrated a vicious murder just under four hours ago.

"No one has seen what you are going to see - the evidence being too fresh for prior consumption.

"Therefore we are taking a gamble that the victim built a visual memory record leading up to her murder.

"If it was a short sharp attack you will probably not witness key murder details, but you will still be able to experience at first hand our Memory-Camera breakthrough. Hopefully we will be able to unlock the case and give you the guilty head that so ruthlessly cut short Julia Venison's life. If this is possible, you will be convinced. Convinced that this research baby is the biggest scientific discovery since the dawn of mankind. I must point out that the demonstration will probably uncover distasteful material, and if anyone feels unsure of the calibre of their metaphorical stomach, I would advise them to leave before the display wall behind me recedes in one minutes' time and the demonstration begins".

No one left.

The display wall sank into the floor to reveal an extension to the Lower Chamber. The extension was powerfully illuminated once again and it echoed the semi-circular shape of the chair pattern in the main Chamber. Everyone's eyes went to the focal attraction in the extension.

Lying naked on a marble slab was Julia Venison. Her flesh was pallid with blue bruising appearing on her mouth and temple. The blood had been washed from her and the fatal knife wound looked relatively innocuous without evidence of the deluge of blood that had passed through it. Her eyes had been closed as Mason felt it was more appropriate with regard to the respect the victim deserved. To Venison's left was a large laser recording screen, behind her was an array of digital gadgetry and on the slab close to her head was the 'Vault-Splicer', a conception created by Vain. As some of the assembly audibly drew their breath, Vain approached the marble slab and took hold of the Vault-Splicer. This instrument was three inches in length and resembled a king-sized needle with cables threaded through the eye to the digital power base behind Venison. Vain broke the apprehensive silence.

"What you will see now is the Prototype featuring crude edges and obvious penetration. What will follow in subsequent months will be subtle in comparison - a sensory stimulus that won't even break the skin. Well here goes, let's go Vault hunting!".

Vain drove the Vault Splicer into the cerebral hemisphere. He knew through tests the exact region that would stimulate Vault response. The previously unexplored Cerebral Vault was his baby. He had located the netherworld that others had overlooked. Now it was all down to his placement and Venison's storage capacity for HVs - heightened visuals.

The lights dimmed and the laser screen took precedence.

The first image to appear on the screen involved three glasses of red wine placed upon a wooden bar surface. Pub background noise accompanied this visual display. The image of a uniformed bartender next appeared on the screen and the crowd heard a woman comment...

"...That's right Harry, the fusty air in your old pub really brings out the body in your over priced red!"

The screen temporarily blackened but after a few seconds illuminated an open hand with a necklace in the palm.

A male voice commenting, "excuse me, return dreamer, is this yours?" accompanied the image. The assembly were then taken through Julia Venison's introduction to Sandford-Everett, with the Memory-Camera revealing Everett's appearance to the full. The Godalming Lady reference appeared as did most of the initial dialogue the two had shared.   The sequence closed on Everett's card, displaying his name and professional involvement.

The blackness returned, to be replaced after three seconds by an image, which drew excited gasps from the invited assembly.

There on the screen was Julia Venison herself, preening her hair that was reflected in the glass covered bar wall behind the optics. All eyes flitted between this visual image and the corpse. The reflected image showed an attractive face without bruising, and this fuelled the desire of the watching assembly to fight her case for her and give her murderer the retribution they deserved.

A range of faces appeared on the screen next, cross cutting with each other, accompanied by a dialogue involving congratulations for Julia and a monologue of self-interest. Julia's MC selection had made an excellent job of illuminating the shallowness of the mutual admiration society that had broken her privacy.

The 'rain in the streetlight' sequence provided a bizarre scenic interlude on the screen. This sequence led up to the pivotal top range Jaguar visual. Julia's Memory-Camera had managed to record the infamous plate number in its entirety. Everett was then 'framed' leaning out of the car with his lift invitation being recorded for all to hear.

A murmuring briefly started amongst the assembly, as the more vocal guests started to voice their suspicions concerning Everett's probable role in the murder.

The smiling friendly face of Everett left the screen, being replaced by an opposite portrait highlighting a sneering mouth and enraged eyes. The assembly recoiled as Everett's verbal tirade began. The heads shook when they heard the "don't feel special" references, and this disgust turned to anger as the malicious character that made up Royston Sandford-Everett turned increasingly more perverse.

The Tamala-Motown CD appeared as it had been intended as a sick joke, and when the Memory-Camera ventured outside near the fir copse, Everett's tribute to the aesthetic quality of the landscape firmly established the insanity of the man. The walk to the fir copse offered images that were too hard to discern due to the lack of an adequate light source.

The "illuminate my noble face" comment caused one woman to shout "bastard" at the screen, and the leering portrait was captured in the spotlight Everett's vanity had demanded.

Everett's chilling departure line "You have a choice now bitch. Shattered, tattered or battered" forced an awesome silence from the assembly. The crowd knew that an air of finality had sealed the delivery of the words and the last recorded image, although not a frame of clarity, showed the descending fist that turned out to be the coup de grace.

Julia's Memory-Camera had blocked any recordings of the knife that sealed her execution and the assembly considered this to be a blessing in the context of so much suffering, hoping that she wasn't fully aware of its existence in the moments that led up to her death. The screen went black - the show was over.

17

The lights were returned to full beam and it was obvious that the assembly had been moved by what they had seen. Some of the crowd had buried their heads in their hands, some stared blankly ahead of them, not being able to confront what they had just witnessed and a few broke down in tears overcome with repulsion. After allowing a couple of minutes for the assembly to recompose themselves, Leif Denison proceeded to the front of the Lower Chamber extension. He wished to pay his tribute to the MC Project team.

"This assembly represents some of the brightest minds of Medical Science, Defence and Criminal Intelligence in the Western world. It is fitting that you were selected to bear witness to this historic discovery. What we saw represented the heightened visual selections made by the late Julia Venison leading up to her murder. We climbed inside a supposedly dead brain and extracted all we needed to place Royston Sandford-Everett where he belongs - prison. The image continuity tells us that the Memory-Camera doesn't capture everything we see. It doesn't store useless images but keeps visuals of heightened meaning intact and available. A glance at the screen counter shows a totality running time of thirty-four minutes - DEAD! Julia Venison subsequently communicated to us after her short life had been so cruelly terminated. She had stored all we needed. My Team's research obviously re-examines the concept of brain death, and I would like to take this opportunity to briefly detail the operations of the research team who pioneered this discovery.

"I bear the ultimate responsibility for team organisation and control. Doctor Gregory Vain, the Team Leader, broke through the mystery surrounding memory just over five years ago, with his controversial discovery of the Memory-Camera Vault.

"Located deep within the cerebral hemisphere, the MC Vault records key heightened images that represent significance to the viewer. As you have witnessed tonight, this vault initially survives death, staying intact like an encased film awaiting development. That development arrived in the forms of Professor Mishimo Ko-Chai and Doctor David Tavini.

"Professor Ko-Chai leads the field of Laser Extraction and Doctor Tavini is an expert in the field of Digital Conversion. Between them the team have devised the technological apparatus that unlocked what you saw tonight.

"I know Mr Voight is keen to get the details surrounding Everett's arrest organised so I will close shortly, but before I do close I have three important points to detail.

"Firstly a method to elicit confessions has been formulated without breaking the news of our discovery at this moment in time.

"This leads us nicely into my second point. All of you have taken oaths of secrecy and your complete silence regarding this discovery is strongly advised.

"The final point concerns the future - the exciting future!

"The team have discovered that the MC Vault has an extension. It is their view that this extension might contain images of the minds' eye, our thoughts - our imagination. If they are proved correct, then the living mind can be explored to a degree beyond our wildest expectations! Remember secrecy is paramount, you will be kept informed, goodnight".

TWO

An overcast August morning usually annoyed Gregory Vain, making him feel cheated by the seasons. This particular morning did not disturb him unduly however, as he was mentally immersed in the dramatic events that had taken place at Designation B. Vain's team had stayed overnight in the demonstration building and it looked like they had enjoyed the rare privilege that a lie-in afforded. The ornate clock on the wall showed quarter past ten, and Vain felt impelled to check how Mr Voight was progressing with the organisation behind Everett's arrest.

After hurriedly washing, Vain put on a casual suit and used his internal bedside phone to contact both Ko-Chai and Tavini. He told them that he was going to check on Voight's progress and arranged for the team to pay a collective visit at half past ten. Both Ko-Chai and Tavini seemed content to follow Vain's decisions, and they had never expressed any noticeable resistance to Vain's Team Leader tag or indeed the way he led the team.

Ko-Chai was the first to arrive at Vain's room. His courteous morning greeting had it's customary warm tone and the mini bow which always accompanied its delivery, whilst initially seeming quite humorous, now properly finished the greeting ceremony. Vain liked the fifty-six year old Korean to a degree whereby he considered Ko-Chai to be his best friend as well as one of his research team members. Ko-Chai, although having a higher qualification to his name was always respectful of his leader calling him "my boss-man" to fully establish the high esteem he felt for Vain. Ko-Chai became a naturalised American in the early 1970s and his laser exploration work had kept American Microsurgery in a very healthy state since he became an American citizen.

Ko-Chai had expressed deep regret to none other than Leif Denison about how saddened he was that the rest of the Vain and Ko-Chai family members could never be introduced to each other.

Denison had replied that the tightness of the security restrictions couldn't allow the loophole of harmonised family friendships breaking the cordon of the project's blanket discipline - it was too bigger risk to take. Ko-Chai was not convinced, and he had seemed to bear Denison at a distance ever since.

Ko-Chai was in love with the Anglo American Memory-Camera Project because of the potential it seemed to possess in relation to the illumination of the criminal psyche. Ko-Chai was overjoyed that Julia Venison's Memory-Camera had revealed so much and he was particularly pleased that the team were going to be able to witness the arrest of Everett. In thirty-four dead minutes, Ko-Chai along with the rest of the assembly had learnt to like Julia and despise Everett. He thought that it was particularly fitting that the team could witness the arrest and see the outcome of their research.

A second knock sounded on Vain's door and David Tavini entered the room. Whilst Ko-Chai was only marginally over five feet, Tavini had the height of basketball proportions. Six feet four would be a conservative estimate, and Tavini's athletic build seemed to accentuate his height even more.

His greeting was not quite as formal or warm as his Americanised colleague. A jargonized "Yo. What's going down fellas", was Tavini's way of asking for the game plan concerning Everett's arrest.

Whilst Vain didn't consider to rank Tavini amongst his best friends like Ko-Chai, he nevertheless liked the tall American and couldn't wish to work with a more skilled Digital Conversion expert. Tavini had majored in Athletics in his College days, and had only discovered his potential for Digital Conversion when he reached his mid-twenties. Once this was realised, there was no stopping the 'All American Boy' and he sailed through his doctorate by the time he was thirty-one. Tavini, now thirty-five, was two years younger than Vain and he was very much a man in the mould of Denison.

Vain spoke to both members of his team simultaneously.

"Well guys, if yesterday was D-Day, today won't be boring in comparison. Mr Voight told me last night that we could witness the arrest of Everett at first hand and I arranged for us to drop in to the Lister Room at around ten thirty. So let's go and check out Mr Voight's method for eliciting confessions".

The team greeted the security forces outside the Lister room and after completing the required security checks, were shown into Voight's base room.

Voight extended his usual formal warm welcome proceeding to detail the team members who would be involved in the arrest of Everett.

"We are arresting Everett tonight at 21:00. Surveillance have researched his intended movements and have concluded that he will be socialising in The Vernet Gentleman's Club adjacent to New Bond Street at this moment in time. Tonight's retribution team will consist of the following personnel;

"The MC team will be present to a man, but will not enter into any dialogue with either Everett or any of his associates. They are there to bear witness to the outcome of the research which is responsible for this initial arrest. It is of paramount importance that they should see their hard efforts rewarded and coming to fruition with the desired criminal head being presented on the metaphorical platter.

"I will oversee the operation and will subsequently bear full responsibility for the precision surrounding its execution. I will not enter into dialogue either initially, being a silent witness like the MC team. Blyth Carson will represent the C.I.D at tonight's arrest and Brynley Stowles is there to represent M.O.D interests. Both these gentlemen will partake in verbal dialogue with Everett bearing 'dumb' testimony that Everett will have no problem in answering.

"Both these gentlemen have a role which involves acting as a proverbial foil for Ms Marcia Levene of the C.I.A who will turn the screw upon Everett in her rehearsed attack role. It is important for all present to realise that at no time will Carson or Stowles proceed with a formal arrest scenario.

"Carson and Stowles will act as the decoy for Levene, who will anticipate formal arrest procedures. After she has injected her words, Everett will confess. Using this approach we will get a confession straight from the lips of the guilty party, and the Memory-Camera Project will not have to be evidenced in the criminal trial that will ensue. It is our prerogative to keep our research hidden at this moment in time, and as you know we have ensured that we are not obligated to reveal our exposition tactics surrounding this crime. The judicial systems of both Britain and America are in the dark concerning the MC Project

23

and that is why the devised method to elicit confessions involves verbal confession in the presence of witnesses. Once we have got Everett's verbal confession tonight I will administer his formal arrest and then unenlightened Law enforcement staff can extract the motivating factors behind the case. After we have done our work the criminal can be returned to the conventional system for them to execute sentence.

"I realise that the MC team members will be a little in the dark with regard to the actual implementation of our confession extraction method, but tonight's arrest will eradicate any doubts you may have.

"It is true we are dealing with a very bright murderer in this instance, a Harvard Legal graduate, a multimillionaire who has many of the brightest Legal minds in this country and overseas in his pocket. It is true that the rain obscured tyre tread details that might have built a suspicion and it is true that Everett's Armani clothing is now as we speak being cleaned to a degree whereby murder connection details would be lost.

"We know in our enlightened position that both the dead body of Venison and the living body of Everett carry enough DNA evidence to make the identity of the murderer an absolute certainty, but we only know this through Memory-Camera Hindsight. Without our MC apparatus, Everett would be beyond suspicion. After all, he only had a brief conversation with the victim and Julia's MC didn't register any people witnessing the pick-up. Small fragments of information might have been gathered, but that would have given Everett time to build a Legal Defence team powerful enough to ensure the case never came to court.

"Without our MC breakthrough, Everett would have remained a free man, a free and extremely dangerous man.

"Our seven person collection squad will depart this venue for the Vernet Gentleman's Club at 21:00 with the MC team and myself in one car, and Levene, Stowles and Carson travelling in a second car. We will be escorted by four cars, two front and rear, that contain additional security staff. These escort staff know nothing of our research. They will follow us into Central London until two kilometres from the New Bond Street vicinity. At this point they will scatter, to re-assemble at 22:10 outside the club. Our 'method' does not anticipate opposition to Everett's arrest, but if this did materialise, the sixteen chosen extras would cope with any disturbance very efficiently.

"Well, gentlemen and Ms Levene, I look forward to meeting you again when we re-convene at 20:55 outside the main entrance of this designation. We are obviously 'house-bound' until the reconvention".

Vain was generally pleased with the selection criteria that had governed the arresting squad. He had a great deal of time for both Stowles and Carson. They had shown sustained enthusiasm for the MC Project since they had been made au fait with its objectives three years ago. Stowles was hunched and looked quite unkempt in his appearance. He didn't represent a High Ranking MOD stereotype on a face value level, but his intellect and drive firmly put him into the brightest minds category in relation to the totality of project staff.

Carson had fought hard against any racist discrimination that had tried to bar his way in the C.I.D. He had risen to the top through sheer industry and had preserved a sense of humour that made him one of the most popular project members.

His first words to Vain had captured his spirit perfectly...

"...Hiya, I'm Blyth; black, bright and according to my wife, beautiful!" Carson's up-front humour didn't intrude upon the dogged determination he showed when addressing the parameters of the criminal mind. The seminal work he had done in relation to the exploration of criminal psychology had made him an excellent choice for the project as a whole, the devising of the arrest method and the options for that nights arresting squad.

Vain was once again pleased with Voight's pivotal role with regard to the arrest and he was most satisfied that his MC team had been chosen-to a man. If Vain alone had been selected it could have ushered in divisions through the team, and possibly have set back the Anglo-American co-operation that had so far been one of the greatest strength areas in the project.

The only shadow area involving arrest team selection seemed to arrive in the form of Marcia Levene. That morning had been the first time Vain's MC team had met the woman, and whilst she had seemed to register Voight's words with admirable intense scrutiny she represented a 'new face' at a time when everyone's mind was upon the arrest. She was to a level, through no fault of her own, an intrusion - someone who had disrupted the collective concentration of the 'familiar face' interactions. Before this morning Natassia Overson had represented CIA female involvement and her project commitment had seemed beyond dispute. Vain presumed she had been taken ill, because she wouldn't have missed the arrest execution for the world!

The afternoon passed slowly for the MC team. Tavini had challenged Vain to a game of Real Tennis in the court on the Lower Floor, and had proceeded to hammer the Englishman without breaking sweat. Ko-Chai had immersed himself in an eighteenth century novel detailing Rococo French aesthetics, before witnessing the Tavini massacre in its latter stages. None of the team could concentrate enough to continue their research. Their minds were on that night's arrest and they knew that their vault extension work, whilst approaching completion could wait a day or so until after the initial criminal scalp had been pinned on the door!

The team members took a light meal together at 19:00 before they retired to their rooms to attire for the 'main event' that would shortly take place.

The team arrived collectively, shortly before the reconvention deadline. Voight, Carson and Stowles were already in readiness as were the escort party. Marcia Levene was the last to arrive, appearing with Leif Denison. The latter proceeded to wish the seven good fortune and finished with a line of typical Denison delivery - "go get that head folks. This one's for Venison".

The arrest squad departed Designation B and progressed toward Central London. No one spoke because all minds were fixed on their impending encounter with Everett. The escort cars scattered at the appointed place and all seven of the arrest party knew that their quarry was now a matter of minutes away. Vain wished Voight good luck as their car slowed to a halt outside the Vernet Gentlemen's Club.

The seven arrest party members proceeded through the club's main entrance at 22:01 and Voight approached the door staff flashing his high-ranking credentials badge. As one of the door staff asked for Voight to pause for a moment while he read the badge Voight snapped...

"Read it but be quick. You aren't going to hold up this momentous event with your remedial education. Now, where can we find Royston Sandford-Everett?"

Taken aback, the door person replied...

"Er, he's in the Trevallier Cocktail Bar, Sir. He won't be very pleased, Sir. He has invited some very eminent guests tonight. I wouldn't advise you to..."

Voight cut in.

"Bollocks. The Trevallier is sign posted over there, let's go".

It was the first time Vain had heard Voight utter a word that bordered upon expletive fare, but he saw the glint of determination in the mans eyes and realised that nothing would get in the way of his handling of the arrest, especially time wasting advice from a well meaning member of the club's staff. Vain was pleased that the organisational side of the arrest was in such capable hands.

The arrest squad entered the Trevallier Cocktail Bar and were greeted by a sight that illuminated Everett at the peak of his vanity. His words dominated the whole Bar and a crowd of eleven drooling associates hung on his every word...

"...and I didn't choose that moment to illuminate my prowess in that merchandise realm. I merely waited until the ignorant fool had given me enough ammunition to fully hang, draw and quarter him! I mean what ignoramus would engage in a dialogue with me on the merits of a transportation method that is so archaic that it renders the extoller positively Bronze Age in comparison with MSE. I mean..."

Stowles, speaking from the squad's position on the fringes of the associates cut short Everett...

"Mr Royston Sandford-Everett we would like you to accompany us to our investigation station to answer some questions concerning the murder of Ms Julia Maria Venison".

Everett didn't flinch in his retort...

"Does your rudeness know no boundaries? First you interrupt a private dialogue at this private Gentlemen's establishment and then you have the audacity to associate me with a crime I know nothing about, concerning a woman I've never heard of. I thank you not!"

Carson added support to his partner's request...

"It is in your interest to accompany us Mr Everett. We merely pursue an inquiry and have to address every avenue in our attempt to eliminate the innocent and find the guilty".

"Oh, so it's a team effort - the hunchback and the black man. Well that just makes things worse, doesn't it? I mean you could have sent a well-presented delegation to ask me to talk to you about your ludicrous hypothesis, but no! Instead you send Quasimodo and an excuse for a man who I can't fully discern in this half-light. Now look around you and you will see four of the most eminent lawyers in this country who will block this pathetic initial arrest attempt and then turn the tables on you when I sue for defamation of character".

Whilst Everett's attack on the arrest squad continued, Vain felt the anger welling up inside him. He hated Everett even more now. Not only had he cruelly illuminated the poor physical condition of Stowles in a malicious fashion but he had added to this by his pathetic racist attack on Carson. Everett's 'yes men' associates had added a background of sustained laughter during the course of his condemnation.

It was that moment that the previously quiet Marcia Levene chose to play her and the team's trump card. Speaking from the shadows she commented...

"You have a choice now Royston, shattered, tattered or battered?"

Everett's smug face changed in an instant.

Then, thinking his actions had been physically witnessed, he returned to the raving wild-eyed Everett of the previous evening.

"You were there! You bastards. Why didn't you stop me? For Christ's sake you let me do it - you bastards!"

With Everett's confession the giggling yes men physically withdrew and Voight's team encircled Everett. They locked their arms around a man who was screaming his outrage. Turning to his associates he cried...

"They let me do it! They let me do it! Look, you've got to help me gentlemen. Pearce, you'll help won't you? For Christ's sake Philbey, Hamilton help me, help me...!"

His pleas fell on deaf ears. The associates were already departing. Everett was dragged to the awaiting car and a smile flickered on Vain's face as he saw Julia's tormentor roughly forced into the security vehicle. Vain picked the neckerchief up off the pavement. RSE was woven into the garment and it seemed to be a fitting souvenir for their first operation concerning MC retribution.

THREE

Leif Denison had called a Review Meeting in the Lower Chamber for 09:00. The purpose of this gathering was to assess the Everett arrest, comment on how the conventional MC-ignorant police force were handling the case, divulge the ensuing plan of action and conclude by detailing the social function that would take place that night in Designation B. All bar one of the England-based MC-Project staff would be in attendance.

After the thirty-eight staff members had taken their seats Denison addressed the assembly.

"Congratulations. The Memory-Camera Project team have triumphed. Our dedication and endeavour have been rewarded with the first sick animal being placed in the long stay sick pen.

"I feel 'sick animal' is a fitting description for Royston Sandford-Everett, and my only regret concerning this case is that Britain fails to utilise the death penalty for this type of offence.

"Mr Voight's method of arrest proved flawless with the Carson-Stowles foil perfectly setting up the Levene hammer-blow. I know that some of the initiated doubted whether the guilty would crumble when their own words were thrown back at them, but the quick thinking Everett was hooked as soon as Ms Levene had quoted his evil 'shattered, tattered or battered' option.

"Mr Voight's method is foolproof. We don't always need words to elicit confession, and could for example pick upon a non-verbal action or mannerism the killer displayed when they perpetrated their crime. In both verbally and non-verbally determined instances we merely need to select the correct 'tactical' hammer-blow. The hammer-blow that we could not have seen or heard without our MC breakthrough, and the hammer-blow which makes the killer believe they were physically witnessed while they were slaughtering their victim.

"Everett was handed over to the British Police Authorities at 22:22 last night. He had to have a Lawyer appointed for him because his usual Legal associate Mr Dorian Pearce had been present at the Vernet Gentlemen's Club, had heard his confession and had consequently refused his services. Our inside sources have informed us that Everett has been refused bail, has opted to plead guilty and has been sedated because he collapsed at 06:04 this morning when he was undergoing sustained questioning. A motive has not been established and it appears at this initial stage that Everett simply hated women.

"You are probably wondering how we know so much in such a short space of time! Well my friends, the answer will illustrate to you how well networked the MC Project is. If you look around the Chamber, you will work out that we are a person short. Yes, we are one person down, and that is because the thirty-ninth MC Project member is, as we speak awakening Everett ready to carry on with his role as the appointed Lawyer for this murderer!"

The Lower Chamber erupted in laughter, with the project members not being able to hide their amusement when imagining Everett being defended by one of their number.

"Before collapsing, Everett repeated time after time "they were there, they heard me" but each time 'our man' reminded him that the issue was murder not an imaginary audience!

"Our man is going to apply for Diminished Responsibility in court, but we all know that the Prosecution will tear that to shreds in this instance, successfully applying for premeditated murder in the first degree. When he is found guilty the judge is likely to opt for a twenty-five year minimum sentence. The Judicial system of this country normally award lenient sentences when the rich offend in relation to drugs or tax evasion, but this leniency will be replaced by vengeance when silver spoon killer Everett stands in the dock. He has let the Higher Classes down, betrayed them, and the judge will consequently go for his jugular!

"This first test case has been exciting, fulfilling all our expectations and justifying our belief in the MC Project. Now the intensive Memory-Camera operation really gets going. Tomorrow, most of you will be relieved of any duties for a ten-day period. This rest represents the calm before the storm. You will need time to relax, to see your loved ones and to gain strength for when we reconvene. After the ten-day lull period is over, the onslaught will start. For three weeks we will stay based around London, and then for the next five weeks we will relocate our operation to Designation J in Chicago.

In both locations we will be uncovering more Everetts and scoring more 'instant hits'. Before we reveal our MC findings to a global audience, we need to have a proven track record of success, of undisputed criminal scalps pinned to the door. In both locations, the project team will be split into three functional groups.

"Gregory Vain's team will continue their research on the MC Vault extension and apparatus modifications. Barring sleep, the only time they will suspend their research is when a victim arrives and they have to implement direct MC operations.

"Mr Voight will be placed in charge of both internal and external security in London, although in Chicago his American counterpart will handle affairs. Both men will work in liaison with Ms Levene.

"Paul Mason will work with his American parallel, Dwight Richards. Together they will monitor surveillance, selecting victims and liaising with security to organise the collection of victims, the mapping of desirable routes and the reconnaissance of venues where a 'hit' is to be made.

"All of you are going to be exhausted when the two months is over. All of you, apart from the active service arrest squads, will be restricted to the Designation site where you are in residence during this time period, and every team member will understand what the word teamwork really means after this intensive operation. Two months is a long time to be parted from loved ones, but you knew that when the squeeze came that this would be a factor. The squeeze is ten days away!

"Tonight we have a function that has a dual purpose. We should eat and drink to celebrate how far we have come, and we should socialise with MC Project members who we haven't previously associated with. We are a family, holding the key to a new world. Once the MC discovery is broken to the world things won't ever be quite the same again. The same for the global population and the same for you my friends. At this moment in time we are a small intellectual niche who know something everyone else doesn't.

"Once knowledge of our discovery is shared by the world you will experience a sense of loss despite the praise that you will enjoy. This loss will involve the floodgate factor. Part of you will always be reminiscing back to the beautiful world when only the few knew! Savour the moment. I'll see you tonight. Good day my family".

The MC Project team rose to a person and applauded. It was a spontaneous reaction never partaken of before. Denison was an excellent orator and this reaction had been on the cards for a long time. It was this moment that finally released the collective admiration.

No one clapped louder than Gregory Vain did, but despite his enthusiasm for the moment, three factors lodged in his mind offsetting the admiration he felt for Denison.

Despite the enthusiasm of the man, despite the opportunity that Denison had presented for him, and despite the warmth he seemed to feel for the whole MC Project staff, there was a darker side to him, something that Vain couldn't pinpoint but a disturbing subliminal trait none the less.

The second issue that bothered Vain during the applause concerned the further absence of Natassia Overson. No reason had been forthcoming to explain this and Vain knew that the MC Project wasn't one where leaving was an easy option. Each individual knew too much and Vain was glad that he loved the work.

It was the final factor that really disturbed Vain. While the applause reached its climax he became aware of a pair of eyes - beautiful dark eyes that surveyed him intently.

For the first time he saw the white skin and dark hair belonging to a different woman, a beautiful woman who had proffered a cold half smile as her gaze seldom left him. For the first time he had seen Ms Marcia Levene in a different light!

The Review Meeting closed and Vain was left to reflect upon the subtle networking that the MC Project was protected by. His thoughts dwelled longest on Marcia Levene, pondering how he could have been blind to her attraction before. Vain wasn't hooked on her image yet but he was curious. There was something about her presence that made her enchanting - the dark eyes that beckoned him, and the almost vampirical pallor that suggested a power above her slight frame. Vain loved Tanya deeply, but Levene's gaze had sown a seed. Her eyes spoke to him with the power of the only verbal address he had so far heard her utter - that fateful hammer-blow sentence to Everett!

* * * * *

The Banqueting Hall was laid out to sumptuous proportions with the red and white table decorations blending well with the dark wooden wall panels. Denison had decided that the celebration meal would adopt the format of European Nouvelle Cuisine. He hated the vulgar eighties translation of this concept, preferring to mirror original Nouvelle practice. The courses would subsequently be minimal in proportion but vast in quantity. The obligatory wine would appear with each course. Vain cast his eye down the menu, looking at the nine courses that made up the celebration meal and realised that the whole event would take up to six or seven hours to reach its conclusion.

When Denison did something he didn't do it by halves!

The Memory-Camera Project team were now there in their totality, with the Legal insider appearing to make up the full complement. He had worn Everett down when compiling his supposed defence, and while the guilty now rested he had taken his leave to partake in the celebration.

In addition to the MC Project team, the forty-six people who had been present at the Venison demonstration had been invited. A collection of twenty-five musicians had been hired to add a classical musical mise en scène to the evening's proceedings. Their presence was the reason that the phrase 'Et In Arcadia Ego' appeared in gold embossed lettering at the top of the menu. This Latin phrase signified in this instance that death as far as the project was concerned was everywhere, especially when one's guard was down and the wine led to 'good times'. Each MC Project member and each of the forty-six guests knew its presence on their menu meant that there was to be no mention of the project inside the Banqueting Hall and no dialogue at all with the 'alien' party - the musicians. The musicians understood their paymaster was the C.I.D and they were fully primed with regard to the format of the evening and their role as aesthetic support. Voight would keep an eye of scrutiny on them none the less.

Leif Denison speaking from the head of his table extended his usual 'le mot juste' greeting.

"When you are proud of your family, you share the moment of celebration and invite your close friends to extend their homage in communion. Tonight we are celebrating and I hope you will enjoy the food, drink and musical entertainment that we have provided.

"I will for once limit my words, and after my greeting toast you may commence your meal.

"The Champagne tastes best when it is toasted to those dear to you and so...

"...to Family and friends".

"To Family and Friends", the collective response echoed. The meal began.

Vain was seated next to Mr Voight and Ms Diana Fearston, one of the invited assembly who had impressed Denison with the work she had undertaken whilst graduating from the Sorbonne.

Her specialism concerned exploring the déjà-vu phenomenon and she held Vain in great respect for his MC findings. Fearston was a very pleasant woman who was a good raconteur in relation to a wide range of disciplines. Denison had personally recruited this American feeling that once she and Vain started to collaborate the collective potential would prove salient to their research.

Vain, for his part, was looking forward to drafting Fearston into the 'fringe' team after their Chicago placement had reached it's conclusion.

The Et In Arcadia restriction had blocked any references to the project, but Vain enjoyed the human sandwich he was positioned between, as the dialogue was wide ranging from extolling the merits of German nineteenth century Romantic paintings, to debating over who had the most comic prowess, The Marx Brothers or Laurel and Hardy. Mr Voight had still operated his security obsessed gaze from time to time but he had played a full part in the discussions offering a critical type of assessment that proved to have regulation potential as far as any debate was concerned. He had a 'casting vote' role, which pleased him immensely.

A break of twenty minutes was built into the evening's schedule after every three courses and the assembly could utilise this rest period to sit nearer the musicians or walk around the vast floodlit gardens that made this designation so palatable to the eye.

Vain didn't take advantage of the first break option, being too immersed in the discussions which he, Voight and Fearston were enjoying. After the sixth seafood based course had been consumed he felt it was a fitting moment to take advantage of the break facility and proceeded to slowly walk around the main lawns.

Voight and Fearston had taken the opportunity to survey the musicians from a closer proximity, and thus Vain was alone enjoying a few moments of contemplation to himself.

Vain's thoughts turned to Tanya and his children. The ten-day rest period would be a blessing, enabling him to spend more time with his beloved family, but the succeeding two month absence would represent the longest period of separation Vain and his family had experienced so far. He felt Tanya deserved to know more, to learn a little about the work he was undertaking and understand the reasons why his employment was so secretive in the process.

Vain was standing at the bottom of the main lawn with his back to the Manor looking downward at the illuminated terraced gardens that fell away gradually, culminating at the edge of the distant boating lake which in daylight was one of the Designation's most attractive features. He was on the point of turning back to the Manor when a voice broke his contemplation.

"One can revel in the mysteries of darkness can't one, Mr Vain?"

Standing twelve feet behind Vain stood Marcia Levene, resplendent in a black shoulderless evening dress.

Feeling underdressed in comparison, wearing the same casual suit that he had worn for the past three days, Vain responded in a hasty and slightly defensive fashion.

"Surely the profusion of illuminated lights dispels any mystery, doesn't it?"

"Well doesn't that depend on what you are actually seeing Mr Vain, doesn't that depend on whether your eyes or your mind's eye paint the image on your memory-canvas?

"You see Mr Vain, you know better than anyone what people really register, don't you? I mean what would you store, what would you keep for access purposes if this black dress dropped to the lawn beneath me with it's owner lying naked on the dew covered grass and you Mr Vain, lying on the said grass with your face between my legs. What would you keep?"

Vain rose to the challenge.

"I would keep two images, Ms Levene. One would be governed by my eyes and would highlight your illuminated face from an angle where the viewer is looking through the cradle of your legs, past your breasts to your facial region. This image would show your shut eyes and your mouth, which is twitching slightly in the left hand corner as you approach a state of ecstasy.

"The second image is determined by my thoughts. It shows the part of you that I can't see but which my tongue can feel. This image highlights what I am doing as opposed to what I am seeing. This image burns brightest because it is essentially the most intimate. Does that answer your question Ms Levene?"

"It is an able answer forcing my hand into my next move, freeing the shackles that clothing presents in such an instance. I…"

Vain cut her short.

"What you really need to know, Ms Levene, is that both images are held in bondage by a more powerful series of visual and mental images; images that illuminate the physical appearance of Tanya Vain and display a montage of devoted wife recollections, in addition to this face-value, visually inspired portrait".

"Well resisted Mr Vain. I congratulate you upon your loyalty. Good evening Greg".

Vain watched Levene glide back across the lawn to the Manor. There was something almost feline in her gait.

Gregory Vain had been tempted. He had resisted her advances - just.

FOUR

Gregory Vain walked down the drive of his residence in a determined fashion. His mind kept referencing the pivotal developments that had taken place in the last few days. His Memory-Camera kept illuminating the defeated Sandford-Everett, the ecstatic Denison and the sensuous Levene.

As he neared his house his thoughts turned to Tanya and the children. He was grateful for the ten-day respite because despite the love he had for the MC Project, it had a wasting capacity that rendered team members exhausted in quite a short time period. Vain, Tavini and Ko-Chai would receive understudy support once suitable individuals had been selected and trained but they were currently the only 'front line' team that the project could call upon. This front line demand meant that Vain's team was constantly in the spotlight and thus the MC Project extracted the proverbial pound of flesh from its three leading lights.

Whilst the ten day rest period represented a blessing, a 'serpent's kiss' factor sealed this arrangement, with the project members having to break the news of the impending two month separation that would follow this effective 'holiday'. Vain and Tanya had been split up before during the MC Project's research stages, but an eight week separation would represent a radical increase with regard to the amount of time the two were parted.

Vain felt sure that the strong bond he and Tanya shared would not be reduced by this lengthy separation period but he also felt that it increased her claim for 'right to know' factors surrounding his employment. As he opened the front door, he made the decision that he thought he would never make - to give Tanya an understanding of the 'basics' pertaining to his MC team's work.

He felt it was time to add a little colour, a little definition to the greyness that hung over his absences.

"Daddy, you're home!"

Rachel was usually the first member of Vain's family to register his presence when he returned from his MC business, and this occasion did not prove an exception. The girl proceeded to give him her legendary 'war hero returning' welcome with a melodramatic flood of emotion and then she started to fill her Daddy in with regard to the 'highs' he had missed in his absence.

"...and I lost my blazer so Mummy bought me a new one and so now I've got two 'cos I found my old one afterwards but Mummy's one is best and she says I can wear it on Tuesday because..."

"Slow down darling. You can tell me everything when I've got my coat off. Daddy's home for ten whole days so I can spend all my time with you, Gary and Mummy".

"Ten days with my Daddy, ten days with my Daddy..." chanted Rachel to a fictional tune she had composed on the spot.

"Only ten days this time, Greg?"

Tanya Vain made a svelte like descent of the staircase and tenderly started to cuddle both her husband and daughter.

She had been watching the ecstatic reunion from a vantage point on the first floor landing, and after she had let her daughter perform her usual welcome routine she decided to utilise her favourite method of greeting - the 'staircase glide'. The daughter's exuberance was a perfect foil to her mother's choreographed precision.

"Yo Tan - it's seemed an age. I guess the milkman's a permanent resident now eh?"

"It's only been a few days Greg, but yeah - it's been too long. Ten days sounds great initially but there's a catch love - I can see it in your eyes. Still, that can wait because Gary is hiding upstairs waiting for you to find him. He's doing his 'Omen' routine!

"I thought you hid that video, we've had Damien impersonations since you've been gone!"

Vain went upstairs to find that his son. Gary's greeting was one of mock attack, and Vain kicked himself for leaving his old horror video collection in a place where his kids could find them. Gary had performed his part well, combing his black hair forward in a style reminiscent of the Anti-Christ in the said film.

In the afternoon, Vain and his family went into London and had the 'family day out' that both he and Tanya worshipped. The Museum of the Moving Image thrilled the kids, McDonalds went down well in a party sort of fashion, and the shopping trip to Harrods sent all three of the Vain clan into raptures as 'Daddy' was always Mr Generous when selecting his presents. In the evening Vain settled the children down for the night and then he was alone with Tanya.

The Vains proceeded to make love with the spice of lust and this act honoured the intimacy shared between Tanya and Greg. Their lovemaking was never dull and Vain's absences heightened the mutual attraction shared by the couple.

In the warmth of post coital intimacy, Tanya chose to ascertain how long the inevitable separation would be following their ten-day 'holiday".

"Eight weeks Tan. Sorry, this one's kinda special, things are moving at lightening speed and yours truly is one of the leading lights".

"Eight bloody weeks, Greg. It's August love, not April. Are you fooling around here or what?"

"Sorry Tan, no joke I'm afraid. We're in the London area for three weeks and then the project is to be based in Chicago for a five week residence".

Tanya was rendered silent by the time period involved in the latest separation, and Gregory Vain felt that this was the right moment to reveal more about the MC Project.

"Okay Tan, you deserve to know more. I can't hide our work forever can I? The project work I undertake involves advancing the 'Memory' work I researched a few years ago. My team includes two other guys as well as myself, one a leading light in laser extraction and the other a genius with regard to digital conversion. We look inside the mind Tan, at the moment dead minds with visual platforms still intact".

"Platforms intact? Break it down Greg, for us lesser mortals!"

"Sorry Tan, yeah okay. By platforms I mean areas of the brain that store images - important images that we all keep - at least for a while. At the moment my team is calling up images from dead human minds!"

"Sorry Greg, but this sounds science fiction to me. Are you saying that a brain stores images after death?"

"Precisely. The brain is like a camera film in this context, and my team have the developing key for want of a better phrase".

"What about brain death and decomposition then Greg?"

"Both were seen as the end of the visual story in the past, love, but our work changes that, it knocks it into the past in terms of relevance. Yeah some parts of the brain rot - all of it in time, but other parts are impregnable remaining fresh and useful to my team for some days after death has been diagnosed. You see Tan, humans store HVs, visuals of significance in the area of the brain we are investigating, and our team can access them - call them up and even play them back!"

"Exciting but rather freaky, Greg. What do you want to achieve with all this?"

"Catch murderers for a start, darling. You see, sight *is* a camera".

If Tanya had been a little bit unsure of the relevance of Greg's project initially she now recognised a great validity in her husband's research work. Vain continued to explain general areas of his team's work, missing out firm names and locations. The one name Vain divulged was Julia Venison. He related the events surrounding her thirty-four minute HV screening and the circumstances leading up to Sandford-Everett's arrest, referencing him as 'the killer'. Vain decided to emphasise the organisational power surrounding the MC Project, as he was already feeling a bit uneasy with regard to what he had revealed thus far. He trusted Tanya fully as far as confidentiality was concerned, but despite this he felt impelled to dwell on implications surrounding security as he envisaged the dire consequences applicable to anyone who broke MC Project secrecy.

"You see, the MC Project involves the full range as far as security is concerned, Tan. We've got a British crew containing individuals from both the MOD and the CID.

"In addition to that, the project's ultimate power base is secured by the Yanks - the CIA to be exact. I also think that both MI5 and the FBI might know a thing or two with regard to the project, but those two organisations haven't been referenced to us as active parties - yet! We're well networked too, Tan, with regard to Legal systems and medical cover. The bottom line basically involves an Anglo-Americanised power base that is immense in terms of its collective strength.

"This power factor explains the 'shadowing' you've noticed on occasions. You see, the security blanket around the project deems nobody to be beyond its parameters of surveillance. Oh and one more thing, love, I suppose it is patently obvious how powerful our project is. If it got into the wrong hands, it could be abused - you see we're reinventing science here!"

"Will the wider world ever get to know about the project Greg, or is it going to stay hidden?"

"We've got to prove our work with more concrete successes than just the Venison demonstration, hence the two month absence, Tan. Once we've got more Venisons in the bag we will be better positioned to let the world know. There is another very important factor though, love. I can't say too much about it, but lets just say that whilst Venison was dead apart from her visual retention, our work is nearing a stage where the living mind will be able to be accessed - mindsight, not just physical sight recordings - we're talking thoughts here Tan, what your minds-eye sees!"

"Sinister Greg! What you did with Venison's visual retention was brilliant. If your MC work can put away bastards like her killer then you are doing wider society a great service, but if your work is approaching the stage where it reads living minds, all kinds of heavy negatives seem to surround it! I mean who would be tested? Why would they be tested? I mean, what we think isn't always what we'd do is it love? If a person's mindsight were played back, wouldn't a sick picture get shown on the screen on occasions? I'm sure I've had thoughts that aren't exactly morally perfect - What about you, Greg?"

"Yeah, we all think things that we'd never actually do but mindsight could still be useful to dip into. I mean we could use it on a medical level to help people with psychological neurosis".

"You're a very clever man with a kind heart but jeez, sometimes you can be Mr naive! I've got a funny feeling that a couple of those organisations you quoted earlier might find other uses for trapping a person's thoughts!"

"Well anyway Tan, at least now you know the reasons for all the secrecy and the unspecified periods of absence. I was in two minds whether to tell you about the project or not, but now I've actually related the basics to you I'm kinda relieved. I'm sorry you had to wait so damn long but I guess I was a bit scared about the consequences of such a revelation".

"Oh come on Greg, I'm not exactly Mrs. Gossip now am I! 'Consequences' is a heavy word though - any chance of firmer elaboration here, love?"

"Exactly what you were thinking earlier, Tan. You just mentioned about alterior motives surrounding some of the organisations controlling the project - the bottom line is power. These people don't want the world to know just yet and I'm sure they'd kill to preserve project secrecy".

Tanya and Gregory Vain continued to talk about the MC Project for an hour before both drifted off into a relatively calm sleep.

Vain had finally exorcised what had been hidden too long.

The ensuing nine days were greatly appreciated by the Vain family. Tanya initially felt more comfortable now that she knew some specifics pertaining to her husband's work. The family spent four days in Yorkshire at a Hotel, which was situated in a scenic rural location, and when they returned to their home they had several London based outings.

They spoke about the project on occasions, but Tanya didn't press to know any further in depth details until she was alone with Gregory Vain on the eve of his departure.

"We've had a brilliant ten days Greg, but one things been on my mind since you told me about the MC Project. What could happen to the kids if you were suspected of betraying the secrecy of the project?"

"The only way they'd know would be through you, Tan".

"Well I obviously wouldn't tell anyone about your work deliberately, but couldn't situations arise where information could be forced from you revealing your revelations to me? Once both physical sight memories and mindsight are further tested, isn't it feasible to argue that team members could be screened for their loyalty with regard to their secrecy, or lack of it as the case may be? You see, what we've discussed since you got home is firmly embedded in both our Memory-Cameras isn't it?"

"Yes, we've both stored a heavy number of heightened visuals and the respective sounds that went with them. I hope you're wrong about team member testing, but if that did take place love, I'm sure that even the guy who heads the CIA project involvement has let some project information slip.

"We're only human aren't we - they wouldn't touch any of us Tan - especially the kids.

"The kids know nothing. Nothing would show on their MCs, so what threat could they represent if they were tested?"

"I hope you're right Greg, because otherwise you just might have told me too much".

"That's a bit unfair, Tan. You frequently tried to ascertain details surrounding my work. When I finally tell you, you start insinuating I should have maintained the secrecy that you hated so much. Catch fucking 22 or what?"

"Sorry 'Saint Gregory', but your information just might have been a loaded gun mightn't it? Very nice of you to tell me and all that, but I'm fucking terrified about the possible consequences of what I now know! I've had ten days to mull over your work and all the connotations that go with it and it's left a bad taste – there are too many powerful organisations surrounding your project. Maybe you've messed around with science too much here, maybe murder's favourable to reading people's minds. I'm so fucking scared, Greg!"

Tanya Vain collapsed into Vain's arms sobbing like a frightened child. Vain managed to comfort her and she eventually slipped into an uneasy sleep. Vain didn't sleep until much later. He kept worrying about the pressure that had shown itself so overtly in his wife, and he wished he could reverse his decision to tell her of the MC Project.

He had never seen Tanya so scared in their marriage up to this point in time and her anxiety had made him wonder about any darker side lurking within the confines of the project's organisational ranks.

Tanya had stored her fears up, not wishing to spoil the family holiday they all had enjoyed and subsequently her fears were expelled in an outburst - with Vain getting the full extent of her anxiety.

Tomorrow Vain would start active work on his project again but he was returning with the curse of a man who had possibly said too much to the person who was dearest to him.

FIVE

"Welcome back, Vain".

The voice belonged to Leif Denison. Vain had just entered the underground London Designation that would be the project's residence for the next three weeks. He was quite surprised to encounter the project leader around the entrance area of the Designation. Denison usually remained out of sight until he addressed MC Project staff, but apart from ten security personnel he was the only front line presence apart from Vain in the said area. Vain had arrived an hour early, a factor consistent with his character since a young age. When he was a teenager he would arrive at football grounds as early as he could so he could build the atmosphere to a level where his enjoyment of the match was embellished by watching the stadium gradually fill and hearing the crowd noise increase in volume. As an adult Vain maintained this character trait, and he preferred to be one of the first project members to assemble in the various Designations used for their work. After Denison's greeting he ushered Vain away from the entrance area to a side room. He had some pressing news for Vain's three-man team.

"I'm dispensing with the usual formal re-assembly greeting today Greg. You see our first specimen for want of a better word has beaten the project team to our Designation. The corpse is fresh - Mason intercepted it from local police at 05:02 this morning in the Isle of Dogs area. She's a bit on the messy side with severe head injuries. I don't know if the parts of the brain you need will be affected or not, but you're the expert there Greg, and I'm damn sure you'll try your utmost to release some HVs. It's a bonus Greg, giving us an opportunity to carry out MC work straight away!"

Vain followed Denison down to the mortuary, and as they arrived Mason extended his usual subdued welcome. This team member only seemed to come alive with regard to social skills when he was describing 'causes of death' details to team members. The majority of the MC team found the irony in this personality transition quite humorous. A few didn't find it that amusing feeling that Mason was almost 'turned on' by corpses. Tavini had labelled the man 'Mr Nechro' and when the MC team were together this was the name he utilised for Mason. Ko-Chai was a bit more reserved with regard to finding the applicable humour in Tavini's description but he had to admit that a comic irony did exist when a man displayed most life-force when describing death!

"Well gentlemen, I hope the good breakfast I trust you had won't make a reappearance after witnessing this victim! I don't know her name or age but have settled for 'Charlotte' for initial categorisation purposes. I think she's young - 16 or 17 but as you'll see in a second it's really quite difficult to be precise at this point in time! I think death did her a favour here - she was a heroin addict - hardly any blood left in her left forearm. Her veins were like a sponge through repetitive injections!"

Mason opened the ice compartment that contained Charlotte, and both men were initially taken aback by the guignol sight that greeted them. The diagnosis began.

"As you can see, Charlotte had a particularly painful death. The epidermal structure of the skin has been removed to a ratio of about forty percent. Large chunks of flesh have been removed from both facial cheeks, the small of the back, the breasts and the stomach. The tongue and lower lip are both missing and the left eye has been removed with some force - almost like a drill in its intensity! The hair is matted with blood - I should say her own - about two pints worth. Parts of her lower intestine have disappeared and one kidney has also been extracted. The…"

Vain cut in.

"What the fuck did this to her?"

"Dogs, loads of them. Big dogs, but not animals that were well cared for. Their teeth left scum all over her body. She was bitten with such ferocity in the small of her back that parts of domestic food garbage were sunk into her spinal cord! The teeth that ripped her apart left their calling card all right".

After he was sure he had answered Vain's question with enough in-depth precision, Mason continued. He carried on detailing the savagery of the attack, paying particular attention to the more macabre details.

Leif Denison directed another question at Mason.

"A druggie getting wasted by stray packs - happens every day in the States, and I'm damn sure it happens here too. Are you sure we're looking at murder here Mason - seems like a shut case - young girl leaves home, falls on bad times, does drugs, dies - end of story, mate".

Mason was rather indignant at this second interruption regardless of the powerful source that made it.

"My team have intercepted twenty-odd corpses from areas of deprivation in the last couple of months.

"In terms of product relevance we scored blanks.

"We got au fait with what a junkie's body ends up looking like and early this morning I thought, 'here we go again'. This one's different though. As luck would have it and coincidence for that matter, I think Charlotte can help us! Even for a girl who liked injections so much I feel a strychnine injection to the back of the neck implies the presence of another - a murderer. The dogs just finished her off and had their junk food. She was murdered - you've got your required murder victim Mr Denison. What she has held visually will be in your team's hands.

"Mr Vain, Are Mr Ko-Chai and Mr Tavini in residence yet?"

"They weren't when I met Mr Denison but I expect they are here now. Are you going to clean her up a bit Mason? Ko-Chai's stomach is not exactly impregnable you know!"

"How can you clean up a rag doll Mr Vain? I'll do my best to fill in the blanks so to speak".

Vain met both Ko-Chai and Tavini together. They had met close to where Vain had encountered Denison. After exchanging greetings Tavini took the lead, saying what both he and Ko-Chai thought.

"You look like you've seen a ghost man. There's pale and beautiful and she's always the ultimate in female, and then there's you Greg - pale and fucked. Have you spent your ten days in Chernobyl, buddy?"

Ko-Chai looked a bit embarrassed by Tavini's dark humour but Vain took it in good faith, realising it was just part of Tavini's showmanship. He broke the news of the imminent duty awaiting the MC team.

"If you thought we might get a gentle run in to our explorations in this Designation fellas, I've got some interesting news for you.

55

"I've seen our next corpse - she's here, and take it from me, she isn't exactly a pretty picture!

"I know that you found Julia Venison's wounds slightly graphic Mishimo, but in comparison, 'Charlotte', as Mason has christened her, is a 'Jack the Ripper' construction!"

Mishimo Ko-Chai physically withdrew after Vain's words.

He was not squeamish when Memory-Camera extraction work was actually being undertaken, but the build up to the explorations often caused him to be physically sick. After his convulsions he was fine and this was the reason Vain had utilised a melodramatic victim description.

Vain knew that he had to adhere to this 'cruel to be kind' formula on occasions as far as Ko-Chai's MC preparation was concerned. Everyone benefited from a relaxed Ko-Chai, none more so than the man himself. Ko-Chai asked to be excused to visit a toilet, which was in close proximity to their location.

The three MC team members proceeded to the exploration area. The said area was more cramped than the 'grand scale' demonstration arena in Designation B where Venison's HVs had been recovered, but there wouldn't be a sizeable audience on this occasion like there had been on the seminal exploration. As the MC team entered the exploration area Vain was quite surprised to notice that only four MC personnel were ready to view any HV's Charlotte had built. The four in question represented project power to an optimum level though, numbering Denison, Levene, Voight and a tall powerful looking white-haired gentleman who was unfamiliar to Vain's team.

Levene welcomed the three team-members and Vain was sure that her eyes hung on to his for a fraction longer than the gaze one would associate with a fellow professional. She introduced the white-haired gentleman who was unfamiliar to the team members.

"Gentleman - please meet Mr Fray of the FBI.

"He has been recruited into our project ranks with direct responsibility to Mr Denison. He has parity responsibility with regard to myself".

The silver-haired gentleman smiled in greeting the MC team but it was a cold gesture, as his eyes didn't echo the warmth of his upturned mouth, remaining cold and piercing in their intensity. His voice was very muted in tone, almost gentle in comparison to the tone Vain had expected to emanate from this man.

"I salute you, gentlemen. Having seen the Venison demonstration second hand and hearing about the subsequent arrest method of Sandford-Everett, it is a pleasure to be involved with the leading edge nature of your scientific explorations. My chief role will involve global security and communications. Whilst Mr Voight performs his internal security role with admirable precision, I will be involved with the outside world, and when the time is right I will be co-ordinating the Global revelation pertaining to our project. I wish you luck with regard to your imminent exploration".

After thanking Fray for his complimentary words the MC team went into action.

Mason had tidied up the victim considerably, even inserting a temporary padding to fill the vacant recesses of the facial cheek area. Vain inserted the vault-splicer, and after Ko-Chai had set up his laser extraction equipment, Tavini installed the digital conversion devices that translated the visual signals encoded by the vault-splicer.

The laser screen became the dominant focus for the four project members in attendance. The images that appeared on the screen were understandable, if a little grainy in their texture.

Charlotte's Memory-Camera was rather unstable in its operation. The images alternated between panning sequences of inner city ruins and almost abstract visuals that involved the Memory-Camera looking repeatedly upwards towards the sky. It soon became apparent that Charlotte's HV retention was going to be one of discord in comparison to the flowing visuals that were a feature of the prototype demonstration.

The visuals involved an intermittent delivery being broken with a black screen resolution on frequent occasions. Charlotte's Memory-Camera had obviously been effected by her heroin intake, and when the screen count showed the storage counter had reached 5 minutes of HV's, the sky staring preoccupation started to take a dominance that made the team members wonder if they were going to unlock any relevance to help them with the murder of the young girl. The accompanying sounds to the visuals were not significant either, with snatches of distant traffic and the comparative ambience of birdsong being the only two dominant sounds to emerge from the girl's MC. Tavini voiced what the team were collectively thinking, albeit in his own maverick style.

"Is this girl playing for real or what? If these are HVs then I'm Queen Anne fellas. I know heroin fucks you up, but this is ridiculous!"

More irrelevant visuals appeared on the screen and then the team were rewarded with an image of clarity that disrupted the pastiche of sky gazing.

The man approached Charlotte's location, with determined steps that implied he had a firm purpose in mind. Charlotte's Memory-Camera scanned him in good detail, and his screen portrait illuminated a man of average height with fair hair and dark green eyes. He wore faded jeans and a casual black shirt. His words illuminated a psyche that was at odds with his innocuous appearance.

"Hi Leah, how's things? Look I'm going to give it to you straight babes. Your clients are pissed off - two years ago you were their golden girl but you know how times change love, don't you?

"You see, Michelle and Becky are in demand right now and people are queuing for 'em. We're small right now love, there's little money and we've gotta..."

The screen returned to darkness. Tavini couldn't contain his frustration."

"Oh come on girl, for fuck's sake. Don't black out on us now - tell your story girl - damn you!"

Ko-Chai felt impelled to interject with a more pragmatic explanation with regard to the lapse of images.

"She may have died, David. Your project enthusiasm is well regarded by one and all, but at times you seem to forget moral niceties in your treatment of others".

"Get real Mishimo man, we'll all weep for her later. This girl was finally coming up trumps with..."

The girl's HVs returned to the screen and the mans voice was still evident.

"Hey stay with me now, Leah. Come on, I've got you a little special something to let you know how much you really mean to me and the guys!"

Leah's voice was the next sound to be heard with a fixed HV of the man accompanying its rendition.

"You gotta still need me, Dave - you simply gotta. I mean I know I'm still clean. Yeah I need my scag but I'll cut down Dave, honest I will - you've gotta believe me Dave, once I'm back man, I'll stay golden - no I'll be even better Dave.

"I'll do fives man, and learn to keep it all down man - all down. Just give me some scut end or a nub because I'm your girl Dave - I wander man, but I'm your girl".

"Leah you're always my golden one and to prove it I brought you something special. I'm just going to give you a little taster in the back of your neck love. It's liquid ice - a new kind of paradise. Now just lie back and relax. I owe you a holiday - yes you're still my golden one".

The screen temporarily returned to darkness and then Leah's HV's returned.

"What you doing, Dave? Who are they, man?"

"Just lie back, Leah. I told you it was good stuff. These are two of my mates - Eddie and Felix".

"Why are they putting them bones down near me, Dave. They're fucking scummy man. Where are they from - London fucking zoo?"

"Relax, Leah honey. The lads are just feeding a couple of my doggies for me. You can feed 'em if you like, they'll be here soon - nice little doggies".

"Okay Dave...see I love dogs...see I used to..."

The images left the screen and the team hoped they wouldn't return, as they had seen Leah's corpse and could anticipate the HV outcome if she died at the hands of the dogs before the strychnine could finish her off. Despite this realisation they were still taken aback when the next slightly diminished HV did hit the screen.

Less than three feet away from the parameters of Leah's Memory-Camera stood a large dog, bedraggled but powerful in it's front quarters none the less. The dog was salivating with it's top lip curled and blood was splattered around it's mouth region. The HV was made particularly guignol as traces of a flesh like substance were rapidly being devoured by the said animal, and on the strands of the flesh in question hung an eye - a human eye! The morsel disappeared down the beast's throat.

Leah had regained consciousness after the dog had gouged her eye from her!

The growling of the dog which had been a consistent acoustic commentary was suddenly drowned out by a scream which reverberated around the exploration area, such was it's guttural magnitude. Leah's final words built her epitaph.

"No - Jesus God - no. Dave I need you. Dave I need you - help me - my fucking eye - no!"

The screen showed more dogs running toward Leah's spatial area. The camera then died visually, but the sounds of screaming and canine growling continued for a period of eleven seconds. It was the longest eleven seconds Gregory Vain had ever experienced, and when the girl was finally 'counted out' in twenty-seven minutes and eight seconds, all present uttered an audible sigh of relief. Case two had delivered the required murderer, but the team wished that the strychnine could have taken the girl before the victim had witnessed Dave's method of 'cover up". Mason rewound the gathered images. He preferred his choice of name for the victim. To him she was more of a 'Charlotte' than a 'Leah". The team members thought it bizarre that the man was bemoaning the unsuitability of her real name after the horror pertaining to the images they had just witnessed. Mason was weird in the eyes of most MC team members. As the team recovered, Vain made sure that the case study reference card was changed to reveal the young girl's real name and not Mason's choice.

Denison and Fray left the Demonstration area with the MC team, and all five entered a side room to discuss what had been visually extracted.

Denison directed his initial comments to his new FBI recruit.

"So there you have it, Vance. This show wasn't quite as polished as the Venison display but this girl was on the bottom rung - a junkie - and we still dragged enough visual information out of her mind to be able to operate the arrest method I told you about! You see what she gave us, Vance?

"We know the guy's first name, his face and we know two of his acquaintances by sight. The guy's operating base must be close to where Leah's corpse was found. A primed arrest squad will find him in no time".

"Which line are we going to sink him with, Leif?"

"No need for a line this time Vance. This guy won't have the type of legal back up Everett had. It will be a quick fire arrest and bang up, with the fucker DNA'd the following morning. He'll have his one phone call and our crew are going to be on the other end! Getting a confession out of this bastard is going to be a breeze, and we'll have more than enough matched up evidence when we finally hand him over to non-project security staff. What did you think of the horror film anyway?"

"When the screen resolution dipped a bit, I first thought it was a technical shortcoming. Then I saw the eye! I mean that's the stuff of nightmares guys - it firmly shatters that 'man's best friend' crap! If the visuals had carried on with the sound near the end that would have been one sick showcase - it would have been like we were getting mauled guys with the dogs right on top of us! Pretty gruesome Mr Denison, but compulsive viewing - in a funny way I didn't want it to stop! I mean this is the ultimate scientific discovery fellas!"

Denison then released the MC team and they headed off to a recreational area within the

Designation. Tavini was particularly impressed with the choice of decor prevalent in the expansive relaxation lounge, and as he proceeded to extol the virtues of the Art Nouveau style trappings. Tavini was composed of almost schizophrenic character traits.

On the one hand he was the brash larger than life American, and yet occasionally he displayed a cultural sensitivity that was quite introverted in its application. It was when Tavini displayed this more reserved character facet that he and Ko-Chai were closest. As the two debated the merits of the lounge's colour scheme, Vain was left to reflect on what had been another successful MC exploration. He was deep in thought when Marcia Levene arrived on the scene.

"A drink Greg. Well done - two in the bag already! I was wondering if you wanted to see the garden?"

"Cheers for the drink Marcia. The garden? We're underground here, and I always thought Denison operated a twenty four hour 'stay down' curfew when we have to work in one of the underground Designations!"

"Who said anything about breaking the curfew, Greg? Come with me.

"This Designation was initially earmarked as a fall-out protection venue in the event of a nuclear holocaust, and it was set to house the elite. Obviously they have newer sites for that purpose now, and so our project freed up this location for our research.

"The good thing about this Designation as far as relaxation is concerned involves what was left behind, Greg. Come and see my micro-paradise!"

Levene ushered Vain away from the relaxation area and he proceeded to follow her down several flights of stairs. At the bottom of the last flight Levene quickened her gait, eventually stopping in close proximity to a large black panelled area which had widened considerably in comparison to the narrow corridor they had previously been walking through. She turned to Vain and with an impish look made the following comment.

"Well Greg - time for a surprise!"

Levene inserted an identity card into a decoding panel on one of the wall sections. The applicable section withdrew, receding downwards into the floor. What was revealed seemed like a visual Arcadia - especially being placed in the confines of such a claustrophobic Designation.

Marcia Levene had not been melodramatic with her 'micro-paradise' description. Her words had been a faithful pragmatic definition. The other side of the wall had revealed an ornate garden – about an acre in size. Vegetation from a variety of climates grew side by side with a compatibility that denied nature in terms of geographical location. The bias prevalent in the creator of this aesthetic construction involved a predomination of plants from tropical regions, and yet despite this, sections of a 'quintessential' England were in evidence on occasions. A small strip of dark green lawn was the most noticeable section of 'little England'. An artificial brook meandered through the garden and a selection of classical statues were located along the sides of the marble pathways which marked the boundaries of Levene's paradise. Vain was surprised at the scale of the garden complex. Trees of considerable height stretched upward to the complex ceiling and a rain forest type foliage was the most consistent presence in relation to the wide spectrum of the plant life. The temperature was artificially regulated and although the tropical vegetation dictated that the level of heat reflected tropical climes foremost, the overall environment was balanced to a degree of comparative comfort. Levene paid testimony to her paradise.

"Pretty therapeutic isn't it, Greg? When our project decided to take over ownership of this Designation, one of the salient reasons concerned this aesthetic complex. The prevailing line of opinion felt that in an underground locale, staff would need outlets.

"The curfews impinge upon a person's liberties and they could subsequently tarnish one's ability to perform efficiently. It was felt that we should retain this complex, as it added an ambient ingredient to an otherwise claustrophobic Designation. The nature of the design is interesting too, Greg. You see a lot of the respective flora and fauna isn't actually real, being composed of a variety of plastic-based materials. A hybrid creation like this one couldn't possibly survive in our 'real' world and so whilst the tropical elements are largely natural, the majority of the vegetation from cooler geographical regions is artificially constructed".

"Surely the lawn's real isn't it, Marcia?"

"Sorry Greg - your little slice of England has been artificially installed on sporting surfaces for years!"

"How come you know so much detail Marcia, so much surrounding the minutiae of the complex?"

"I make it my business to look deeply into things that I am likely to have frequent contact with, whether my focus is a place or a person. The complex was easy to examine - all I had to do was ask Leif the specifics pertaining to the design. He's a proud man Greg, proud of every area surrounding his project, and it may surprise you to know that there's a softer side to him, one that involves a man who comes into his own when visual aesthetics are the applicable subject being discussed".

The pair entered the garden area and after a short period of contemplative silence Levene directed a more personal question to Vain.

"Tell me about your family, Gregory".

"I thought team members weren't meant to enter into dialogue surrounding their dependants, Marcia?"

"We're human Greg, aren't we?

"Those sorts of rules are token issues that surround any security-based project. Let's melt the ice of formality".

Vain proceeded to tell Levene about his wife and children before returning the question to his CIA colleague.

"What about you Marcia? Is there a Mr Levene, or any children?"

"Neither Greg. I'm married to our project - for want of a better phrase. Don't get me wrong, I haven't lived in a life of celibacy, and I don't hate men or anything weird like that. Let's just say that my sights are set on career horizons right now. I survive predominantly through fantasy as far as incarnated relationships go - although I've had one night 'no questions asked' flings with a few twenty-something fellas back home in Seattle. You're a good fuck Greg - at least in my mind!

"Don't worry 'once bitten, twice shy' Mr Vain, I'm not going to make that mistake again!"

Vain was quite taken aback by the frank nature of Levene's reply, and to an extent his guard was down. This showed itself in Vain's riposte.

"Maybe I've fucked you from afar as well!"

His words suffered from a slightly hurried execution but their intent was fully registered by Levene's eyes, even though the sentence had been uttered almost subconsciously.

The pair continued to walk around the garden in a good-natured silence. Neither felt embarrassment in relation to their short verbal exchange, and each felt as if their proverbial cards had been put on the table with regard to the type of attraction the two had for each other. As the couple retraced their steps, Levene once again took the lead with regard to dialogue.

"Well Greg maybe we'll fuck in closer proximity one day!"

"A couple of weeks ago I would have said something similar to what I said when I encountered you on the lawn at Designation B, now I'm not so sure. Thanks for showing me paradise - I'll be seeing you Marcia".

The next two weeks seemed to pass relatively quickly for Vain and his team. Four other victims were forthcoming, and each one had stored enough heightened visuals to enable quick arrest procedures to take place. Whilst the MC team were pleased with the results of their work, they had in effect seen two extremes of HV quality in the first two victims that they had examined, and thus whilst they still enjoyed the challenge of locating Memory-Camera footage, their sense of awe couldn't recapture the pique of the excitement generated by the first two demonstrations.

The MC team had undertaken vault - extension research in the time between the arrival of suitable corpses and this had enabled understudy involvement to take place. The three understudies would become an effective fringe team after the Chicago based MC testing, but they were initially given the opportunity to further their areas of specialism in the London Designation.

In the idle hours between victim explorations and research, relaxation or sleep became the order of the day. The respite time was particularly conducive for social bonding surrounding both MC teams, and this factor pleased Denison immensely.

The bonding period gave Vain the chance to assess the two fringe team members who shadowed

Ko-Chai and Tavini - Hannah Nichol and Marco Sant respectively.

Diana Fearston, Vain's understudy, had proved extremely popular with all three 'first' team members.

The two comparative newcomers had to earn their colours as far as scientific ability and congeniality were concerned. Both fringe team members fitted in well with Vain's front-line MC team and whilst neither Nichol nor Sant had a personality as warm as Fearston's, they both passed the unofficial character tests prevalent in the minds of the main MC team.

Ko-Chai and Tavini both came into their own with regard to social bonding - albeit in quite different ways. Tavini challenged Sant, his understudy, to a variety of sporting based activities, which were possible in their underground Designation, and Ko-Chai built a cultural bond with Miss Nichol, sharing a communal interest with regard to architecture. This left Vain with time to further the research that he and Fearston were undertaking concerning the membrane structure that separated the main MC vault from it's extension.

When Vain had occasion to relax he would visit Levene's garden or one of the many relaxation sections of the complex. He spent little time in his personal quarters beyond the four hours he allowed himself for sleep. He and Levene had rare conversational exchanges but they no longer had the guarded intimacy they experienced when Vain was initially shown the garden. Vain thought of Levene quite often during their 'incarceration' and while part of him felt guilty for this mental infidelity, another part of him longed to make incarnate the desire that they both had for each other.

The time spent in the London Designation was proving very fruitful until three days before their departure date to Chicago.

Tavini broke the news that Vain had always inwardly dreaded.

"Yo Greg, brace yourself man, our room 101 has just arrived".

"You what Dave?"

"Another victim mate, but he's a minor so I guess things are going to be a bit tougher with regard to the exploration. I know you and Mishimo have kids - you've both let that slip, and whilst I haven't got any it doesn't mean I don't feel, you know".

Tavini was unusually ruffled by the fact that the next victim was a minor. When Tavini reduced his streak of showmanship it immediately heightened the significance of the applicable area in focus. Vain had been inwardly devastated by the news that Tavini broke to him. In the past his research had involved experiments on minors but none had been murdered, and Vain could tell by Tavini's face that murder was a likely ingredient in this instance. He spoke as naturally as he could.

"How old, Dave?"

"Seven years, man - seven fucking years old!"

"Cause of death?"

"Strangulation. At least that's what Mr Nechro reckons but there's a big problem here, Greg. The boy was only partially sighted and I guess the HV's are going to suffer. Leah's Memory-Camera was a bit patchy to say the least but now we've got one that's going to be well and truly fucked up!"

"Oh Christ. Let's go and see Mason and get all the cause of death details, David. If he gets all ghoulish with the description this time, you may have to hold me back mate, because you're right, this is our room 101 all right!"

Mason preserved a respectful decorum when he detailed the nature of the child's death.

If he had become theatrically intense when he described Leah's death, his chosen method on this occasion favoured the reserved dignity that the MC team had hoped for.

Tavini had been correct with regard to Mason's initial diagnosis concerning the child's death, and the latter spent a long time reviewing the likely effect that partial sight could have on the exploration. Vain directed a question to Mason.

"This lad looks well cared for, Mr Mason. Our first six victims were either adults or individuals who were isolated from their immediate families and so project staff could intercept the corpses quite easily. Surely we can't hold this child for long. I mean, there's going to be a community up in arms over the murder of a seven year old, isn't there?"

"Yes Mr Vain, that would normally be the case, but Christopher went to a special school in Harrow, North London - a school providing care and education for partially sighted children. His parents both work in Namibia and whilst they have now been informed of the child's death, we have been given the transit time Mr Vain. Both parents will be back in this country in thirty-six hours and our work can take place long before this deadline. We will be able to have the case wrapped when we hand the lad back to regular Law enforcement officers tomorrow morning".

Unfortunately Mason was tempting fate on this occasion. Up until this point the MC Project explorations had always delivered a guilty party. The Memory-Camera work had consistently extrapolated images and sounds, which enabled convictions with ease. When the guilty were handed over to non-enlightened conventional security staff, the project 'plants' within these areas played the DNA card and thus the project's blanket security was maintained.

The immediacy surrounding MC explorations built a collective confidence and MC Project staff had thus become almost blasé with regard to the apparent infallibility surrounding their work.

Mason had warned the team that the applicable twenty percent sight factor would disrupt the usual quality surrounding visual flow, but even he couldn't have anticipated the HV's that ensued.

Christopher's Memory-Camera had spoken a visual language that only he could understand - a beautiful language that was akin to the 'northern lights' without any discernible images. The HVs were almost ambient, with blue and purple hues entwining over a base colour of silver. Until the actual exploration, Tavini had maintained that sound would assist the team if the visuals were unhelpful, but the team were to be thwarted here as well because the victim had abridged his own sound - a sound to echo the visuals that were on the screen. Christopher gave the MC team nothing to build a profile of his murderer. How he encoded his visual retention could have been linked to his partial sight, but his acoustic composition was beyond comprehension. The sounds were slightly reminiscent of the sonar calling made by whales although nothing could be linked to indicate pain or fear. As the screen eventually returned to blackness, the MC team had realised that Christopher had called the shots with regard to the screening. He had retreated into his own visual world in the build up to his murder, and his ability to control both of his senses made the team feel humble in comparison.

When the Global revelations of the MC Project takes place in the future, Christopher will have a lot to say with regard to psychological and medical practice.

His MC storage would pioneer subsequent research and in that respect, he would not die.

Christopher's murder would have to be solved by conventional investigation methods and this factor served as a reminder to the team - that their work was brilliant and leading edge in it's nature but it did have a fallibility to it. As Vain's team reviewed the exploration, Mishimo Ko-Chai seemed almost pleased by what had been witnessed - what could not be explained.

"Well my boss-man and David, I guess this young boy has taught us a thing or two! We assumed that sound was just automatically linked through the same environment, as a back up to the dominant visual register. We were wrong, my friends - we were correct up until now - yes, but Christopher has added a new dimension to our explorations. This child 'coloured' over his partial sight capabilities blocking out what he didn't want to confront, and what's more he uses sound in the same fashion. He was found in a park in North London and yet what do we get - whale sounds or something similar! Don't you see how significant our findings are here - a boy with severe sight problems is capable of controlling laser type images to block out what he doesn't want to see, and in addition to that, he changes sound to probably block out what he doesn't want to hear. Christopher may have had some visual disability but his sensory capabilities were far more advanced than those with A1 sight. This boy was a real find, a prodigy. Surely his capabilities come from a higher source. I'm sad the child's dead but I feel enlightened, rejuvenated even refreshed!"

Tavini proceeded to play down Ko-Chai's excited exclamations.

"I'm pleased to hear of your spiritual experience Mishimo, but we can't really gloss over failure can we? I mean we fucking lost here, guys. This boy gave us a show for sure - a real trip, but the arrest squad are going to be just a bit hard pushed to make any sense of what we saw. Who are they going to look for here - a bunch of fucking killer-whales?"

Ko-Chai was angered by Tavini's narrow-minded approach and he appealed to Vain to validate the scientific relevance of what they had witnessed.

"You tell him, Gregory. Our work involves a wide spectrum of scientific research doesn't it?"

"Well fellas, you know I don't usually like to sit on the fence, but this time I've got to. Yes Mishimo, our project does embrace scientific areas that transcend our usual MC findings and yes, Christopher illuminated some far-reaching differences with regard to the type of visual storage we've uncovered so far. However, like Dave I feel a bit disappointed with regard to the initial use we can make of what we saw and heard. You see, part of the success surrounding the MC Project involves the pace at which arrests can unfold. The conventional forensic DNA gang are going to solve this one. Yeah Dave, we lost on that count".

"Short term thinking for you, Gregory. I am surprised. I trust that a disabled victim has the same rights to a quick MC service as an able bodied victim?"

"Of course they do Mishimo, but you're going a bit over the top here, my friend! We've got Mr Denison assessing our every move, noting down our successes with a keen eye. He's a man who prefers to deal with clear results and right now, with the clock governing our every move, we are encouraged to think like him. When we break our MC findings to a global audience, we are going to need as many direct hits as possible. Christopher's MC show could have a Achilles heels here.

"His images don't represent visuals we are familiar with and some quarters could imply they are manufactured. To a level Christopher's visuals could be self defeating to a wider audience. At a later date we could utilise them but initially, they would just add a greyness to our achievements if we accessed them along with our clear cut successes".

"Look Mishimo-man - the world's going to really kick most of our findings but today's HVs could fuck things up quite a bit you know!"

"Your language seems to have deteriorated of late David, quite limited in its expletive reliance".

"Stop, my heart bleeds, man!"

Tavini and Ko-Chai continued to verbally spar with each other. The line between their differing viewpoints and direct insult was occasionally blurred, and Vain felt that this occasion marked the clearest instance of a major division between the two. The MC Project itself was the factor which kept Tavini's rampant ego in check and it also stopped Ko-Chai reacting to the excesses prevalent in the taunts of the American.

Vain had felt more affinity with Tavini's line of argument on this occasion, but he was worried about the thin ice that underpinned communication between the two.

The MC team had another successful exploration before departing for Chicago, and whilst this ensured that the project staff travelled on a winning streak, Ko-Chai seemed distant, dwelling in his own private world.

Vain hoped that Chicago would re-strengthen the bonding between his team although the city of gangster culture found them housed in one of the most uncomfortable Designations - an ill-lit structure which was underground once again but without any aesthetic sections this time.

Before the MC Project took control of Designation J, it had housed some of Chicago's criminally insane, and this factor seemed to echo the overall feel of the venue. The Memory-Camera work carried out in London had been very auspicious, with the exception of the blank drawn concerning Christopher's HV delivery. Chicago subsequently had quite a hard act to follow with regard to successful MC completions.

SIX

The 'windy city' would provide the project base for the next five weeks and the MC team awaited their incarceration in Designation J. For the initial two days all project staff would enjoy a rest period a hundred miles north of Chicago in a country retreat owned by the project. This relaxation had a two-fold purpose. Initially it was included so that all the project members who had partaken in the London based explorations could unwind in the grounds of the said venue. A further reason concerned the mental preparation that was needed with regard to the second curfew that would be forthcoming. Curfews in outside Designations, that offered the chance to walk around the parameters of the physical structure housing the MC Project, enabled team members to temporarily escape the claustrophobic hold prevalent in the underground venues. Two underground placements so close together marked the longest period of subterranean curfew that the project staff would have collectively experienced. This factor fully tested the resolve of the team, and morale would have to remain of an optimum level in order to preserve the good working relations synonymous with the various sections undertaking MC operations.

Mishimo Ko-Chai had found the rest period quite useful as his mind was still recalling the scientific complexities witnessed by the team in Christopher's exploration. Indeed, he had found it difficult to concentrate on other issues and he still harboured some resentment toward Tavini for the American's dismissive polemic.

Ko-Chai took advantage of the pleasant gardens that were a highlight of the team's rural retreat and when he was walking through the grounds on the second day, he encountered Levene.

He had been trying to organise this type of encounter for some time but he had sensed that this project member preferred to bear him at a distance. Levene spoke first.

"Mr Ko-Chai, are you enjoying the calm before the storm?"

"Very much so, Ms Levene. It gives me time to think - to consolidate. We are racing ahead so quickly that we seem to pass by anything that isn't dealing in the same visual language as the MC demonstrations, which lead directly to quick-fire arrests. I am a scientist, Ms Levene and want to look at the fuller parameters of our research".

"You're still upset by our decision to stall research into Christopher's visual condition aren't you, Mr Ko-Chai?"

"Yes".

"Whilst I share some of your concern, I feel impelled to agree with the decision Leif made - to proceed onward in our hunt for more corpses that help stockpile our success ratio. I agree that our work foundered with regard to an individual with a twenty percent sight factor but what the hell could anyone expect? We can't live in the past Mishimo, we've got to work for the many, not get held up by the few!"

"Your point seems to be the prevailing position doesn't it, Ms Levene? I understand that you are likely to follow that thinking. As the highest ranking female on the MC team your hands are tied to an extent, but are you as project loyal in other areas or does your libido impede your loyalty?"

"Very direct, Mr Ko-Chai. Can you elaborate on your libido reference or must I draw my own conclusions? Either way, the remark seems right over the line in terms of the decency expected from MC team members. Can you please be more explicit with regard to your intended meaning?"

"Gladly, Ms Levene. I feel that your attraction for Gregory has become so overt that some project staff have started to speculate on your relationship, building their own conclusions in the process. It is most important that you don't distract Mr Vain's concentration, as he is still the linchpin on which our successes hang. He is also married Ms Levene - married!"

"You can stuff your moral Puritanism up your Korean arse, Mr Ko-Chai. Greg and I have a professional relationship and your inferences are ludicrous! Old men often confuse social niceties with foreplay don't they, Mr Ko-Chai - it's their way of still getting it up! Keep out of things which don't concern you, Mishimo".

Although Ko-Chai was close to the mark with regard to the truth, he had lost the ensuing verbal battle with Levene.

As Levene walked away, he was left to muse over his last few days. He felt strongly that Levene was making sexual overtures to Vain and he would still like to widen the project's research scope, but he had crossed swords with some powerful team members in the process of making his feelings known. He decided that a low profile was the favoured course of action for the next few days. The MC team was transported to Designation J later that evening. Mr Fray undertook the welcome speech to project staff and he revealed that seven corpses had already been received earlier that evening after a gang fight disturbance. The scale of the Chicago research was going to up the quantity considerably with regard to the flow of suitable research material, and project members would be able to select a wide range of corpses to carry out explorations upon. Age and gender would be the two main criteria that determined selection. Mason and Vain's team would be in action for the majority of the five week haul, and whilst all four of the individuals in question were daunted by the workload awaiting them, they also realised that this intensive period would be the best possible type of training for their respective understudies.

After Chicago, two front line teams would be in readiness to undertake the explorations and this factor would make the workload more palatable. The initial exploration was to be implemented at 03:00 the following morning, and Denison had decided to let Vain's team select the corpse that they would work upon. Selection would take place at midnight and Mason would brief Vain's team about the relevant causes of death. It was envisaged that the body count would rise quite dramatically in the hours leading up to the midnight selection, and thus Vain's team were expecting images, which would be macabre on occasions.

In the period leading up to the selection, Vain's team walked through Designation J and assessed its potential as far as exploration space was concerned. They also looked at the relaxation areas, hoping to find therapeutic inclusions similar to the last Designation they had been based in. The team were disappointed with regard to both areas.

Designation J bore the hallmarks of the depressed South Side area in which it was situated.

It was an underground structure that echoed the vulgarity of the prefab housing projects above it.

This Designation was ill lit, dirty and spatially cramped. A concrete fixation meant that the decor was sparse and 60s minimalist. In effect this structure was the kitsch of the Designations used by the MC team. Tavini encapsulated the team's feelings with regard to their new base.

"What a fucking hellhole to end up in, guys!

"I apologise that my country constructed shit like this".

The team undertook some MC vault-extension research after they had viewed the Designation, and then they retired to their respective sleeping quarters to rest before the midnight liaison with Mason.

Mason was waiting outside the area that housed the corpses. He looked rather ominous, dressed in black and appearing more gaunt than usual. He spoke with his usual succinct precision.

"Good evening gentlemen, we've had some more deliveries - in fact Chicago's spoiled you! She doesn't usually throw up nineteen corpses in less than twenty four hours, but the glorious South Side gang territories and a couple of RTA's have helped boost the overall body-count to a figure way beyond the average quota on this occasion. It isn't clear yet whether any of the RTA's involved murder but our salvage squads secured them just in case. I'm afraid that one of the RTA victims won't be able to help you at all - an eighteen-wheeler has squashed his head to pulp. Unfortunately one side of wheels literally rolled over his body from nipple height upwards, so you can imagine what he looks like.

"The salvage squad that brought him in were on their first run, and as you know, we don't send them out primed with corpse criteria until they have proved they have the right calibre for our work. Every squad has sent in some duds and only three crews know any specifics pertaining to our MC Project. MC specifics are closely guarded and only released to the selected few at this moment in time. Until our Global revelations take place in the future, the salvage squads will always be 'fringe' project members and this will be secured by their ignorance.

"A couple of the gang-fight victims look a bit doubtful as well. One has received two headshots from an Uzi and the other received a direct headshot from a Magnum type pistol - thus two fifths of his head are absent! I thought I would give you the background to what you are going to see, because you probably wouldn't have anticipated the number of corpses. The way the bodies are collectively laid out makes the room look like a scene from a war film. The RTA victim is particularly graphic, Mr Ko-Chai - it might be wise for you to look away when you pass his bed. Okay gentlemen, shall we enter?"

As Vain's team entered the makeshift mortuary, they were initially taken aback by the stench of the preservatives that had been applied to some of the bodies. Whilst all the corpses had been located within the last twenty-four hours, not all of them had died within that time period. Indeed, two of the victims had gone into advanced stages of decomposition, making their appearance guignol in the extreme.

The range of corpses backed up what Mason had said about the fluctuating levels of project knowledge evident amongst the selection squads. Some of the dead were beyond research suitability, having gone past the three-week period that would keep the MC relevant sections of the brain fresh, or having received terminal injuries that physically damaged the aforementioned cranium areas. Tavini had shaken his head in disbelief as he passed one victim.

The said victim had been decapitated and the head was absent. His comments pertaining to this particular corpse injected a wry black humour to the proceedings.

"Well guys, I guess a blind school selection squad picked up this one!"

The MC team examined the range of corpses that were laid out for them and they quickly devised an initial short list of suitable individuals. Their primary judgements were based on the external condition of the bodies and yet the internal condition was the key factor in ensuring a positive MC visual display. Each front line project member knew that the real test of victim suitability could only be determined once the vault splicer was embedded within the brain. Mason had a medical background that made him useful for identifying suitable victims and whilst he didn't have the specialist skills of Vain's team, he had developed a 'sixth sense' regarding corpses that were ideal for MC explorations. Each of Vain's team turned to Mason for advice on occasions and he seemed to warm to this leading light role.

After fifty minutes the MC team and Mason had narrowed their shortlist down to three individuals. The four men were just about to make their final selection when Mr Fray entered the room and expressed his desire for the team to select one of the gang-fight victims. He was obviously better informed than the MC team and knew something they didn't. His opening words were clinical in their tone.

"Good evening gentlemen. Explore Marco's mind. He's the fella with the Raiders jacket. One shot through his neck, two through his legs. He doesn't present any problems for exploration does he?"

Vain confronted Fray.

"We were just going to select the victim Mr Fray. We'd narrowed things down perfectly. Surely one of the two twenty something females will strike a chord more with global audiences when we show off our successes - they have more universal appeal for empathy generation than what looks like a South side crack dealer!"

"Things aren't always what they seem, Mr Vain. Marco Uccelli didn't hit the ground with the crack boys.

"He was dead three hours before that rumble! No, Marco used to be one of our best, a top FBI man. Then he made a couple of bad decisions with regard to the faith the FBI had in him and he became an embarrassment - a serious security threat. The word went out that it might be better if Mr Uccelli wasn't around any more and for fourteen months he subsequently went into hiding.

"My boys were placing bets on who could nail him and two of our best guys were on his tail today - not teamed up, but two crack individual units. If you look at Uccelli, you will notice that the shot he took in the front of his neck has caused considerable damage, and yet we're certain that it was fired from a gun that only does substantial damage at close quarters. The chances are that he will have 'framed' his assassin in his Memory-Camera and we will be able to reward the individual that finally got him".

"Does it really matter who finally pulled the trigger, Mr Fray? I can't see the big issue here. I mean the guy's dead just like you wanted - case closed, surely?"

"No, you've got to understand the intricacies of the situation here, Mr Vain. Once the word goes out concerning the removal of an ex-FBI boy, the top guys are put on the case, and several prefer to operate as individual hitmen. Yeah, the bulk of them are teamed up, but Jensen and Mace preferred to work alone. Both of them have been in there from the start, with regard to locating Uccelli and you can bet your bottom dollar that both will claim the scalp. One will have won and the other lost.

"True, the FBI will see it as a bonus either way but now we actually have a chance to possibly prove who fired the fatal neck shot. We'll play the exploration back to the guys and if it's a good 'take', the 'who killed' question will be sorted beyond any doubt. You see, these two guys had one focus - Uccelli. They ate him, slept him, fucking dreamt him I shouldn't wonder. It's no surprise that both are going to claim his head. They were both pumped high on the end of the chase, and the bravado is going to take over. It's no good spouting team effort bullshit to them because both were wild card operators who worked as individuals. Uccelli is their exorcism. The guy who didn't fire the fatal shot will have convinced himself otherwise by now, and soon we'll get to the confrontation stage where the two will clash with each other. I want to eradicate this stage Mr Vain, as cancer in the ranks fucks up the whole operation. Seeing is believing, and Leif and myself want this issue clarified. I'm here on his behest, so your selection has been made for you. Right guys, the lesson endeth. This could be one fucking shoot out - I can't wait!"

Fray took his leave and left the four men alone to discuss the change in selection policy. Tavini spoke first, paying tribute to Fray's style of verbal delivery.

"Jeez, that guy sure knows how to win over an audience, doesn't he fellas? He walks in here, changes our plans and swans out - job done! He and Denison are golden, two of the same breed.

"I know he's not quite your sort of leader, Greg and Mishimo, but even you have got to admit that his presence is pretty commanding".

Ko-Chai answered.

"Yes David, the gentleman does indeed have a commanding presence, but he also has the power to change our selection decisions and I'm not likely to celebrate that factor am I?"

"I'm with you there, Mishimo. I mean what is the purpose of our exploration going to be here? To settle a rather infantile squabble between two FBI hitmen?"

"You're not reading the situation correctly, Greg. Fray was dead right about the tension that builds when two FBI guys are after the same goal. Someone's got to win and someone's got to fucking lose. Our role here is vital because this isn't an infantile squabble, it's life or death mate! Both those guys were over a year in the hunt and if you let the rumours build, the pressure could make one crack. Ask yourself, what kind of guys these two are? They're the kind who are trained to kill, the kind that live on their nerves and the kind who compete with each other to the most intense level. What we uncover will add a degree of clarity that will hopefully close the matter once and for all. FBI inter-faction fighting is a bitch fellas, and what may initially seem a trivial war of counter claims could leave a guy on the slab if it wasn't for our project".

Mason seemed content to relinquish the spotlight he usually had when selections were taking place, and Tavini had managed to win over both of his fellow exploration team members to a fair extent. The exploration might not clarify things fully in terms of the visual awareness captured by the victim but everyone recognised the potential for illumination prevalent in MC Project work. Vain's team commenced their exploration.

The ensuing exploration featured exactly the kind of visuals that Fray had been hoping for.

Initially Marco Uccelli's Memory-Camera highlighted both FBI men firing from mid-distance on adjacent street corners. The two were not together, firing randomly in the direction of the Memory-Camera, and our viewing position by extension. The visuals were delivered in a jerky, fragmented style as they were determined by an individual who was running for his life amidst the ruins of Chicago's South Side region.

The proverbial darkness broke the visuals on occasions when 'heightened' images weren't in evidence and after twenty-two minutes the screen only registered the presence of Jensen pursuing the Memory-Camera's position. Jensen was running very fast and whilst gunfire had been returned from the MC position initially, now just Jensen's gun was active.

Cries of pain suddenly rang out from Marco and the Memory-Camera dropped to a ground level perspective. Slowly Jensen approached Marco's fallen spatial position. He held a pistol in his right hand and he brandished it menacingly in our direction. A bloodied hand wiped Marco's eyes, although it distorted the visuals for a short time as a red smear temporarily distorted the approaching Jensen. After Marco's MC lens cleared, the assembled project members witnessed Jensen being 'framed' in close-up, standing twelve feet away from the Memory-Camera position. He was revelling in his empowered position and when he spoke his words were music to Fray's ears.

"You've got ten seconds, Marco. Start counting out loud - you never know, I might change my mind!"

The gun appeared on the screen, from an ominous high angle.

"...five, six, seven..."

The bullet sunk into the man's neck.

"I lied, seven's my lucky number!"

The MC images didn't die instantly on the screen but lasted a further three minutes, featuring a concentration of sky gazing shots similar to Leah's visual display. A choking sound accompanied the images and when the death rattle finally sounded the images slowly faded off screen. Jensen hadn't administered the 'coup de grace' and had even taunted the man as he lay dying. "I'll check out your wife" were Jensen's last words to Uccelli.

Fray was enraptured by Marco's HV retention and he proceeded to backslap each MC front line team member. He behaved in a fashion akin to a child receiving the present they had hoped for above all others at Christmas. His words were as ebullient as his actions.

"Stuff *Mean Streets*, stuff *The Godfather*, stuff *Reservoir*, this is the real thing, fellas! Yo, what a display. Jensen is a living De Niro here. I guess this is the ultimate way to solve a 'hit' dispute - what a precedent!"

Mason spoke from the margins of the explorations room.

"How are you going to display Uccelli's HVs Mr Fray. I mean, surely project security dictates that you can't have a mass departmental screening? Those in the know project-wise probably still number less than a hundred, and you have over three hundred persons in your FBI departmental area alone!"

"Don't worry Mr Mason, the screening will essentially be a private affair with Jensen and Mace being welcomed into the project fold after they have witnessed Uccelli's HVs. Seven other members of my FBI departmental area will also witness the event as they are already working within the MC Project.

"Question answered, now let's have another look at 'cool-boy' Jensen - he was worth a fucking Oscar!"

The Chicago precedent had been set on the first night as far as selection was concerned. In the first three weeks the MC team did select some corpses themselves for exploration work, but more often than not Fray or Denison would choose a victim that was relevant to either FBI or CIA operations. Vain had started to feel that British involvement in the MC Project was being pushed further into the margins as far as staffing was concerned. In London no new British project staff were forthcoming, but in Chicago new American recruits would arrive on the scene in pairs or trios on a daily basis.

The success ratio pertaining to the Chicago explorations was excellent and by the end of the third week, the MC team had been involved in over twenty productive explorations, with only one failure. The latter exploration failed because the victim had died due to a blow to the back of her head without building any HVs or trapping any useful supporting sound. In effect the killer had left nothing to indicate their presence and the victim's Memory-Camera couldn't subsequently register their existence. The MC team had been disappointed by the failure, but the victim was killed on impact and was denied any chance to visually capture her killer. Vain found this second negative demonstration more palatable to accept, as the victim of this lethal attack was unaware of her circumstances due to the blind-side factor which led up to her death, and thus she would not have suffered the way other MC exploration victims had.

The MC team workload had been so arduous during the initial three weeks that Vain had wondered if all three would survive it. His thoughts were mainly focused on Ko-Chai, who had experienced heart problems three years previous. Both Vain and Tavini were very healthy in comparison to Ko-Chai, but even the athletic Tavini had looked jaded in some of their recent explorations. Vain fought this fatigue by snatching sleep when he could and partaking in the occasional walk along the lowest corridors of Designation J. He had met up with Levene twice in this area of the Designation, and on the Tuesday of the fourth week both encountered each other for the third time.

"I hoped you would be here, Greg. This bottom corridor that we walk through is over a kilometre in length you know!"

"You're a mine of information, Marcia.

"How the hell did you come up with that stat?"

"I've told you before Greg, I need to know as many project-related details as possible. It's become a habitual obsession for me, and when we're in a tomb like this Designation it helps fill any vacant time. Looking at Designation J architectural plans with Mr Denison were one way of enduring our subterranean existence! The key word is survival here, Greg. Being down here could induce a condition similar to the 'coffin effect' experienced by some submarine crew members. I mean we're all crying out for fresh air - it's the collective wish of all project members at this moment in time".

As the pair proceeded through the corridor, they gradually became closer physically and when they reached the end of their only route, Vain turned to face Levene.

She spoke to him unguarded, with regard to her choice of words.

"Hold me Greg - like there's no fucking tomorrow! That's all I ask for, nothing heavy, and nothing to break your marriage vows, just a sign of warmth in this godforsaken hole! This is my living hell you know, Greg. My phobia's been claustrophobia since I was eleven, after my brother had locked me in a cupboard under our stairwell. Please hold me".

Gregory Vain saw Levene's request as a genuine cry from the heart.

Tears had been in her eyes when she uttered her words and Vain felt impelled to comfort her. He cradled her in his arms and her face sunk into his chest. Vain was surprised by the intensity of the feelings he suddenly felt for this rather beautiful woman. Gone was the fatale style that had previously enshrouded Levene, and in its place appeared an almost childlike dependency. Vain slowly lifted Levene's face and saw two lines of mascara based tears falling unevenly down her cheeks. Their ensuing kiss encapsulated their mutual thoughts, speaking a thousand words in the process. Vain's tongue probed Levene's soft mouth and his hands translated his mounting passion, as his nails gently marked the small of her back. After a couple of minutes he broke away, as his guilt became overbearing and family recollections dominated his mind. Levene didn't react with hostility to the disruption of their kiss. She had anticipated this initial passionate gesture between them would induce feelings of betrayal in her married project partner.

Vain put his arm around Levene's back again as the two of them retraced their steps back to the main Designation area. His guilt trip was short-lived in comparison to the duration he initially thought it would have lasted, and whilst either of them could have laughed off the gesture as 'just a kiss', both knew that it signified the deeper attraction that was evident in both individuals.

The dye had been cast. As the pair parted, Levene whispered her thanks to Vain and lightly kissed him on the cheek. Vain was left to reflect on their meeting, and as he settled down for a three-hour sleep period his libido was still working overtime.

Gregory Vain awoke and was initially confused as to why he had beaten his alarm signal.

Usually Vain was almost robotic in his three-hour sleep shifts, awakening either a couple of minutes before the signal or after hearing the electronic shrill sound. On this occasion Vain was awake for fifty minutes before the signal and he knew that something was amiss.

An acrid smell started to drift through Vain's sleeping quarters and as its presence escalated, Vain hurriedly put on a shirt and jeans. As he dressed the Designation fire alarms went off simultaneously. He raced out into the adjacent corridor and was met by a black smoke and fumes.

Vain choked on the fumes as he proceeded toward Levene's sleeping quarters. He woke the sleeping Levene and pulled her into the corridor. She had managed to grab her long coat but was naked underneath. Both project members ran towards the Fire assembly checkpoint but encountered flames just short of their intended destination.

"Come on Marcia, let's try the mid corridors - this way's a ticket to the fucking undertaker!"

As the pair raced through the mid-sections of the Designation, they heard screams and Vain initially hesitated. Levene helped to focus his thoughts in the panic pertaining to their situation.

"Move it Greg, they're fucking doomed, you know!"

"Who are, Marcia?"

"Only a couple of selection squads in the 'sealed' confine sections".

"They're going to fry alive, Marcia. We've got to help them!"

"They already are, Greg. Fuck them. Come on let's move it, or we'll join them!"

Levene temporarily took the lead and pulled Vain closer to the assembly area. When the pair finally arrived at the said area they were hurriedly packaged into the waiting lift by Fray, who was overseeing the Designation evacuation. His instructions were as concise as ever despite the pressure the fire had generated.

"Marcia, Greg. The MC gear's safe. When you get up top, stick with Leif's crew. He's waiting for you up there now. You may need these because it's South Side scum-land up there and MC staff could well become targets for the criminals that are going to arrive when they see the fire vehicles.

"Don't engage in any verbal stuff; just shoot any bastard that gets too close. I'll be up in a short while. See you up there".

The pair were not prepared for the scene that awaited them when they arrived at ground level. Denied any seasonal context for over three weeks they were initially surprised at the severity of the weather conditions. Early November snow was quite commonplace in Chicago, but the last time the pair had been on the surface in their rest period location the elements had been very mild, carrying the last throes of summer. Now ten inches of snow lay heaped on the ground, and a lurid light emanated from this white covering amidst the darkness of a 02:00 Chicago morning. The fire vehicles' electric blue lighting contributed to the almost surreal atmosphere, with the snow reflecting the blue strobe in a chaotic style of its own construction. Sound was similarly discordant, with sirens and agitated voices competing for dominance.

The project members had not been primed by media reports concerning the meteorological conditions as all forms of extrapersonal communications were banned in the Designations barring the MC display screens. The reason for the media blackout was linked to the maintenance of the insular concentration that was collectively important for all project staff.

The gunshot shattered Vain and Levene's transient contemplation. One of the firemen fell dead and Blyth Carson's voice suddenly dominated the environment.

"Hit the fucking deck guys, some 'ghetto-posse' boys have started shooting".

As the project staff took cover, Fray and Denison took control of the situation. Denison's voice became the most dominant.

"Stay down, project crew. That scum smelt our presence. Just keep away from the fire guys dousing the Designation entrances. Keep your fire trained on the two north-western high rises and don't worry - those guys are gonna be in for one fucking surprise in a couple of minutes!"

Vain fired back into the said buildings, and the collective MC Project guns sent back traces made by bullet trajectories which added an almost aesthetic spectacle to the gun battle! Another firemen took a bullet in the shoulder, and Fray made sure security staff added more bulletproof cover to corral the fire fighters.

Two of the forty who had witnessed the Venison demonstration fell dead near Vain and Levene, with head shots that pumped blood on the snow. One of the dead had fallen with his head turned towards Levene and Vain. His dead face was mask like, having a frozen expression that was akin to the 'tragedy' muse in its appearance.

It seemed to look straight into Levene's eyes.

The gunfire continued for ten minutes and then Mr Fray's surprise arrived on the scene.

Three armour-plated vehicles with rocket launcher rear sections sped past the MC staff and reversed towards the buildings that housed the ghetto posse. Then there ensued a synchronised intensive fire volley from the respective vehicles, and the lower stories of the buildings were all but totally destroyed.

Not content with this devastation, Fray gave the order for two of the vehicles to intermittently blast the upper sections of the structures with 'surface to air' type missiles. If the gun battle had been closely fought before the arrival of the vehicles, it was now a totally one-sided confrontation with no fire being returned toward the MC ranks. Internal explosions started to occur within the buildings, and when the MC Project vehicles temporarily paused for realignment purposes, the first inhabitants emerged from the two buildings. Many had been severely cut by flying glass, some had been badly burned and a few had lost limbs in part or whole. There were a minority of posse members, but the overwhelming majority of individuals were not armed, some of them being families.

Fray then selected his next stratagem and raced into action. Leading a contingent of eight FBI centred MC Project members, Fray charged toward the survivors of his blitzkrieg. He started to unload his machine pistol into the ranks of the former occupants and was assisted to a 'right hand man' level by a project member whom Vain had not seen before. In the midst of the chaos pertaining to this kind of situation, one individual didn't usually stand out, but Fray's accomplice was no ordinary project member.

The said individual was a giant of a man who wore a heavy-duty combat uniform. He was often ahead of Fray with regard to the massacre that was taking place, and after a short while he discarded his military style helmet as the opposition had been quelled.

This factor didn't stop the shootings though.

Denison started ushering the MC staff into a project transportation vehicle, which was in readiness for the evacuation of MC Project staff. Designation J had been written off, but another site in Michigan had already been set up for such an eventuality. This would shortly be the new project base, and as Vain and Levene slumped into a double seat, both had a short time to survey the scene outside. Two things dominated Vain's Memory-Camera with regard to his final look at the battle zone.

The first was an image of the silver-haired Fray and his black, giant of a man, second in command, laughing as they surveyed a group of corpses and the second was an image of a child clambering over the dead body of it's mother, crying and touching her face.

Chicago had been a hell on earth.

SEVEN

The journey out of Chicago was undertaken at high speed, and the MC Project ranks preserved a uniform silence due to the collective fatigue that had taken its toll on all staff. The hurried nature of the Designation J evacuation had meant that the project members were in varying states of dress, ranging from semi-naked like Levene to the immaculate attire of Denison. Vain wondered if the MC Project leader ever slept. Gregory Vain's mind kept on replaying the key events pertaining to the night's events and his thoughts were only interrupted when the sleeping Levene murmured in her uneasy slumber. Her words were not readily discernible, but her body language was occasionally suggestive in its execution with her hands reaching out for Vain, stroking his chest in the process. Vain didn't wake the woman, but he was glad the pair had located one of the vehicle's rear seats, because her posture would have incited rumours amongst some of their fellow project members.

The Michigan replacement Designation would be comparatively ambient after the claustrophobia that had characterised Designation J. Although project members would have preferred to leave in less frightening circumstances, tempers had begun to fray, and the transference was thus a blessing in disguise to a fair proportion of the MC Project staff.

The Michigan site - Designation S, had been used by the MC Project in a training period three years prior to the actual exploration work that they were now undertaking, and it was a favourable ground level venue.

The Designation had adjacent grounds, which the project members could utilise in their relaxation periods, and although Michigan was likely to have more snow than Chicago, most project members were going to put up with the elements in favour of venturing out on occasions. Thus, if Chicago had given incarceration, Michigan offered the potential for temporary 'escape.'

The MC Project staff were going to be given two days to adjust to their new environment, and on the third day Denison and Fray were going to address the project ranks. Project staff were eager to know the causes of the Designation J fire and the scale of the casualties in the ensuing gun battle. These two issues would be clarified in the assembly on day three.

Every project member took full advantage of the two-day rest period and although Designation S had an excellent leisure complex built on to it's main section, extended sleep was the most preferable form of relaxation. The staff who took their places in the Assembly room on the third morning were thus more refreshed than they had been for some time, although the 'culled' project totality was evident in the number of chairs provided. Denison mounted the speaker's podium and commenced his address.

"Today, it is my sad duty to report the deaths of eleven Memory-Camera Project staff and before I deal with the events of Chicago, I want everyone to stand and pay homage to our lost friends, with a minute of silence".

Denison checked his watch and bowed his head once all the assembled ranks were upstanding.

The sixty seconds were observed in unanimous silence and then the group sat down again.

"Words are pale substitutes for lost friends, and although not all those who died would have been familiar to project staff, nine of them had sweated blood in the name of the MC Project.

"It is true that five of the eleven never knew any specifics pertaining to our work, as they were rookie 'selection squad' members. It is true that they died in the sealed-confinement section of Designation J, and thus it is also true by extension that they were burnt alive for a cause they never really knew. Those five were due to be taken into full project confidence when the Chicago work had culminated, so all of them had the guts to be up to the macabre duties performed by the selection squads. They had nearly 'passed out' and their deaths are thus a great project loss as well as a personal loss.

"Some of you may wonder if locked confine approaches are really the correct way to house fringe project staff after this tragedy. Some may feel that this form of incarceration is barbaric, even Dark Age in its application, and some may feel that the deaths of these five young men takes the edge off our achievements. I say to you my friends - we were right to operate this form of separation.

"The project is bigger than anyone, and everyone is expendable, from myself to Mr Vain to fringe selection squad members. You see, our project is going to save thousands of lives each year.

"When we reveal our findings to the global public, people are going to be overwhelmed by what secrets the dead mind stores. There will still be a proportion of murders but most individuals are going to think twice because the cliché still applies - 'seeing is believing.'

"Until the time of revelation, the protection of information is our God, and hence those who are being tested for project suitability will remain on the periphery, locked away from those who know. Imagine what damage leaks to the media would do to our work? We can't take any chances with fringe staff and that, my friends, is why those five men died. We did, and will still do, the right thing. They were thus martyrs to project secrecy even though they died clothed in ignorance. I salute them".

Denison's words made sense to the project ranks in front of him. Even the selection squads who had been taken into full project confidence nodded in agreement with him on occasions. They had proved themselves, and as they sat amongst the full parameters of MC Project staff they felt a collective pride. Denison continued.

"Six other project staff died that night in Chicago, and I honour four of them as professional staff members who will be hard to replace. Two of the four died in the Designation, and ghetto scum shot the other two when they surfaced. All these individuals had been handpicked for their medical and scientific brilliance, and their baptism into project awareness took place on the night of the Venison exploration. Their services of support for the fringe front line team had just reached completion and their relevance to the project cause will never be forgotten".

Diana Fearston bowed her head in sadness as Denison talked about the deaths of some of those who had helped train her. She had been particularly close to the two men that had fallen next to Levene and Vain in the Chicago gun battle. As the project leader spoke, her mind hung on to the dissolved friendships.

"You will have noticed that I hold the utmost respect for the project fatalities that I have talked about thus far, and I wish I had the same kind of feeling for the two other victims. The truth is that their deaths were brought about by their own misguided and thoughtless actions. We are well rid of them. David Turner and Heather Maddox were also members of the forty who were baptised upon witnessing the Venison display, but thankfully their support duties were less important than some of the aforementioned fatalities.

"They made the mistake of getting too close to each other, negating their professional responsibility in the process.

"Everyone felt the heat of Designation J. Everyone hated the close confines of the fucking place, but it seems that these two couldn't endure things like the rest of us. They had to do something about our choice of venue. They were our 'fire-starters'. Just how infantile can one get? Just because they didn't have an external venue like Designation B to mask their romance, they thought fire was the remedy! Self centred, petty juveniles - that's what those two became. They also killed other loyal project staff by their actions, and so I'm damn glad they went to the wrong evacuation point - it was poetic justice that their fire wiped them out! The idiots had been tracked on our close circuit cameras anyway, so their punishment for arson would have almost certainly resulted in their death. They did us a favour".

Vain and Levene had cast each other a glance when Denison had referred to close circuit surveillance.

"I'd like to pay my compliments to Mr Fray for the way he dealt with the ghetto posse who took us on. He and Jess Wheeler's small crack unit gave that scum the only mediator they really understand - the bullet. Plenty of 'em, come to think of it fellas - nice one!"

Denison continued to praise the efforts of Fray's crack unit response during the gun battle, and as his verbal address approached its closure he enquired as to whether there were any questions from the assembled MC Project ranks. Usually there were none, as Leif Denison's oratory ability was so conclusive that he answered any points of query that his staff may have arrived with. On this occasion however, Gregory Vain did feel impelled to ask one question that he felt his project leader hadn't encompassed.

"I feel that the crack unit response in Chicago was rather zealous in its execution, Mr Denison. I saw families hit the deck in that encounter - unarmed mothers and fathers. Whilst I didn't see any children actually killed, I saw them clinging to their slain parents, and that was a factor that tarnished the strides we have made in our research, in my opinion. All of a sudden I felt we stopped being the 'good guys'; dropping down to the scum level of the ghetto posse we had engaged in the gunfight. I didn't see any blaze of glory once Mr Fray's rocket-launcher vehicles had put paid to the fighting, all I saw were a range of sitting duck, innocent targets getting gunned down. I feel the MC Project staff are collectively owed an explanation concerning why our line of fire was directed at innocent people escaping the burning buildings. What the hell were we trying to prove here?"

"I think your line of argument suffers from melodramatic toning here, Gregory. In the heat of that moment our guys weren't aware who was actually hitting the deck. It was a simple them or us situation, and how could Mr Fray and his charges have separated a posse member from a civilian? We all owe them a debt, our lives. We owe them everything.

"Rather than attack them for a misguided line of fire, we should applaud their efforts that night. Think about it Mr Vain, which would you rather be - a saint in a coffin or a 'leading light' MC Project operator? We're still the 'good guys' to quote you Mr Vain, but we're human at the end of the day, and morality is way down in terms of importance when a gun battle is the event under scrutiny. The survival quest rightly stamped on any limp-wristed chivalrous ethics that night, and I'm damned glad it did too. You owe Mr Fray and his colleagues an apology Gregory, and when your moral indignation has subsided after you have re-examined your words in hindsight, I trust you will make that apology".

Jess Wheeler glared at Gregory Vain as the project congregation took their leave. As the two of them passed each other near the assembly room exit, Wheeler quietly muttered his resentment concerning Vain's speech.

"Nice one, Mr Vain! You can deal with any fucking bullets yourself next time, man!"

Vain had time to contemplate the comments of Denison and Wheeler during the remainder of the Michigan placement. His mind kept recalling the method by which his words were shot down. Denison had knocked the stuffing out of Vain in public, and Wheeler had applied the metaphorical killer blow in a more private fashion. Whilst Vain hadn't been won over by the two men as far as their opposing viewpoint was concerned, his defeat had felt total as the exchange had been witnessed by so many of his project peers. He was afraid that some of the assembled ranks would have been swayed by Denison's superior orator ability.

The exploration work at Michigan was more spasmodic than the frenetic supply of corpses that were evident in Chicago, and the outdoor placement of Designation S added an aesthetic quality to the relaxation periods. Vain occupied his time between explorations with vault extension preparatory research, front-line team interactions and walks in the pleasant Designation S grounds. On occasions Levene would accompany him, but since Denison's comments pertaining to team-based liaisons, the couple had reduced their paired - up contact. On the penultimate day of their American placement, Vain took a solitary walk around the grounds and encountered Blyth Carson, partaking in the same form of relaxation. Vain greeted his fellow project member warmly and asked about the whereabouts of his usual partner - Brynley Stowles.

"Hiya Blyth, good to see you.

"How come Brynley missed out on America - I thought he wouldn't have missed the American explorations for the world! Is he still London-based?"

"Yeah he's still in London Greg, and you're right, he was real cut up about missing out on the States. He's back in Designation B along with Mr Voight. They're both laser-formatting the English Explorations in readiness for when we 'let the world know.' It's his own fault, poor guy. Before his **MOD** work he worked in film packaging and distribution! Talk about your past coming back to plague you!"

EIGHT

Brynley Stowles stubbed out his cigarette and proceeded to spill coffee over his bedside table. This careless act seemed to sum up the way he was feeling perfectly. Stowles, to put it mildly, was annoyed.

Most of his MC Project colleagues had departed for Chicago four days ago, and he had been selected to remain in England to assist Mr Voight with the laser disc formatting of the initial explorations undertaken by Vain's team.

Stowles knew that his previous experience in the film distribution industry did mean he was ideal for such a task, but he was an individual who thrived on taking part in front line developments and he felt that exploration formatting was very 'backline' in comparison. Blyth Carson, his regular MC partner had gone to America, and Stowles was left to work in the small team headed by Voight. Whilst Stowles got on quite well with his section leader, he had never managed to really achieve the kind of bonding he and Carson shared. Voight was a very 'distant' project member with regard to his personality and as his expressionless eyes looked at a person during verbal interactions, it was difficult to ascertain if he was really thinking about the subject being discussed. Voight unnerved Stowles to a level.

For an individual with quite bad physical difficulties, Stowles had looked the world in the face and battled hard to succeed. Being hunched had given him a disadvantage in life but he had disregarded his physical appearance and concentrated more on furthering his heightened mental ability. He saw himself as a winner and he tried not to let sarcastic jibes pertaining to his deformity drag his spirit down. It was true that the 'street-callers' did sometimes sting his pride, and Sandford-Everett's 'Quasimodo' reference typified what the man had to endure quite frequently. Brynley Stowles however was deemed to be a salient MC Project member, and this factor enabled him to rise above such petty-mindedness. He had loved the project before being left out for the American explorations - it had been a great strength, his one real goal in life. Now the project had let him down as far as he was concerned and he had been taken over by a bitterness that was usually alien to his character.

Stowles was still in a pessimistic state of mind on the fourth day of his formatting duties. Voight had delegated him to make 'visual register' lists pertaining to the stored explorations, barring Christopher's bizarre image retention. These lists were very intricate in their construction, listing every visual development, indicating time and space continuums in the process. Stowles was working on Leah's exploration on this particular day, and as he logged visual developments an idea came to him which had foundation in his past and validation with regard to his current circumstances. For the first time Stowles had seen the explorations in a different light - they were marketable as a niche based film commodity!

During his years in the video film distribution sector, Stowles had seen thousands of films, from dominant Hollywood stables to smaller, independent Arthouse practitioners. The latter had occasionally involved images which severely tested the borders of conventional taste and whilst some of the filmic fare were deemed too graphic in their horrific content, some of the more subtle offerings that interspersed mutilations with surreal aesthetics were accepted. Stowles remembered how the distribution company where he worked had initially been very cautious about their acceptance. The films traded off 'snuff-movie' poor quality influences, but they added a post-production visual gloss that made them leading edge with regard to their style. A niche audience soon developed - very loyal in their buying frequency and content to keep buying the same regurgitated filmic recipe. They bought because they believed that people had actually been hacked to death in the film, and the distribution company soon overcame their initial caution as sales soared, spreading their own rumours that ascertained that some of the films were indeed for 'real'. The films were eventually forced out of the marketplace because their ill wind alerted influential public figures and 'obscenity' rooted law suits were being prepared to end the operation of the distribution company.

The films had proved that a market for the grotesque avant-garde existed, and Stowles felt that he could fashion many parallels in the MC Project explorations he had in close proximity to him. These would be different though, even more subtle.

The 'camera' would die in the films he could distribute.

In the lower levels of Designation B there were state-of-the-art editing facilities. These were primarily used for packaging the explorations in terms of titling and time count displays, but Stowles knew that the potential for his own post-production alterations did exist. He would keep his project colleagues satisfied by producing laser-discs of the explorations but he would also operate his own 'hidden agenda' involving the generation of video cassette master copies. Voight left him alone to work most of the time and he rarely visited the bowels of the Designation where the formatting took place. Laser disc formatting seemed beyond Voight's comprehension and Stowles assumed that this was the reason he didn't closely monitor his work.

Stowles had kept in close contact with some of his former distribution colleagues and one of them had left their former workplace to operate a chain of capital-based video retail outlets. He felt sure that Max Yardley, the aforementioned colleague would be very interested in distributing the kind of video he could compose from the explorations. He and Yardley had been closely involved with the distribution of the 'mock' snuff videos and both had been disappointed when their distribution agency had to pull the plug on this type of film.

Yardley knew nothing of the MC Project work undertaken by Stowles because Brynley had honoured the secrecy prerogative applicable to project operations to the full. Now however, Stowles felt let down by the American snub and he decided to make some additional revenue out of the work undertaken by project ranks. He would not hand over copies of the laser discs as they would reveal the names and dates, which would, if located by project security forces, inevitably lead to his execution! Instead, Stowles was going to employ post-production methods to mask MC Project identity.

He would soundtrack the build up to the death of exploration victims and would add digitised colour toning where he felt it was appropriate. Stowles was going to include the exploration visuals generated from Julia Venison, Leah and Michael Stark, who's death had been the fourth successful exploration uncovered by the MC team. Stark had been garrotted after a long chase across London and Stowles felt that his storage of heightened visuals were 'too good to miss' as far as his video was concerned.

Brynley Stowles was particularly looking forward to composing a title for his work. He was initially tempted to opt for 'The Eye of the Beholder' because it encapsulated the most extreme visual instance - where Leah's one eye registered the devouring of her other eye, by one of the dogs that so ferociously attacked her. Stowles liked the black irony located in this title. His video would have a running duration of just over 73 minutes.

As he commenced work upon his video, Stowles felt a twinge of guilt. He didn't need any extra income as the MC Project paid him an excellent salary that made him want for nothing. Stowles was producing his video as an act of revenge, and this quickly removed any feelings of guilt he had.

Stowles started to soundtrack the Venison exploration using a hybrid of musical styles, ranging from Michael Nyman's repertoire to 'Techno' driven dance rhythms.

When characters spoke, the music was brought down in the mix and when Sandford-Everett played his Tamala-Motown tape in his car stereo, Stowles reduced his other musical tracks to a very mute level. Stowles chose to further heighten the visuals when Everett had punched Venison in the mouth and when his face was illuminated to eerie effect by his lighter. In both cases he reduced the visual clarity of the background and intensified the contours of Sandford-Everett's face. His reasons for these changes concerned his desire to isolate some images in a more filmic style. Such minimal changes were carried out in relation to all three explorations and the end result kept the rawness of Memory-Camera storage, whilst adding a sharpness with regard to visual clarity. Stowles completed both his project-orientated work and his own master video work within a month. Voight inspected the exploration laser discs and commended Stowles for the work he had undertaken. Then he had a surprise for Stowles.

"Take ten days off now, Brynley. We are not obligated to a tight curfew as we would be if we were undertaking front-line explorations. Mr Denison has given me permission to give my section a break once formatting and other research is completed. You've undertaken your duties to an excellent level and you are fully deserving of the rest period. Spare a thought for the rest of us my friend - our research isn't finished yet!"

Stowles was taken aback. The break would give him time to contact Max Yardley, but he had deposited his master-video in a 'locked confine' section of the editing suite and he had programmed it 'locked' for another two weeks. He had decided to utilise the 'D39 codicil' option for storage and Denison and Fray could only break into this form of security as far as project members were aware.

Stowles met Yardley the day after his Designation B departure and although he didn't have any video-based visuals to show him, his description of the applicable imagery did greatly interest his former distribution colleague.

Stowles didn't confide any MC Project information to Yardley but concentrated on describing the drafted visuals that he had drawn when he got home. Being a fair artist, Stowles could convey the images to an accurate level and he had even 'touched in' colour to make his rendition more aesthetic. The three chosen images consisted of Sandford-Everett's 'wild' face in close-up, the dog with Leah's eye in its mouth and two of Stark's tormentors closing in on him.

Yardley had continued to monitor the niche Horror market that he and Stowles had discovered at their previous place of employment and it had grown considerably, being strengthened by animated Japanese offerings of a macabre nature. He did trade some mock snuff movies through 'under the counter services' and he felt that the visuals that Stowles could supply would be ideal for this type of selective demand. Yardley was particularly taken by the idea surrounding the 'camera's death.' He felt this more subtle approach moved things forward in several ways. He liked the idea of selective gore as opposed to the 'bloodfest' type of film that was so abundant in the marketplace, and he felt that the suspense build up prevalent in the visuals Stowles had described would increase the retail potential of this type of stock. He and Stowles preferred to refer to this new type of video as 'executions' instead of films, as this phrase seemed to encapsulate what the visuals represented to a better level. On occasions Stowles found it hard to keep quiet about his MC Project work but he managed to resist firm workplace details, referring to his supplier as 'Phase 9'. Yardley didn't care who actually supplied the material. He was just content to envisage the high income levels that would be generated by this type of merchandise. Before leaving Yardley's house, Stowles agreed to hand over the first video-master to Yardley within a month. He couldn't be precise in his arrangements because he was unsure about the project commitments that would await him when he returned to Designation B. Yardley's parting line promised Stowles a healthy return for his supply.

As Stowles returned home on the Jubilee Line, his thoughts turned to his chosen method for retrieving his video from Designation B. MC Project staff had to enter and leave Designations through screened areas where staff inspected their clothing and luggage. One in every three personnel was chosen for a holistic X-ray on random occasions, and thus Stowles deemed the risk element too great to ignore. He hadn't been through the X-ray scanning for some time and the likelihood of being chosen was increasing on each occasion. Concealing a small videocassette within his body would also be physically dangerous and Stowles felt that he had suffered enough physical torment in his life without trying that risky option! Stowles planned to survey the internal perimeters of the Designation B gardens during relaxation periods when project operations resumed because the exits to the grounds were unscreened, and he felt sure he could establish weak links in the surveillance camera monitoring that fed twenty-four hour pictures back to the security nerve centre.

Stowles became increasingly desperate in his logistic thoughts with regard to getting his video package out of the Designation, and when he started envisaging himself throwing the package over the security fences into the adjacent woodland he realised that a more secure method must be devised! He still felt that the Designation grounds held the answer concerning the successful extraction of the video from the site, but as yet he was unsure about the precise application pertaining to any plan. Stowles felt sure that time was on his side though, and he was confident that the precise mechanics concerning an extraction method would be determined by him in the next few days - albeit with him working from afar in his St John's Wood residence.

Stowles disembarked at St John's Wood underground station.

He enjoyed living in this affluent area of London for a variety of reasons.

A central factor concerned the relative silence which pervaded the place. Although the St John's Wood region was a 'stones throw' from the city, it was a temporal retreat in many ways, being blessed with an atmosphere that was more akin to a village or small town. Stowles lived in a majestic three-storey residence which was situated quite close to the tube station. The house was way beyond his needs space-wise, but it was useful for his huge collection of films and 'point of sale' cinema displays - these were his family in effect. During inclement weather Stowles took a taxi to his house but on mild October evenings like that night, he would always walk the short distance. As he commenced his twenty-minute walk, Stowles felt far more positive than he had done for some time. The therapeutic silence of St John's Wood eroded some of his project determined bitterness to a level. Stowles glanced at his watch, which registered 21:33 and he then became aware of some footsteps a short distance behind him. The sound had cut the silence and they were the only human presence that Stowles had encountered since leaving the station. He partially turned round to see if he could discern the identity of the individual in the streetlight but the figure was further behind him than he had envisaged, and all Stowles could determine was that the individual was very tall in their build. They wore dark, probably black clothing.

Stowles then heard a second series of footsteps approaching the road he was walking down, from a side street some thirty metres in front of him. He started to feel a bit uneasy. Out of the silence had arrived two fellow pedestrians and Stowles crossed to the other side of the street in a bid to create some distance between him and the two other walkers. As he looked back across the street, the second person came into view - albeit through streetlit illumination. This man was shorter than the first figure but he was powerfully built and his determined stride seemed aggressive in its intent. He crossed to the pavement that Stowles was walking down and the fugitive broke into a half-run.

Stowles was impeded quite considerably by his disability and all the pursuer had to do to keep up with him was increase his gait to a brisk walking speed. Stowles was starting to perspire when his pursuer spoke.

"Nice video, Brynley".

For the first time in his life, Stowles ran. Fear was his spur as he raced down the road like there was no tomorrow. As he increased his speed he felt a series of sharp pains in his back, which were agony to endure but he kept going, not fully registering the pain. Stowles knew that if he was caught, he would feel a far greater pain, and so he made a courageous effort to maintain his speed as the pursuer started to close the distance between the pair.

The MC Project didn't forgive, and as the pursuer started to close in on Stowles he envisaged the praise he would receive for bringing to ground a project traitor. He was just about to jump on the hunched back of his quarry when he was stopped in his tracks by a blade!

Stowles had turned with an agility that belied his poor physical condition and had thrust the blade of his four-inch pocket knife into the chest of the man who had raced after him. As the man started to staunch the blood from the clumsy wound inflicted by the knife, Stowles took his chance and sped into the corralled environment provided by an adjacent building site.

Stowles had hated this development when it sprang up, but now the cover it provided could be his lifeline!

The residence being built was complete with regard to its shell, and Stowles made his way upward to the fourth level. The building was similar in design to the other adjacent properties in the neighbourhood but it was taller than most, subsequently providing Stowles with more cover. As he sought refuge in the upper section of the building, Stowles cursed his bad luck. It was now patently obvious that other MC Project staff apart from just Denison and Fray could break into the D39 storage method.

Stowles assumed that Mr Voight had examined his locked confine area when he had left Designation B for his ten day leave period. The man who Stowles had stabbed was one of Voight's security team and although Stowles didn't know him by name, he was quite a familiar presence around the British Designations. Stowles knew that what he had left behind in Designation B was enough to offset his execution. The commercially packaged nature of his video, with it's titling and post produced visuals could only mean one thing - that Stowles was aiming to commercially trade the explorations. The use of musical soundtracking was a third factor, which indicated the video was being designed for 'public' consumption. Voices from outside disrupted the reflections of Brynley Stowles. Voight's voice dominated proceedings.

"...just dead damn you. I don't care about guns with silences, without silences, knives - I really don't give a fuck! I want his head. That's the bottom line. I want the Fuqua's head - literally. Brynley is a popular team member and if we leave his corpse intact, old 'goody two shoes' Ko-Chai is going to want us to perform an MC exploration on the bastard when they return from the States. If Stowles is decapitated we will have eliminated all visuals pertaining to our role surrounding his death. We'll leave his body but incinerate his fucking head. You see guys, some of the project ranks are a bit soft really. Some would draw conclusions that our treatment was too harsh and project divisions would start to emerge. Leif will obviously get to know of our sentencing method and both he and Mr Fray will back us to the hilt but Ko-Chai, Vain and a few others are going to lose their trust in the security operations surrounding the project".

Stowles froze when he heard the men plotting his method of execution. There were now several hushed voices debating his execution. One of the men put a logistics based question to Mr Voight.

"A decapitation isn't going to be the easiest method of execution right now is it, Mr Voight? I mean it's not as if any of us have an axe or anything, is it? Wouldn't it be better to take him to the Designation to perform the execution, once we've caught him?"

"Jeez - Look around you Brookes. He's holed up in a building site for God's sake. You're going to find a range of objects capable of decapitating a person here. Stop bloody worrying, will you? We've got the guy surrounded, and if any local police show an interest my security identity badge will render them history in a matter of seconds".

The snatches of dialogue could be discerned for several more minutes, although the voices had become muted in their tone and thus Stowles could not discern any further specific information. He knew that things weren't going quite as planned. Voight's security operations usually went without a hitch and yet so far the attempt on his life had been a catalogue of mistakes.

The initial two pursuers had been too obvious in their tracking and had aroused his suspicions immediately. The usually flawless attack plan had fallen apart as well, being thwarted by a hunchback with a pocket knife! Stowles felt that Voight's methods indicated his state of panic and it give him a degree of hope. If the mistakes continued he envisaged that he might yet escape his pursuers. A pregnant silence pervaded the location.

Half an hour went by and Stowles heard no sounds associated with human approaches. Two staircases led up to his top-floor position and Stowles kept glancing at both in turn, expecting Voight's men to ascend through the moonlight. The silence started to cause beads of sweat to form on his brow, and every breath uttered by the man seemed to him to be amplified in volume. The partially tiled roof allowed the moonlight to stream through the uncovered sections directly above Stowles and a bizarre type of patchworked shadow was created as a result. Despite his fear, Stowles was briefly distracted by the effect the streetlight and moonlight rendered upon his location. For a few seconds Stowles was off guard. It was enough.

"And now your end is near!"

As the figure dropped down from the roof scaffolding, his leading arm punched the knife from Stowles's hand, and in one move Brynley lay disarmed in an excruciatingly painful judo hold. The connotational entrance line had been whispered as his pursuer administered his stealthy attack. Stowles had seen nothing with regard to the approach of his assailant. Stowles was then punched very hard in his face and as he struggled to remain conscious, his attacker bound his arms tightly behind him. As blood started to role down his left cheek, Stowles was laid out flat on the floor and he was kicked with great ferocity in his testicles.

The excessive pain made Stowles lose consciousness for a couple of minutes and when he came to, he saw Voight and two of his security team looking down on him. Three other security staff were searching the skeletal top storey with torches illuminating their movements. Voight gazed down in hatred at Stowles, his face illuminated to a malevolent degree by the torchlight. His words, when they came, had their usual measured precision with no hint of the panic inspired utterances he had made outside the shell of the building.

"So you thought you could make a pound or two out of Ms Venison did you, Brynley?

A shame Mr Yardley never got to actually see your hard work. All he had were your rather sad sketches and now he won't see anything, will he? God I hate treachery".

An excited exclamation interrupted Voight's rhetorical address.

"Fortune shines on the righteous, Mr Voight!"

One of Voight's men arrived on the scene carrying a stone cutting angle-grinder with him. The tool was anchored to a mobile power point and an extension cable meant it could be utilised throughout the length of the top floor. Brynley's eyes widened in horror as he realised he was looking at his own customised guillotine!

Voight spoke to Stowles once more - his final castigation.

"We're going to leave most of you here Brynley. They'll know it's you through your fingerprints but no one's going to really give a damn after they've been to your house. Our guys are stacking it full of kiddie porn right now.

"Your decapitation will go down as another unsolved scumland killing. You will have fallen foul of fellow kiddie-porn distributors.

"Who the hell is going to weep for you? Your head? Oh, your head! Well after Charles has severed it from your body, we're going to incinerate the damn thing! Do it Charles".

The angle grinder was activated and as Voight's man approached Stowles, the latter, lost control of his bowels. The grinder raced through flesh and muscle and the gagged Stowles breathed no more as the blade severed his neck like it was made of paper. The whole cut had lasted just five seconds.

As Voight's men descended the stairways the head was thrown from man to man. Occasionally it was dropped, causing the security personnel to break into unanimous laughter. Even the usually reserved Mr Voight couldn't contain himself. St John's Wood echoed to the sound of laughter.

NINE

When Vain arrived back in England, he along with his project colleagues was given a ten-day recuperating period to spend with his family. America had been beneficial as far as explorations and research were concerned. Indeed, Vain's front line team were now ready to 'test demonstrate' their work upon the extension to the MC Vault. The equipment to enable the recovery of visuals had been radically modified to enable the living 'thinking' mind to be tested.

The vault-splicer was now unrecognisable in comparison to the crude, 'inquisition' type device used upon corpses. The new device wouldn't penetrate the skin at all, being composed of small micro-fibre pads that absorbed sensory signals from the brain. The two pads were positioned fractionally above a person's temples and they were wired up to digitised laser facilities. The new vault splicer looked quite mundane, an almost basic piece of equipment, and yet it was a 'mind reader' in effect!

Despite their research successes, America had exacted its toll on the project staff and several of their number had been killed in Chicago. As the Designation J pressure had intensified, the bond between Vain and Levene had strengthened beyond just mutual attraction. Both felt something deeper, something more powerful - a feeling of trust and intimacy.

When Vain returned home to his loved ones, he was genuinely pleased to see his wife and children, but his mind did frequently conjure up the image of Levene. Whilst his love for Tanya was very evident, his lust for Levene made him slightly more 'distant' than usual. This aroused his wife's curiosity but he had told her about the events in Chicago and she assumed the loss of some of his friends had made him more withdrawn than usual. Tanya still found it difficult to comprehend the infrastructure of the project Greg was involved with because she was still denied the names of any of Greg's colleagues and could not establish any chain of command. She knew that both Britain and America were involved in the MC Project, and it was clear that America possessed a power dominance. She also felt that her husband had a close female friend amongst project staff. Greg had a face which betrayed what he was thinking on occasions, and Tanya knew when his thoughts were racing beyond his dialogue.

When he had described the Chicago fire he had stated that he and a colleague managed to scramble out of their project venue and when he had uttered the word 'colleague' he had avoided firm eye contact with his wife, looking down for a brief moment. This gaze avoidance reminded Tanya of an instance that had occurred shortly after her and Vain had commenced their relationship. Greg had been invited to a party which she couldn't attend due to work commitments and so he had gone alone.

The event had been organised by one of Vain's ex-girlfriends and when her partner returned home at 05:00, he was too drunk to reveal how the party had gone. When she tackled him about his behaviour at the said event in the afternoon, he was initially very careful to avoid maintained eye contact with his partner, looking at her side on or staring fixedly past her. It later transpired that his avoidance of eye contact was due to the fact that he had indulged in a bit of heavy petting with his former girlfriend. Vain's avoidance of direct eye contact had subsequently signified his guilt. When he mentioned the Chicago fire, the same look had been there - just for an instant. She decided to tackle him head on about her suspicions.

"Dark hair, tall and thin I should imagine love - is that about right?"

"You what, Tan?"

"Your fellow escapee, Greg. I bet she looks like that, I mean that's your ideal type love, isn't it?"

"Oh leave it out love. I was running away from a bloody fire, not copping off with elegant women".

"So she was elegant then, Greg!"

"Just a turn of phrase, Tan. I haven't even said my fellow escapee was female for goodness sake".

"Your eyes have, love, and I bet your Memory-Camera can paint quite a vivid picture of her".

Vain and Tanya indulged in this form of verbal sparring quite frequently during their ten days together and whilst a full blooded row never materialised, a tense atmosphere was generated by the air of suspicion that pervaded their house. The holiday was definitely spoiled by this factor, and Vain was almost relieved to return to his project duties when the ten days were up. He was amazed at the perceptiveness of his wife and although he hated admitting it to himself, a lot of her comments were correct deductions.

* * * * *

When the project ranks were reassembled at Designation B, Denison didn't waste any time in relating the death of Brynley Stowles. Mr Voight had informed him of the true story and he had indeed complimented the British head of Security for the fast, effective manner in which he tackled the treachery in question.

In his speech however, he ran with the 'planted' kiddie-porn scenario.

"Project friends, my welcome is tempered by some bad news concerning one of our number on this side of the Atlantic. In Chicago we lost some excellent committed MC Project colleagues and a few who abused our trust in them. Unfortunately Brynley Stowles's death is another occasion where an MC member of staff will have few mourners".

As several project members shook their heads in initial disagreement with Denison's words, Blyth Carson stood up and mouthed his discontent.

"Fuck you, man. That guy gave his all for this project. I know, he's been my best buddy for the last five years".

Mr Fray interrupted Carson.

"I think once you've composed yourself and sat down, Mr Carson, you will be able to listen to what Mr Denison has to say to us. I think you might change your opinion of the deceased. After all, I believe you have a couple of children don't you?"

Blyth Carson was confused, he sat down and Denison continued.

"There is absolutely no doubt that Brynley Stowles did work exceptionally hard for the MC Project. However, if I had known five years ago what I have now found out about the man, I would have shot the bastard there and then. Yes it's true, much as I love this project, there are some things that no moral person can endure. Child pornography is one of them, and unfortunately it seems that Mr Stowles had a double life. On the one hand, Stowles was the dedicated colleague we all knew and admired but on the other, he was a distributor of obscene films featuring the sexual abuse of children. He also distributed publications of an equally obscene nature. Obviously Mr Stowles was investigated by security before he was selected for MC Project work and his assessment report found strength after strength with just one negative trait being evident, involving a morose side to his character on occasions, that could possibly obstruct his teamwork. There was absolutely nothing to indicate the perversions that plagued Stowles.

"Distributing filth like the merchandise Stowles traded in is a very dangerous practice, as you are probably aware. Child pornography creates a market just like respectable products do, but violence and death cement the rules of market competition here.

"Brynley Stowles was a small-time player in this sick industry, and it seems he upset one of the big Taiwanese cartels who trade this form of obscenity in Britain. He was subsequently executed".

Mishimo Ko-Chai raised his hand to ask Denison a question.

"Things don't seem to add up, Mr Denison. Brynley was a workaholic with regard to our project. He simply would not have had the time to operate the distribution of any product, let alone obscene material. He was also a good man as well; he wouldn't have traded such sick material. I think we owe it to him to carry out exploration work on his MC Vault and see if he HV'd his killers. The parts we need to activate may still be responsive".

"That would be fine if we had it, Mishimo! His body is in the possession of non-project police officers, and when they found the corpse, the head was missing! The police initially thought that Stowles had been the victim of a kind of juju motivated murder and a story was leaked to a couple of twenty-four hour satellite channels giving sketchy details of the case. That was dismissed as garbage though, after police had visited Brynley's residence a day later. When they entered the house, the officers found the aforementioned child porn merchandise and a cartel killing became their logical conclusion. Their findings effectively closed the case. I mean no one was going to waste vast amounts of time looking for the severed head of a guy who traded kiddie-porn were they? Most of our project ranks were in the States at the time as you know, but Mr Voight capably followed the case, shadowing the investigations that were carried out by the 'regular' police authorities. An MC exploration is thus impossible Mishimo - we are denied our raw material!"

A wry smile flickered briefly on the face of Mr Voight, as he remembered the suffering of Stowles. Ko-Chai wasn't quite satisfied yet though.

"Surely the child pornography could have been 'planted' evidence, couldn't it, Mr Denison?"

"The guy was a pervert and we're well shot of him. The truth hurts sometimes and to answer your question more directly, let's just say that there was enough Stowles related DNA evidence found on the merchandise to sink a fucking battleship!"

As Denison left his speaker's podium, he laughed inwardly to himself, as he thought of the genetic duplication work Voight's men had undertaken on the material planted at their former project member's residence.

The meeting had left project members feeling either suspicious or betrayed. Those members who had been close to Stowles dismissed the child pornography allegations, feeling that their friend would not stoop to such depravity. Project members who hadn't known Stowles well, tended to believe what they had heard but it left them feeling 'unclean' by their association with the man. The revelation had disrupted the good working rapport either way, and it was not the ideal form of scene setting for the 'vault extension' demonstration that would be carried out that afternoon by Vain's team.

As Ko-Chai, Tavini and Vain walked around the gardens of Designation B, they discussed the revelations surrounding Stowles. Tavini was rather ebullient, dismissing the issue as 'yesterday's news' but Ko-Chai and Vain felt that the specifics surrounding the death of their friend lacked plausibility. Vain was like Tavini keen to discuss the operations of their forthcoming exploration, but as the trio approached the Designation, he chose to add one more choice comment with regard to the Stowles incident.

"One final thing, fellas. When we split ranks a while back, Natassia Overson disappeared. This time on our return, we find that Brynley is dead. A lot happens in our absence doesn't it, guys? Perhaps Mr Voight would be able to tell us a bit more, after all he..."

Tavini interrupted.

"Leave it alone, Greg. Some stones have shit under them when they're turned over, you know. The man's dead and if I were you guys, I'd drop your detective role. You're alive and well thought of by most of the project staff, but if you rock too many fucking boats - who knows?"

Vain's team had lunch together and then proceeded to the exploration area. In readiness for them were Denison, Fray, Levene and Matthew

Braddock - the project member who had agreed to be MC 'scanned' in the first 'living' exploration.

Once all the protagonists were assembled, the rest of the project ranks were ushered into the exploration room.

Mr Fray had been chosen to make the important introductory speech that would detail how visual thoughts would be created in the volunteer and how Vain's team would expose them. His tone was perhaps less sanguine than Denison's but he was a good speaker none the less.

"If this exploration is undertaken successfully, it will outrank the Venison showcase in terms of importance. We have dragged out 'seen' images from the mind and now we are going to try and record thought-determined visuals.

"This exploration will subsequently ascertain whether the MC Project has the capacity to mind read or not! You will notice that the equipment used to search the living mind is innocuous by necessity when compared to the barbaric appearance of the vault-splicer used upon the dead! Micro-fibre sensory padding has thus replaced barbed edges. I understand that Mr Braddock is quite pleased about this transition".

Fray's use of humour did endeavour to partially raise the spirits of the previously subdued MC Project ranks. Pleased with this rallying effect, Fray continued.

"In a few minutes Ms Levene is going to read to our volunteer. The selected text will hopefully conjure up images, which are beyond visual capture. In short, we should be able to access heightened visuals which are created through Mr Braddock's imagination. If all goes to plan, we will in effect read his mind".

Vain and his team finished their preparation duties and as the viewing screen was activated, Braddock was blindfolded. Greg had found out in his research that the membrane between the MC Vault and the vault extension was gossamer thin in sections, and the chance of overlap between the two sections was possible if Vain's placement of the micro pads was even slightly erroneous.

The blindfold aimed to counteract such overlap and if the 'physical sight' main vault section was accidentally activated all that would be seen would be the uniform blackness created by the utilised screening material. This was the understanding in practice and the digital conversion equipment would attempt to capture the 'imagined' HVs after Levene had read her short passage on three consecutive occasions. The equipment would be activated when Levene started her final reading.

Levene approached the raised speaker's podium and looked down at Braddock, who was laid on a marble slab a couple of metres beneath her. The ensuing silence from the project ranks was almost tangible in its presence. Levene looked resplendent in a black suit. Her hair was drawn tightly back and her eyes were accentuated by a dark eye shadow. She began her reading.

"The horses had heads like lion's heads and out of their mouths came fire, smoke and sulphur. By these three plagues, that is, by the fire, the smoke and the sulphur that came from their mouths, a third of mankind was killed. The power of the horses lay in their mouths and in their tails also; for their tails were like snakes, with heads, and with them too they dealt injuries".

Denison had selected the passage from Revelation because he knew that the subject matter involved a visual register which couldn't possibly be locked into the 'main' visually determined section of Braddock's

MC Vault. If images were located, they would have to be his thoughts.

As Levene started to approach the closure of her second reading, the atmosphere hanging over the exploration area was uniformly pensive. No one moved or spoke and all eyes were trained on the screen.

As Levene referenced the horses for a third time, the wait was over.

Braddock had envisaged the beasts of the Revelation passage to a level of visual clarity that equalled film with regard to the quality level. Occasionally images of Levene's face would become interspersed within the Revelation visuals and thus a bizarre hybrid of speaker and text existed. Braddock's mind had thus activated an image of familiarity amidst the chaotic narrative. One amalgamated image was particularly memorable in its execution.

This particular visual featured Levene's face emanating through the flames, which were being exhaled by one of the beasts, and her eyes cast hatred down to the minions in purgatory below her. In Braddock's visual construction, Levene had thus become as menacing as the nightmarish creatures that destroyed mankind.

The exploration arena went wild with excitement. The quality of the accessed visuals had been so good, that even the most optimistic expectations had been surpassed. The pessimism that had been generated by the death of Stowles, had with the exception of Carson, been replaced with euphoria. Project members back-slapped each other and shouts of triumph added a resounding crescendo. Levene's reading of the short biblical passage had been visually translated by Braddock in a fashion which sent pulses racing and his subconscious insertion of Levene's face had been the crowning glory.

Tavini found Vain amongst the celebrating project ranks.

"Yo Greg, we did it man, we fucking did it! We're mind-readers now, buddy!"

Vain replied in the same enthusiastic tone as his team member.

"Dead right, Dave! I thought nothing could beat the Venison exploration but Fray was correct - this 'mindsight' raid was perfect, - short but fucking sweet. Let's go and see Braddock. That guy's going to go down in history you know - the first person to physically have their mind read!"

The two men made their way through the project throng and eventually located Braddock, who was surrounded by some high ranking project members. One of them was Leif Denison, and when he saw Tavini and Vain approaching, he was ecstatic in his praise.

"Congratulations, gentlemen...

"...with Greg's excellent front-line team and this gentleman's vivid imagination, we've taken our work into another dimension! Meet Mr Braddock, fellas.

"Forget Mr Armstrong, we've just taken one 'giant step for mankind.' These are the guys who exorcised your mental imagery, Matt!"

Tavini and Vain were introduced to Matthew Braddock. They had seen his face before but as he was in Dwight Richard's security section, they hadn't had direct interaction with him. Vain took the lead after Denison's introduction.

"Well done Matthew, you made a brave decision to be the first! Any problems with the sensory equipment?"

"Not really, Gregory. I knew all about the 'laser side-show' that would take place in my head beforehand, thanks to Leif, and so I didn't feel any apprehension or anything like that. I suppose the pads seemed bigger than they actually were at the time, because I knew what they were capable of doing - their capability seems disguised by their mundane appearance! I'm dying to see the re-run though. I heard you guys screaming and applauding but I was blindfolded, remember! Any chance Leif?"

Denison quickly assured his young recruit that the exploration would be re-run for the remainder of the day in the demonstration area, directly after he had addressed the assembled project ranks. The project leader had been pinning a lot on successful vault-extension work because a forthcoming Washington event was in his eyes 'made' for grand-scale extension work. Once the euphoria had died down, Denison took his position on the speaker's podium.

"I'm damn proud of you. This morning was a bitch, but this afternoon has been our greatest moment thus far. All of you have enabled our success and each one of you should feel proud of our collective achievement. Matthew Braddock was willing to let his brain be used for experimental research and this type of indefatigable commitment is typical of the unanimous spirit that drives our scientific research forward. It will soon be time to let the world know, my friends! We have formatted all our explorations that were performed on the dead and we have Mr Braddock's 'mindsight' exploration. However, we need to amplify the 'seeing is believing' ethos by carrying out vault-extension testing on a larger audience who are collectively ignorant with regard to their test involvement. We need a non-primed test audience to silence the type of individual who may argue our MC work is an 'in house' fabricated construct. In twelve days time, we will have the perfect opportunity at the Washington Peace Conference".

The remainder of Denison's speech involved detailing what lay in store for the MC Project team before their departure to Washington.

Vain's team would spend the duration completing the training of the 'junior' exploration team.

They would collectively finish off their guidance surrounding both MC Vault work and vault extension explorations. The focus of the Washington Peace Conference was to instigate a 'First World cradle' of nations, which could be called upon to help Third World nations who were beset by civil wars, famines or military coups. The principles underpinning the event essentially involved the strong helping the weak, and whereas other Global forms of provision had debated this type of help before, the WPC aimed to be far more pro-active in it's attempt to erode Third World conflict.

A proposition had been put forward by the French for a National mentor system that would involve powerful countries nurturing the development of impoverished nations, in terms of their political stability and their raw material utilisation. The idea would basically feature one 'dominant' country taking a Third World nation under its wing. The proposition did not necessarily hold that nations who entered into this type of 'sister' relationship would already have had previous colonial links set in place. The WPC was essentially trying to start from a 'clean slate' position that didn't want history getting in the way. This event was supposed to set into motion a 'new age' of commitment as far as Global alliances were concerned.

TEN

Leif Denison had several surprises for the MC Project ranks when they arrived in Washington. On the third day, all 'key' front line personnel were moved out of the Washington Designation and into 'The Connoisseur' - a magnificent hotel within the 'Dupont Circle' area of the city. He also gave staff a fair degree of freedom with regard to their movements as far as sightseeing 'DC was concerned. Denison wanted to take the accent away from the usual hard industry, to one that favoured therapeutic team bonding in the build up to the WPC. He also wanted to 'spread' the holistic project ranks, because the Chicago experience had unnerved him with regard to the complexities surrounding mass evacuation procedures.

A series of stipulations had to be adhered to in the three days of comparative project freedom. All project members had to move about in groups or pairs. It was thus forbidden to move through Washington alone. No group or pair were allowed to journey into the ghettoised areas of the south-east and north-east districts because of the gang violence culture that abounded in both locales. Denison had installed a nightly curfew which commenced at 23:30 but this was relatively liberal when compared to the 'lock-ins' that had been a feature in both English and other American Designations.

The MC Project members had not been restricted as far as 'social' grouping was concerned in the three-day period, although most individuals mixed in groups which echoed their project work placement. Vain and his team did spend some time together as one social unit but Levene was also annexed to this main front line section, so she and Greg could meet to socialise on occasions to a 'legitimate' level for the first time, as far as project bonding was concerned. Most MC Project members had already realised the mutual attraction shared between the pair, and with a lighter atmosphere temporarily hanging over operations, people talked more openly about the mutual closeness evident when the two were in a social project environment together - albeit amongst themselves and not directly to Vain or Levene.

On the second evening of relative 'free-time', Levene and Vain explored the Georgetown region of the city together. Marcia filled her companion in on details surrounding their chosen destination.

"This area was rejuvenated in the eighties, Greg. Some people found the change rather ostentatious in its effect, but I think that reaction basically amounted to envy in most instances. You see, this area of Washington offered opportunity to the bright young minds of America and challenged stilted archaic attitudes in the process. I guess we'll always encounter the bitter 'better than thou' attitude from some of the forty-plus generations when they see those in their twenties and thirties really letting their hair down - and the bright, upwardly mobile denizens of eighties Georgetown really knew how to party, Greg. I know, I was here quite often!"

"Are many of your previous haunts still here, Marcia?"

"Sure. Not all of them, but enough for us to recapture the atmosphere.

"One of them, 'Alvettis' wine bar is still the ultimate. I thought we could head there first".

Vain quite liked it when Levene took the lead in social interplay. In his previous relationships or friendships with women, Greg had usually been the person who called the shots concerning where they would go and what they would do. His relationship with Tanya didn't fall into this type of passive acceptance category, but Levene's magnitude added a new dimension to his experience of women. When he was with her he preferred to be led. Thus far their relationship had been exciting without excessive physical intimacy, and because the couple had to resist temptation through project requirements and marriage commitments in his case, he had found the attraction he had for the woman growing to unprecedented levels of sensual feeling. When Greg was with Levene he was very much in her spell, and although he didn't fully realise this factor yet, his feelings toward this woman had been complicated since Chicago by the 'need' he had started to feel for her presence. It seemed a long time since Vain had been suspicious of Levene's presence amidst the MC Project ranks. As the pair entered Alvettis Levene cast Vain a very 'knowing' glance. Her power was often reflected in her minuscule facial gestures, and when she playfully bit her bottom lip whilst offering a half-smile, Vain was 'hooked' on each occasion. This was her chosen gesture in Alvettis, and combined with her cold dark eyes, the overall look was essentially her winning formula.

The pair found a table in a secluded part of Alvettis and Levene ordered two-half bottles of the house red.

The primary reason Levene found the wine bar

attractive concerned the Art Nouveau type decor, which established the style of the venue, and this interior design factor also appealed to Vain. The chosen colour scheme of blue, purple and silver added a debonair quality to the place, as it ran through most of the fixtures and fittings, being broken only occasionally by black wood furniture. Alvettis also made good use of stained glass seclusion panels and the MC Project pair effectively had their own 'glass menagerie' of privacy.

As the couple conversed in their alcove, heavy rain started to hammer down on Georgetown. Hail was interspersed with the rain, and a cacophony of sound was generated as the stained glass windows of Alvettis were lambasted by the elements. Vain and Levene sat opposite each other, with a small round black wood table between them. Levene looked exceptionally elegant, wearing the dark suit she had favoured during her recitation role in the Braddock exploration.

The key light source in their vicinity emanated from a small Nouveau designed lamp on their table, and the ornate patterns that were sunk into the glass lamp covering cast bizarre shadows on the faces of the couple.

Vain moved closer to Levene, taking hold of the woman's left hand and gently pulling her towards him. In their dimly lit location, his project partner had a presence, which was almost supernatural in its intensity, and whilst Vain had noticed this factor before, the weak illumination given off by the table lamp accentuated her dark image to a degree some way beyond other occasions. As Greg looked into the depths of her dark eyes, she spoke in a whisper. There was a sensual urgency in her voice.

"Feel me, Greg".

She forced Vain's right hand under the table and directed it through the split in her skirt toward her thighs. Vain didn't need any encouragement as there had been sexual electricity inter-playing between both individuals for some time now, and he greatly wanted to explore her body on a more intimate level. This seemed like a fitting occasion to do just that, and the threat of detection from the table girls who brought drinks to customers heightened rather than diminished this feeling. Her second directive was a more specific instruction.

"Trace me - every line, every fold. Let your fingers talk to me".

As Vain's hand travelled upward toward the vaginal region, he inwardly marvelled at the smooth nature of her skin.

She felt cool initially, but as he approached the favoured region he felt a heat pulse through his hand. The difference in temperature was uncanny and as his fingers contacted her briefs, Vain's libido was further charged by the dampness he encountered through the silken material. His forefinger crept inside the gusset of Levene's briefs and as he gently parted the material, his hand became wet from the woman. He didn't start tracing the curves of Marcia's outer labia immediately, preferring instead to gently knead her small pubic mound and the upper reaches of the areas of skin on her bikini-line. These were shaved with great precision and the underlying softness was a perfect complement to the spiked feel of her pubic hair. Vain's fingers started to work figure of eight patterns through the pubic mound, gradually diminishing the area of coverage in each successive stroke. As Vain's fingers got nearer to Levene's clitoris, the woman uttered a faint cry as she anticipated his touch on her most sensitive area. Levene bit down quite hard on her bottom lip and her eyes half closed when Greg finally touched her clitoris. This touch was the spur for the release of further vaginal juices, and Vain just managed to stop himself from ripping off the flimsy briefs and copulating with her there and then! Slowly, Greg's forefinger started to penetrate Levene, and her minuscule thrusting movements enabled him to get deeper into her. Levene had a compact vagina and yet her powerful vaginal muscles had a strength, which belied her graceful exterior. As Vain's hand became fully covered in her juices, he inserted his middle digit. She writhed to his movements, finding it hard to control her gasps as she neared climax. When Vain believed she was ready to cum, her eyes opened wide and whilst grasping Vain by the wrist of his active hand, she made her third request.

"Taste me, Greg".

"Go down on you here, Marcia! There's only so much we'll get away with you know!"

Pulling Vain's face close to hers, she whispered a bizarre instruction. Her hands held Greg's face tightly, with her fingers spread from his temples to the point just below his chin. Her eyes pierced his, only a couple of inches apart.

"Listen, Greg, you are going to bring me off big time, but I want this first one to be on my terms, okay? On our table there are two objects. The first is the Nouveau lamp which you've probably noticed by now - beautiful, with a vibrant silver, blue and purple colour scheme. The second object is one you probably haven't given a second thought to - the tiny bowl of black cherries. Alvettis pride themselves on their minutiae theme retention, and the cherries do indeed echo the favoured purple.

"I want you to taste me with one of the fruit Greg".

137

"I've lost you here Marcia!"

"Then I'd better nurture your imagination hadn't I, Mr Vain! Take one of the cherries and push it into me. Don't look into my eyes, don't worry about hurting me and don't talk at all. This will be our time, Greg, and I want you to taste the fruit once it's been in me, deep in me".

Although Vain had naturally been quite taken aback at the unusual nature of the request, he was more than ready to comply with her wishes. He was aching to ejaculate himself, but he was curious to see how Levene would 'recover' the fruit once it was inserted. He took a black cherry and he inserted it into her vagina. Her hands tightened on his face as the fruit was inserted and Vain shut his eyes as he envisaged what he was doing. Levene spoke.

"Deeper, deeper - near the womb entrance".

Vain pushed the fruit up Levene's vaginal passage as far as he could, using two fingers to guide the cherry toward the intended region. When she was satisfied with the positioning, she momentarily freed one of her hands from Vain's face and directed his fingers back to her clitoris. Then she kissed him, her tongue lashing around his mouth like a serpent rearing in the wind. Whilst Vain massaged her nether regions, Levene's tongue sank deeper into Vain's mouth.

In a state of frenzied passion, she momentarily bit down on Vain's bottom lip. A small amount of his blood passed between their mouths, and a tiny residue trickled down Levene's chin. No one disturbed them, such was the sanctuary that their alcove provided, but the two would have been oblivious to an interruption anyway, due to the intimacy they were collectively experiencing. As Levene came, she placed her hands underneath Vain's shirt on his back and sank her fingernails into his shoulder blades. With shreds of Gregory Vain's skin under her nails, she moaned quietly into the side of his neck and as she did so, her powerful vaginal contractions forced the fruit down towards her opening. When Levene recovered her composure, she looked into Greg's eyes and spoke softly into his ear.

"Thank you, Greg. I guess you can taste me now".

Vain felt inside Levene's briefs again and as he entered Marcia with his fingers, he soon encountered the cherry.

"Taste the real me then, Gregory, but don't bite down or the fruit juice will blur my presence. Basically you've just got to suck to find my flavour, biting will only contaminate!"

Gregory Vain had not anticipated that the taste of Levene's vaginal juices would be radically different from the other women he had performed cunnilingus upon, but as he flicked the cherry around his mouth he did notice a sweetness of flavour that he had not encountered before.

Her taste did contain the usual musk-like element, but mixed with this was something quite distinct. After seven or eight seconds, the presence of Levene was gone but her taste would live for a long time in his mind.

"What is your verdict, Greg?"

"If I was sampling a good wine, Marcia and you here, by extension, I would definitely allow the waiter to fill my cup. Do you want to carry on in my Connoisseur suite?"

"No Greg, not yet. Don't get me wrong, I've fantasised about you since our first meeting, masturbating to my mental images of you on occasions, and project restrictions have left me feeling desperate to consummate our relationship. In Chicago my sexual urges for you were almost racing out of control, but I had to keep the lid on them and I started to get sexually high on our mutual state of institutional bondage - Christ, I even came when we kissed at the end of one of the lower thoroughfares in that Designation! I want to keep the repression in place until after our global MC revelation. After we have spoken to the world about our discovery, internal social restrictions will be reduced to a fair level and then if we get caught fucking each other senseless Leif and Fray are going to let our indiscretion pass. The Stowles affair hit Leif hard you know, and I was amazed when we were given the semi-freedom we are currently enjoying! If he found out about us now, he'd blow big time. We would definitely be separated in terms of project operations and our every move would be monitored constantly - we wouldn't even be able to visit the bathroom without a damned surveillance camera watching us!"

"I guess you're right, Marcia, but I can't help thinking that it might be worth running the risk all the same. My suite is around the elbow of the corridor the front line crew have been located in, and it is subsequently relatively private".

"You're forgetting that Ko-Chai is your closest neighbour, Greg. He watches us like a fucking hawk, seeing you like a wayward son and me an intellectual harlot! If he did happen to suspect I was alone with you in your room, I'm damned sure that the guy would find an excuse to interrupt us".

"I'm sure Mishimo doesn't think that of you, Marcia. He's often said how important it is to have bright women like yourself in the MC Project ranks".

"Maybe so, but the guy bugs me with his preaching on occasions. He thinks I'm some kind of vamp that wants to suck you in and spit out the bones!"

Levene placed her hand on Vain's arm and assured

him that the wait would just make things better in the long term.

"Think of the waiting as a kind of build up - a pain to gain factor that will make you cum like a river when the duration is run".

Vain eventually saw the sense in Levene's line of argument, and the pair decided to have a couple of Budweisers before they would have to leave to fulfil the curfew deadline. As they drifted into a conversation about the eighties spirit that hung over Alvettis, a woman approached their alcove. Her line of inquiry was direct from the outset.

"Marcia, Gregory, at last we meet! I'm Vicky Lassiter from the 'Washington Vanguard' and I want to ask you about the MC extension testing that is going to take place at the Washington Peace Conference".

Although naturally taken aback by the woman's project knowledge, Levene and Vain adopted the much-rehearsed policy of ignorance, which had to be adopted by MC Project staff in the event of such a security breach. Vain took the response lead on this occasion.

"I'm afraid you've made a mistake, Miss Lassiter. My name is Paul Hedges and this is my wife Sonia. I really don't understand your request; we work in Commodities. I'm sorry we can't help you, but we're not the people you are looking for, and if you don't mind we would prefer you to let us enjoy our time together without any further interruptions - we get precious little time to call our own".

"Nice try, Mr Vain, but please give me a bit more credit for my researching abilities. The Conference Gregory - what are you going to try to prove in MC terms?"

"Look, we haven't got a clue about your damned Conference or the MC thing you keep on about. If you persist in bothering us, I'll have to ask the door staff to remove you".

Turning to Levene, Miss Lassiter continued to try to force a weakness from her quarry.

"Do you speak Ms Levene, or is Gregory Vain your mouthpiece?"

Marcia's reply was instantaneous and it kept up Vain's charade to an excellent level.

Paul and I are equals Miss Lassiter, but our relationship is none of your damned business. You see that stained glass door over there? It's beautiful isn't it? Why don't you use it - good bye".

The woman was made of an indefatigable spirit though, and she persisted with another avenue of attack.

"Oh leave it out, folks. Are you saying you haven't heard of Fray, Venison and the Chicago fire?

"Are you going to remain mute about Stowles, FBI infighting and Braddock?"

Vain decided to show a vague familiarity with one of the names to see if the woman would reveal any more MC Project information. This was phase two of the method of counteracting leaked project knowledge. He had to stall the woman, so that he could assess the potential damage put in motion by the project traitor. This method of counteracting was only known to a dozen high ranking project staff, and thus if she knew it's stages, she would know that 'in-situ execution' or incarceration were the final conclusion! If this was known, the leak would have emanated from one of the highest project sources and all hell would break loose in terms of internal project security organisation.

"I do know a David Braddock from our South African imports Division. Is that the guy you mean?"

Miss Lassiter started to lose her cool - exactly as Vain and Levene hoped she would.

"Do I look like I left my brain on the stairwell Mr Vain, or does your 'never surrender' attitude emanate back to your 'stiff upper lip' English patrimony. Come on folks - lighten up. We all know that I know the inner workings of the MC Project and a fair proportion of the events concerning operations. My unit can break you now, if you aren't co-operative. The Washington Peace Conference will never happen if we reveal all we know about your project in tomorrow morning's edition. You see, Gregory, you can't play games with the media - did you really think your project could hide from us? If I don't get a story, the whole fucking shebang will be on the 'Net' within minutes. If you help us, we'll even break the story after the event, so your best laid plans can stay intact".

As Lassiter spoke, Vain surveyed her intently. She was exceptionally bold in her blackmail, and her face retained a confidence that showed no element of fear or trepidation at all. Vain could thus deduct that the woman was either ignorant of the three stage procedure or had a kamikaze journalistic streak. He concluded the former deduction was the correct one, and he felt pleased that no high-level leak had been made. Neither Vain nor Levene were prepared for the next development that took place in Alvettis.

Mr Fray, Jess Wheeler and two security personnel entered the alcove. Fray turned to Miss Lassiter without looking at the two MC Project staff.

"How pleasant it is to meet you, Miss Lassiter - my name is Fray. I think we may well have a story for you here. After all you already know a great deal about our project, don't you?

"Well, I have been authorised to detail our extension work plans to your paper but directly to the Editor you understand, and so if you would be so good as to divulge their website identity or phone number, I can deal with the matter right now".

Lassiter started to look pale. Her Unit had moved on the MC Project leak without notifying their Editor or any of their fellow newsprint colleges, just as Fray had envisaged. She had wanted her seven strong team to achieve the ultimate scoop and sell the story down the line to the highest journalistic bidder. Her greed had created a cocoon of isolation for her Unit and this played into the hands of the MC security ranks. It was going to be far easier to deal with one discreet separatist group than a holistic Institution. Lassiter answered Mr Fray with a tone that now had trepidation mark its delivery.

"That won't do, Mr Fray. I think he is absent right now, but he's due back tomorrow. My six Unit staff can take your story though - they will all be in attendance in our office corral right now. I think they..."

Fray interrupted.

"Too right they'll be in attendance ready to blow MC Project details all over the Net, if you don't get your fucking story - isn't that what you said? Our surveillance guys sussed you weeks back but you just clarified our one area of uncertainty. You didn't want to share 'Pandora's box' did you? Your greed will build your fucking coffin now!"

Lassiter felt that she still had an ace to play.

"You're wrong, Fray. If my crew doubt my safety for an instant, all your details will be scattered through the Net. It's our survival card - harm us and you go down too!"

Fray put his hands together in mock applause and a sardonic smile appeared on his face.

"You stupid bitch. Hold the CIA and FBI to ransom would you? Jess - do it".

Wheeler broke Lassiter's neck before she even registered his hand descending towards her. The woman slumped forward onto the table but such was the controlled ferocity of the blow, no heads turned toward their alcove. Jess Wheeler had dealt a death blow like others would swat a fly. Fray turned to Vain and Levene, apologising for interrupting their evening with a fake sincerity that was easy to determine.

"Marcia, Gregory, what can I say? Good evening, young lovers, wherever you are. That would have been a better greeting wouldn't it, but we had a killing to attend to and Jess had to work around you - I hope we didn't disturb you too much!"

After the white haired security chief had aired his sarcasm, his mood darkened.

"Alvettis is going to close early tonight. My guys will take the corpse away and the place will be corralled just like standard CIA practice. The mandatory forensic crew will be brought in - you know the white line ensemble.

"Some of the staff and a few customers will be questioned by our back line personnel and I guess that just leaves you guys, doesn't it? Well, someone's been dying to congratulate you on flushing out the press and preserving MC Project secrecy in the process. I'm sure this person isn't that bothered about the odd transgression of security stipulations. I'm sure they think that intimate liaisons in wine bar alcoves don't represent any threat to project security and I'm positive that having a long frenchie across a table wouldn't attract attention! As for the other stuff - well what do you fucking think? Both of you are to wait here".

As the security squad took their leave, Wheeler

couldn't resist a comment to Vain. He had disliked the Front line team leader ever since Vain had questioned the necessity of Wheeler's actions in the Chicago gunfight.

"Try using a chilli pepper next time Gregory - makes a girl squeal like a pig!"

Levene and Vain were rendered silent for a while after the security staff left to close down Alvettis. Whilst they felt both embarrassment and anger over the surveillance of their intimacy, the overriding mutual feeling was one of fear. As Leif Denison approached the alcove, they realised that their relationship was established top-down! When he spoke, his eyes were less cold than Frays but his initial words were just as hard hitting.

"Thank you Marcia, thank you Gregory. I mean that. Your collective movements were so easy to predict in Washington - it was just a matter of researching Marcia's favourite hang outs. We hooked four venues with acoustic isolator capabilities that separate out conversations to micro frequency signals. You were the best form of bait we could possibly have in terms of flushing out the Vanguard threat, both of you being young, good looking and bloody naive in your movements around Washington!

"We knew you wouldn't be able to keep things low-key if we gave you free time possibilities, and we were reasonably confident that Lassiter would follow your movements. I was impressed with your operation of the three stages surrounding MC Project detection and before your castigation I suppose you deserve some credit for this observance". Denison drew his breath audibly before continuing.

"I guess you know you're a pair of fools, don't you? I mean let us examine things here folks. Your attempts to hide your attraction for each other have hardly been convincing, have they? You buddy-up in both UK and American Designation sites, you 'eye to eye' each other at meetings and you faun around Washington like a couple of teenagers awaiting their first heavy petting session! Back in the cold war era, the pair of you would have been a fucking nightmare as far as security is concerned, and I guess we are lucky that some of the current eastern heavyweights haven't locked into the MC Project scent yet. If the latter had happened you would have been expendable Marcia, if you get my drift!

"After Washington, we will break our discovery to the world, if what we envisage in the Peace Conference transpires - that some delegates speak peace with a hidden agenda of take-over. So far we've been very lenient with the pair of you. You've been monitored more closely since Chicago because your attraction towards each other seemed to be escalating. Ironically this factor probably did help us during the fire, because in the mayhem of the windy city crisis you both helped protect each other as well as your quest for self survival, and naturally we were extremely pleased to get two of our brightest project personnel out of that shithole alive. Having said that, you must realise that neither of you are infallible, and as I've said before the MC Project is the real power - bigger than anyone. It turns all we know upside down – Christ, our baby is a new fucking religion!

"A project controller with a more irascible edge to them would have wiped one of you as a lesson to the others, maybe both of you for that matter. You two are damned fortunate that I didn't listen to advice along this line from some of my more - shall we say impetuous colleagues!

"Until we have broken our findings to the world, I want the pair of you to cease all fucking contact with each other, barring work commitments.

"If you trivialise our collective team spirit with your mating game prerogatives, I'll pull the fucking trigger myself!

"This time your security risk status did us a favour but if that hadn't been the case, Jess might have been breaking someone else's neck. You've been given a reprieve this time. Just make sure your future behaviour doesn't load my gun. Come on Mr Vain, you're going back to The Connoisseur. Marcia is going to finish her drink here and reflect on how fucking lucky the pair of you have been not to be going out of here with Lassiter!"

Leif Denison had provided a rude awakening for Vain and Levene, shattering their illusion of safety as far as their relationship was concerned.

Denison had clearly established the threat that his two front-liners had been to project security, and his words had their desired intent as far as the installation of collective fear was concerned. As Vain journeyed back to The Connoisseur in the rear of the project leader's limousine, he had time to mull over the events of Alvettis. He regretted the naiveté that both he and Marcia had shown with regard to the power of the security embryo that hung over the MC Project, as it seemed as though surveillance had followed the couple in their most intimate encounters. He thus realised that when the pair had thought their privacy was unchecked, they had a camera or a recording device chart the progress of their affair. This factor annoyed Vain, rather than make him feel guilty for his security indiscretions and it put the MC Project rein handlers in a new voyeuristic light in his mind.

After his anger subsided, fear returned as he tried to recount what he had said to Levene about project developments and the leading figures that orchestrated them. He felt reasonably certain that unlike Levene, he had directly criticised Denison,

Fray and Wheeler on occasions when the pair had met, and he now wondered what this power triad would have heard him say about them. Alvettis had been the most impressive security decision as far as Vain was concerned and he had to admire the perception with which the security section had anticipated Levene's choice of location in her Washington free time.

As the car approached the driveway to the hotel base, Vain thought about what Denison hadn't revealed. He tried to determine who had leaked project information to The Vanguard, and he wondered what fate awaited Lassiter's 'in the project know' colleagues. These were answers, which Vain would never receive - his security misdemeanour with Levene ensured that.

*   *   *   *   *

When Denison's party entered The Connoisseur, David Tavini greeted Vain in a show of typical exuberance.

"Yo Greg, good to see you, buddy. You gotta skip the cabaret pal, because I gotta take you through the conference set up details. Come on we'll take the elevator to the project rooms - we can talk there".

Tavini had preferred to stay in touch with the organisational details surrounding the Peace Conference, during the free time period, as had Ko-Chai who met them when they disembarked from the elevator. Upon greeting Vain, Mishimo echoed Tavini's buoyant enthusiasm. He even managed to take the verbal lead away from Tavini for once, when they entered Vain's suite.

"The set up makes for quite a show, my boss-man! With speaking delegates, front line aides, back line interpreters and the plethora of body guards, over two thousand people have to be accounted for. This figure doesn't include our own MC Project staff or conventional security forces and so you can envisage the magnitude and sheer volume of the event".

Tavini interjected.

"We've finalised the ten first world nations who are going to put their provision cases forward Greg. The ten are going to be the first nations to take the global media entourage through the cradle support system and their vault-extensions are going to be recorded during their twenty-minute verbal introductions. As the delegates speak, we'll access their thoughts buddy and when Leif gives us the nod halfway through presentation ten, our findings will be illuminated on the huge laser screens directly behind each speaker's podium. Obviously we're going to need you to check the sensory positioning of the padding that is encased in the headgear that the speakers will wear. We've placed the line adjacent to the microphone cables that link the speakers to their respective interpretation crews. Our reception devices are out of sight in a section on the third floor overlooking the arena - we've got space either side Greg, keeping our security without looking too fucking suspicious in the process. The other third floor sections are all media annexes you see and we're hiding amongst them!"

As Tavini paused for breath, his eyes became very excited. His athletic frame moved closer to Vain and Tavini's voice became hushed in comparison to the volume that accompanied his utterances thus far.

"The best news as far as we're concerned surrounds three of the ten speaking nations. We would have been mad to turn the potential gun on ourselves here, and so the Brits and us will have a 'no show' as far as speaking is concerned, but we reckon some of the big guns speaking have ulterior motives surrounding their supposed cradle based assistance. What these guys say could be a fucking mile away from what they would really like to do with the countries they have offered to help!

"The French are on show. After all the conference is their fucking idea, but we reckon their good guy image could be a bluff.

"The French are supposedly going to help Guyana with their depressed economy and raw material management, but our research has indicated that a 'clean sweep' take-over plan may lie behind their offer. Think about it, Greg. They already have control of French Guyana, and only the Dutch owned Surinam lies between what they already control and Guyana itself! A territorial clean sweep would give the frogs one hell of a presence in South America.

"Sure they could milk the metal processing and timber raw materials of these countries, but we reckon their interest in Guyana is more closely linked to the testing ground potential of the tropical environment prevalent in this region of the world. The French have been stepping up their production of organic germ warfare compounds - living weapons that contaminate through parasitic regeneration. One of their latest efforts 'Guerre Ex 20' is a real fucker, breaking down tropical vegetation through an injection of mutant spores that essentially pollute localised oxygen in a region. If people come in contact with the stuff, they're dead in seconds if they're in close proximity, and thus the French need a paradise to play around with as far as testing goes".

Vain begged a question of Tavini.

"Why do the French need Guyana as a test base though, Dave? Can't they get a control programme working in their own back yard?"

"Only through simulation, Greg. You see the nature of Guerre Ex 20 essentially means that it needs a 'living' environment to breakdown. Yeah, a simulated environment would give them a good effect idea, but they are looking for grand scale living landscapes to wreck for want of a better phrase.

"They have got things off to a fine art here. Guerre Ex 20 only fucks up a location in tropical environments, and another creation 'Zed 29' only devastates in high altitude 'thin air' locales. The French have been under scrutiny since they fucked up in Fiji with their atomic testing a few years back, and although Gericault promised a radical reduction to their military programmes when he got elected last year, we know that they've intensified their germ warfare capabilities to an awesome level!"

Vain was intrigued by the possibility of a hidden agenda being the reason for France initiating the peace conference. His love of French style and art had always been tempered by his distrust of their approaches concerning military research, and he was also suspicious of the far right political leanings that Gericault had demonstrated on occasions. Tavini turned his attention to the second of the three nations that the MC Project ranks doubted as far as integrity was concerned.

"We've also got strong suspicions with regard to Germany's offer of support to Burundi. The unstable nature of the military coup-determined Government in this country has meant that the country is a mere shell of the potentially flourishing nation it could be. The Krauts have offered to help stabilise it politically by offering their services as an arbitration type mediator.

"They have also designed a regenerative tourism programme, and a landmine clearance scheme is apparently ready to implement now!

"The Germans have already promised that they wish to nurture the autonomy of Burundi as opposed to transplanting their national culture on the place but the package seems too fucking good to be true doesn't it, Greg?

"You see, back in the late eighties we had some of our research guys out there bluffing on the archaeology front. Their real role was to ascertain whether 'heavy metal' deposits existed in three key regions. They drew a blank, but four years later we know an undercover German party scored a hit, finding quite a rich vein of uranium and slivers of caesium as well. Things went quiet after that because different tribal factions started to use the area as a fucking battleground, but we think that in the light of our findings, the German support offer could be a serpent's kiss rather than a moral blessing!"

Vain put a question to his team members.

"The territorial French case seems very legitimate fellas, but this one is a bit lacking in terms of validity. I mean Germany are an affluent nation - if they wanted substantial heavy metal reserves, they could import South African supplies without skirmishing for them in a war torn outpost! I mean a fourth Reich isn't exactly around the corner, is it? Why would the Germans want to stockpile stuff like uranium nowadays? They're businessmen, not warmongers! The South American Neo-Nazi strongholds make Germany passive in comparison".

Vain's Korean team member offered a wry smile before answering his front line leader.

"How right you are, Gregory. The Germans are indeed businessmen and that is exactly why Burundi appeals to them. They don't have any master race sentiments motivating their offer of support here and they would indeed provide the forms of assistance they have offered, but when Burundi starts to recover economically they would offer the country a bargain it would find hard to refuse".

"A bargain?"

"Yes my leader, a bargain. You see, Burundi would flourish over time if all goes to plan, and Germany would be seen as a pivotal force in the new prosperity. When Germany prepares to pull their support forces out of Burundi, once prosperity starts to arrive, the alarm bells would sound amongst the Burundian people. The Germans would have a whiter than white image after the decade we feel it would take to turn the country's economic fortunes around, and the home country would extend retention offers to their European mentors.

"Burundi would realise that ten years of growth wouldn't kill a vendetta culture outright, and they would fear that the old civil war evils would return to haunt them.

"Germany would be seen as the key to the maintenance of a new peaceful equilibrium, and a retention of their support services would be of paramount importance. Then the Germans would ask the Burundians if they could have the trading rights to any heavy metal reserves they could locate in certain sections of the country. It would now be the right time for the Germans to farm the fields of Uranium, which they had kept secret from the Burundian people back in the eighties. The bargain would be struck and Germany would have a lethal chemical trading post in the process! They would sell the metals through to the highest bidder - without risking fatherland contamination! Oh yes Gregory, the Germans are good businessmen!"

Vain was taken aback by the intricacies his two-team members knew about the nations speaking at the forthcoming conference. He started to realise that whilst he and Levene had been lusting around Washington, his team had been briefed on the gameplan for the conference. He felt guilty initially, although this feeling soon turned to fear. Denison had made Vain realise that both he and Levene had been bait to corner the Vanguard press section, and now in his absence both his front line colleagues had been party to information that would have been conveyed to him first in the past. Vain felt uncomfortable, even expendable to a degree. None of his team had mentioned his liaisons with Marcia, but the rather distanced tone from Ko-Chai and the curious intensity in Tavini's eyes made Vain anxious to return to the ranks of the front-line team fold. The quantity of decent background information that the pair had fired at him in a matter of minutes accompanied the inquisitor-type eye contact, and Vain felt on the rack by their combined effect. The flood of information had rendered him silent, and Tavini saw his chance to enlighten Vain with regard to the final speaking nation that had aroused the suspicions of the MC Project research unit.

"China is the other nation that could well be double-talking on the podium, Greg. They have initially offered to assist Laos with agricultural regeneration. Laos is supposedly a Left Wing Republic at this moment in time, but exist under satellite government control, with their Chinese neighbours effectively making political decisions for them. In this form of mock autonomy, Laos are just a puppet for the Chinese, and the offer to help with agricultural policy was no great surprise. The statement that followed it sure as hell was, though!

"China is going to call for a 'Western' alliance to help consolidate the economic future of Laos. The alliance would be based in Laos, with all the support nations being actively involved.

"The Chinese say that their role would be equal to the support of Western nations, not overriding in its capacity.

"Mishimo and I have been surprised to say the least, at the Chinese calling for a Western aid presence so close to Chinese territory. The economical research and planning that the Western alliance would undertake would inevitably mean uncovering flaws in some of the Chinese-regulated decisions taken for Laos in the past. This form of global exposure would bite China hard. I mean, the economic hardship in Laos is really their work - their dirty fucking laundry! China is up to something, pal. Calling for Western assistance isn't exactly in their nature, is it? Would you want a dozen ideologically-oppositional neighbours sitting on your garden fence, examining your errors and offering corrections - would you fuck!"

After Tavini had finished detailing the suspicions surrounding the Chinese conference support offer, Vain took his leave of his two front line team members and headed for his own hotel quarters. Ko-Chai had given him some diagrams to survey concerning the conference layout, and he had been given the listing order of the ten 'speaking' nations. These countries would initially make a concise twenty-minute speech that would succinctly detail the offer of support that they were intending to make. They would also establish why they had sought to offer help to the third world country, which they had selected.

All mentor pairings had been suggested and agreed upon some months back, and thus the chief function of the WPC was concerned with the illumination of mentor-based help to the widest possible audience. In effect the WPC was hopefully going to be an event with a seminal capacity. It would set mentor support in motion and it would act as a catalyst for other similar conferences to ensue. The hidden agenda of the MC Project ranks would radically alter perceptions surrounding the event, if their suspicions were given visual credence on the wrap-around laser screens, once they were activated.

Denison had decided to record the 'heightened visuals' of the speaking countries as soon as the first nation began their twenty minute verbal address, but the images were to be withheld from screening until halfway through the final speaking nation's address. The Spanish were subsequently the chosen nation who were going to be interrupted by the laser screen HV playbacks. At a sign from Denison, the screens behind the respective speaking podiums would be activated, and the mental imagery of those who had spoken would be displayed for everyone to see.

Denison initially expected a brief confusion to reign but when speakers were confronted with images from their own 'mindsight', a partial realisation of the mind probing that had taken place would follow.

Tavini and Ko-Chai had been briefed by Denison with regard to the organisational details surrounding the conference, but Vain had been shut out to a level, as the MC Project leader wanted to make him feel the pinch that ignorance generated. He still realised that Vain was one of his projects' most prized human assets, but the affair that he and Levene had fallen into had slightly tarnished Vain's image in Denison's eyes. The affair had ironically helped Denison and the MC Project as a whole, because the pair's good looks and powerful positions had helped flush out the 'chasing clique' at The Washington Vanguard. Lassiter's greed-motivated secrecy had been uncovered by her pursuit of the illicit project lovers, and subsequently, her discreet press-unit was expunged quite easily.

* * * * *

Vain was still feeling less informed than his front-line colleagues when he waited for the conference to commence, two days later. Although the event had been a French initiative, the United States had effectively put the idea into motion, and subsequently the American President - Mr C. M. Delavoy, was the individual who was going to open the proceedings. This Western figurehead was clad in ignorance as far as the operations of the MC Project were concerned, and as he began his opening address, his quest for Global Peace moved the ranks of those who were similarly ignorant to the hidden conference agenda.

Vain surveyed the Presidential speech from the confines of the MC Project accommodation on the third floor. The tiered structure of the floors gave the venue a quality that was similar to a huge operatic venue, and as the President closed his introduction, a crescendo of applause rose upward to the press annexes where the MC Project cohort lay in readiness.

The applause continued to a consistent level as the speaking nations took their respective turns on the podium and their mindsight imagery was logged in line with Denison's instructions. No one pre-empted the recorded HVs by recalling material before Denison's signal, and although Leif was elsewhere in the building, Mr Fray was there to outlaw any contravention of his leader's wishes. Some of the project ranks had wanted to check their findings as things progressed, but Denison had been adamant in his refusal, claiming that the MC Project would win either way.

If all the images endorsed the verbal promises, then at least mindsight capture could be illuminated, and if some images were at odds with verbal intentions, as they suspected with France, Germany and China, then 'forked tongue' treachery could be exposed.

Vain glanced down at Delavoy while the crowd heartily applauded the Italian offer concerning third world support. As the presidential hands entered into the ovation, Vain inwardly marvelled at the ultimate power that the MC Project commanded. He was looking at a naive figurehead who was ignorant of the hidden intensity of the occasion, and although other American Presidents had been shunned by security power organisations before, Delavoy had never been approached by either the CIA or FBI with regard to MC Project work. His name would not be seen as a pivotal presence when the history books told the story of the WPC, and he would be relegated as a discarded entity.

The nations under suspicion came to the podium in their allotted order, and the bevy of interpreters translated their respective intent. The French representative made a passionate speech with regard to the raw material expertise his country could offer Guyana, and the German speaker detailed the arbitrary strengths his country could offer Burundi. The Chinese delegation involved a triad of speakers who slightly overran their designated duration; such was their apparent enthusiasm for seeking Western collusion with regard to the future of Laos. After nine nations had made their speeches, the Spanish made their way from the back of the conference hall toward the podium, and Leif Denison entered the hive of expectancy that contained his MC Project cohort.

All eyes looked toward the powerfully built project leader, and after formal greetings were briefly exchanged, a pregnant silence pervaded the control room.

The Spanish delegate began her speech and everyone waited for Denison to fire through the 'all-important command'.

A droplet of sweat trickled down Mr Voight's temple but the man remained undeterred, his eyes looking into the oblivion favoured by those in deep thought.

Ko-Chai eyed the clock intently and Denison was finding a mutual time to set the laser screens in motion. He then started to tap out a discordant rhythm with a pencil on a table edge situated in close proximity to him. This act incurred a piercing stare from Tavini and Mishimo subsequently ceased the nervous affliction. Gregory Vain's eyes fixed on the spectacle-taking place beneath him. His palms were moist, and as he willed Denison to act, thoughts of his children briefly raced through his mind.

Vain looked toward Denison's direction, just in time to see his leader deliver a blow to the 'Vation' unit that activated all the laser screens. As he did so, Denison let forth one of his lines of immortality.

"With this act I thee wed. Nations - here's the future!"

As the screens started to render the stored mindsight images, the crowd was initially confused with regard to the interruption. The Spanish delegate stopped in mid-sentence, and as she surveyed the screen behind her interpretation entourage she became pale; seeing her words of support converted into the imagery she had envisaged. This delegate was the only speaking individual who could witness her own mindsight from the outset because she spoke on the master podium and could thus take in all the delegate screens in unison.

The other speakers could see imagery on the screens behind their fellow speakers straight away, but their screen was situated behind them and thus the visual side-show on offer initially distracted them from looking behind their own section.

This uneasy equilibrium did not last for long, and a staccato cry of outrage uttered by the German speaker set chaos into motion.

The images that caused the German delegation to get upset didn't tally with their definition of support for Burundi. The HVs collected from the German speaker endorsed the suspicions of the MC Project, showing convoys of articulated military vehicles with German insignia adorned on their livery. The vehicles displayed the identity of the various 'heavy metals' that the Germans had discovered in Burundi. The screen then cut to freight trains with the same type of cargo, and shortly after the trains came a series of images which caused the German delegation to stand up and point accusing fingers in the direction of Delavoy. By screaming abuse in their native tongue, they generated a frenzied pandemonium in the space around their section. The images which caused such fury concerned portraits of extreme depravation. Whilst the German speaker had preached his words of support, his mind had logged the real agenda Germany had with Burundi, and his subconscious had supplemented this vision. Rows of wasted maltreated Burundians watched the export trains speed through stations, and these images were the symptom of Germany's real mission in this African country.

The Burundians were spectrally thin in a fashion very close to the imagery surrounding famine and some of them looked as though they were about to fall where they stood. In effect the Africans looked as though they had their life-force sucked from them and one image in particular kept reoccurring fighting the others for dominance. This image featured a frozen close up of the face of one of the Burundian onlookers. This portrait involved a young male Burundian, about ten years of age, who smiled when the trains passed, but this smile illuminated bleeding gums and his eyes were caked in a residue designed by malnutrition. The lad looked as though death would be a blessing, because his smile was forged in lost faculties and the delirium associated with those who are victims to wasting illnesses. The German speaker Werner Schinkell had made what seemed to be a morally sound support speech but his mindsight had betrayed the German offer - right down to the bleeding gums of Burundian persecution.

Whilst his colleagues screamed abuse at Delavoy, Schinkell just sat down shaking his head in disbelief. He knew that somehow, someone had read his mind.

As the clamour of agitation grew, the various security units in attendance shifted uneasily in their assorted positions, and the Burundian delegation started to project lines of suspicious enquiry in the direction of the Germans. Some delegate nations remained quite calm amidst the escalating chaos, and as more nations became aware of their own laser display screen, some speakers started to take the lead with regard to explaining the source of the images behind their delegation.

The Italians were one nation that remained calm despite being a country of vivacious extremes with regard to their political reputation. Their calmness was achieved because they hadn't had a hidden agenda like some of the other nations, and thus visual truth married verbal promises. The most composed delegation were the Chinese - one of the nations under suspicion.

This nation sat in uniform silence as they viewed the consternation around them. Their own laser screen highlighted a consistency of HVs despite the fact that three speaking-delegate minds had been explored. The illuminated imagery showed Chinese politicians, shaking the hands of Western politicians and representatives of Laos were given a central visual prerogative. Crops in healthy abundance appeared on the screen, as did images surrounding education and medical developments. Each group of images featured the presence of China, the home nation and Western support, just as China had verbally promised. The MC Project suspicions concerning this country were subsequently unfounded, as China had not hidden falsehoods within their words. China had nothing to hide - their words had been their bond.

The nation that protested most vehemently was France. Her idea lay in tatters at her feet because of the lies embedded in her offer of support to Guyana. When the French delegate's visuals appeared on the respective laser screen, not even the most suspicious MC Project members could have prepared themselves for what met their eyes.

The French speaker had sold the raw material support France offered Guyana very effectively, imploring the South American nation to embrace the European nation by agreeing to a mentor partnership that would set a seal for a permanent alliance. The speaker's voice quavered slightly as they spoke of the economic hardships Guyana had got used to living with, and as the delegate drew near the close of their address, tears of apparent empathy ebbed down their cheeks. It had been a speech which had won over the assembled nations and the global media entourage who were present to record the events surrounding the conference. The French received the loudest applause because they initiated the idea underpinning the conference, and because their chosen speaker injected so much passion in their oral delivery. When the supporting HVs hit the screen, the German visuals looked almost tame in comparison.

The initial images showed French helicopters spraying the tropical vegetation of Guyana as nationals surveyed the scene from the foreground. The South Americans cheered as the spray hit the vegetation, and a few French soldiers helped co-ordinate a burst of applause as the spray cascaded downwards. Smiling faces abounded and as more spray was discharged, the French led the Guyanans in cheering every time a fresh piece of vegetation was contacted.

The next series of images well and truly shattered the notion of regenerative teamwork. These HVs illuminated gas mask wearing French troops sifting through Guyanan corpses that lay in a devastated tropical wilderness. The speaker's heightened visuals had betrayed the method by which France was going to initially test Guerre Ex 20 in Guyana. France was planning to spray the tropical vegetation of this country in the pretence that the action was linked to the rejuvenation of sections of damaged foliage. The French would tell the South Americans that the liquid sprayed from the helicopters was part of this rejuvenation process and this factor explained the 'envisaged' cheering crowds in the mindsight of the speaker. At this stage in the visual display, the conference audiences who were observing the French screen were confused. All they had seen so far was evidence of a good rapport between France and Guyana and then the corpses. The third series of HVs clarified the treacherous 'cause and effect' links between both sets of images.

These visuals showed consignments of Guerre Ex 20 being transferred from military storage vehicles to the helicopters.

Emblazoned on the side of the said vehicles was the name of the deadly cargo, and as the Guyanan delegation made the very obvious conclusion with regard to what they were witnessing, they turned as one to confront France for an explanation.

The visual show wasn't over though, and whereas the first three batches of HVs had an element of gradual continuity to them, the remainder hit the screen in a discordant, racy fashion. These visuals showed mass graves of Guyanan dead, French execution squads shooting rioting Guyanans, and the French flag billowing over the desolate landscapes of the home country. The image of the tricolour kept reoccurring frequently between the various batches of HVs and this image rightly became synonymous with all the suffering being displayed. Images reminiscent of the Nazis dominated the screen, and the French flag claimed ownership of all of them. The Guyanan delegation broke away from their area, and with the support of their security personnel, they attacked the French delegation. With eight of the ten nations having no ulterior motive with regard to their verbal promises, it became clear as far as the speakers were concerned that the images carried a visual truth. After all, the speakers were looking at their own minds on display! Delegates from different nations snatched moments of partial conversation with each other, and this factor meant that accusing fingers were pointed at both Germany and France, after the realisation of visual truth had started to sink in. Some delegates preferred to carry on surveying the screens in silence. They were overcome by the fact that the 'thinking mind' could be converted to film.

As fights started to break out in the conference hall, American security forces tried to keep a state of order. Delavoy shifted uneasily in his seat. He, unlike the enlightened delegates below him, was still largely ignorant with regard to the motivating factors concerning the chaos that was taking place, and as the violence started to escalate Delavoy was ushered away. The Burundian delegation were assisted by other African nations when they attacked the Germans, and some South American nations helped Guyana attack the French. As one German hit the floor dead, the scene was the antithesis of the peace motive which supposedly governed the conference. Bloodied knuckles and broken chairs became hallmarks of the occasion as the conference degenerated into the universal language of violence. The Chinese remained seated in calm dignity as bedlam reigned around them. They were collectively an ingredient of constancy, and as the American security forces gradually started to restore order, the Chinese took their leave in a uniform departure. They passed a wounded member of the French delegation, who kept repeating "witchcraft, witchcraft" in his native tongue.

Leif Denison turned towards his MC Project cohort. His words were uttered in frenzied excitement.

"Guys - we've made it. Fuck the honesty of China, the other two climbed right into our fucking web. Our mindsight tracking has left the world wondering what the hell is going on. It's time to 'break global' guys - we're gonna let the world know!"

ELEVEN

The Washington Peace Conference shook the world as the MC Project staff had envisaged. Most of the speaking nation delegates had realised the link that the conference had exposed, between a person's thoughts and their recorded mental imagery. The other nations hadn't made a connection that was quite as clear, but words of enlightenment had been exchanged during the event, and thus nearly all the nations left the conference with the knowledge that some kind of 'mind-reading' apparatus had been tested.

The conference had definitely exposed a form of treachery from two powerful European first world nations, and this factor was the chief reason for the violence that forced the event into a very premature closure. Rumours had escalated in the global mass media with regard to what the hidden agenda behind the conference had involved, and truth became camouflaged by speculations of ignorance in the two days after the conference. The French and Germans verbally attacked America, claiming that their respective visuals were a fabricated construction. Both nations carried broadcasts featuring strong Anti-American sentiment on television, and the political leaders of these countries sought 'crisis-talk' opportunities with Delavoy. These were not forthcoming at this point in time though, because the American President was genuinely ignorant with regard to what had taken place, unlike the 'guilty' nations and their media bluff.

Leif Denison enjoyed the forty-eight hours which elapsed after the conference, because in effect he held the American power reins with regard to the global exposure of MC Project operations. The man could hold the world on tenterhooks with regard to this exposure if he so wished, because his elite position was beyond Senate or Presidential control. Denison effectively commanded his own 'micro-empire' and to say that the man enjoyed this position of control would be an understatement - he worshipped power!

The presentational method planned for the 'global exposure' press conference was very meticulous in it's design, and Denison had decided to utilise Vain's team to a person at this event. All three would be named via code-based pseudonyms, but their physical appearance would be shielded from the media ranks, by corralled 'single view' screens. Both Denison and Mr Fray would initially address the global media entourage, and each man would flank the screens concealing Vain's front-line team. Both Denison and Fray would not be 'screened out' but would stand in full view, almost like sentinels protecting the identity of their 'dream team'.

Denison would initially set the scene by acknowledging that a hidden agenda did underpin the WPC. He would then give a brief description on the primary vault research that was undertaken upon the 'dead' mind, and after his words, Fray would activate a laser screen to show visual recordings from the first two explorations performed by the front-line team. After a short duration, the images would leave the screen, and Denison would then explain the full criminal significance lying behind the visuals that had just been witnessed. He would then continue with his verbal address, by relating the exploration work undertaken upon Braddock and the 'living' mindsight capture retrieved from him. This revelation would be followed by Leif's summation of the key events surrounding the WPC, and both he and Fray were going to let the world's media understand how it felt to be to be 'in the know' visually speaking, when the chaotic confusion reigned beneath them, amongst the delegates.

Denison was going to involve some of the Chinese delegation in the press conference, as they had been impressed with how the 'Americans' had achieved 'thought capture', and they obviously hadn't been aware of the initial project suspicions that hung over their nation. The Chinese had maintained a uniform calm as violence reigned around them, and this factor motivated Denison to seek their presence when global media exposure of MC Project prerogatives took place. The Chinese acknowledgement of the 'truth' behind their visuals would in turn condemn both France and Germany, and Denison envisaged that their calm demeanour would be a better way to 'feed' the global media entourage than a reliance on just two 'all American' males. The Chinese delegation had displayed a controlled dignity at the conference, and it was envisaged that their presence would be an effective sedative to conference proceedings. The MC Project leader had planned out the Press conference with Fray's close support, and both men knew that the world's media would expect some 'visual' demonstration surrounding MC Project work - in effect the media ranks would expect a 'performance'.

Denison briefed Gregory Vain's front-line team with regard to the format of the press conference, and after his verbal address Vain directed a question to his MC Project leader.

"What contingency plans have you prepared, Mr Denison, if the media ranks believe the 'fabrication falsehoods' spread by vengeful or ignorant nations?"

"Well Gregory, we hope that our screenings will convince the majority of the media representatives in attendance, but we do realise that individuals who decry the legitimacy of our work will generate some initial disbelief amongst those who may wish to keep scientific development 'checked' in the confines they have gotten used to. We have subsequently decided to have two contingency strategies prepared, to counter this negativity. Our primary response will involve screening the exploration performed on 'Christopher'. You may think that this is a back-to-front way of illuminating our work to the world, but this effective 'failure' on our part will score for us here. It will prove our fallibility to a global audience and our research should command a greater appreciation in the process. Human nature is such that our honesty surrounding an area of failure will soften some of those who may have suspicions regarding our work".

As Denison paused, Vain reflected on the merits of a strategy which used failure to stimulate belief. He eventually decided that this form of contingency plan did have a part to play in MC Project exposure, although he could see that Ko-Chai was having trouble coming to terms with the value of this method. Vain knew that Mishimo's look of disapproval was generated by the word 'failure' being Denison's favoured adjective for the exploration involving Christopher's dead mind sight. Ko-Chai wasn't going to re-open an old wound here by any protestation though. He was keen for Denison to continue.

"If there are still a significant number of nations who doubt the validity of what they see after the screening of the 'Christopher' exploration, we have a final power card to play - the Braddock option! We will offer the opportunity for any individual to have their mindsight read, and although this may seem a bit like a cheap conjuring trick, it will eradicate any dissenting voices for good. Individuals who wish to have their 'heightened visuals' screened will be told to think of very vivid, memorable images and before they are 'geared up' for the extension scan, they will write down brief details surrounding the imagery. These will be distributed to a small sample of media representatives as they survey the set up of the relevant mindsight equipment, or whilst the individual is tested at respective two-minute intervals.

"After the third testing, the imagery will be given the 'ole screen test and those holding written information surrounding the imagery will endorse the truth of what they have seen. If we have to resort to using the mind reading option we'll get 'em. After all, seeing is fucking believing as far as we're concerned!"

Vain had never encountered an individual who could plan ahead to the level of precision that Leif Denison maintained. He would often foresee developments which others would only stumble upon once they were in the heat of a situation, and if his master gameplan was challenged in any way, Denison always seemed to be the master of alternative strategy.

This flawless organisational ability was again in evidence at the start of the global press conference. The event was held in the same venue as the Washington Peace Conference but the assembled media ranks increased the attendance to a figure which was three times greater in totality. The world's media were ready to try and dissect the faction and myth which hung over 'Memory-Camera' operations.

As Denison introduced himself, his face became an icon for the hoards of photojournalists in attendance - he would be their front-page tomorrow.

Vain and his team watched the crowd from behind their one-way screens, and as Denison's words rose to counter the camera noise, the screens vibrated slightly due to the deep tones of the American's amplified voice. The speech favoured by Denison was similar to the one he had made after the Venison exploration, but this time the names of the 'front line' team were changed to protect the trio's real identities. Vain was encoded as 'The Mindfinder', Ko-Chai as 'Laser' and Tavini as 'The Converter'. The MC Project leader then turned his attention to the Venison exploration, working back to front with an initial concentration that involved television pictures showing Sandford-Everett being taken away to commence his imprisonment after his 'quick-fire' sentencing. These images had been flashed all around the world and many journalists had wondered how the accused had been metaphorically 'hung, drawn and quartered' in a matter of just a few days when he had such powerful Legal connections. Fray then activated the display screen, and gradual enlightenment started to dawn in the minds of some of the assembly.

After the screening, Denison pointed out that DNA linkage was used as a secondary conclusive method in establishing guilt. People couldn't refute genetic evidence, and the project leader explained how this factor gave MC Project operations a 'protective womb' to hide behind until global exposure took place. He stressed that he realised that images could be digitally morphed together to a remarkable level in the current technologically-accelerating zeitgeist, and thus he was particularly careful to ensure that MC Project explorations were not understood to be an 'alternative' to genetic determination - he wanted the assembled media ranks to appreciate that work done on 'dead minds' would still be underpinned by DNA conclusions in terms of proof.

The graphic visuals of the MC exploration performed upon Leah were the next batch of images to be screened and some hardened journalists audibly drew their breath as they witnessed the devouring of the eye. Both Denison and Fray explained how the lack of quality in these images emanated from the fact that the girl's Memory-Camera only had a half-power facility!

The assembled media ranks were fascinated by what they were witnessing, and after Denison moved on to detail and screen the 'living mind' exploration performed upon Braddock, several journalists broke into a brief impromptu applause.

Three of the Chinese delegation that spoke at the peace conference then made their appearance. These individuals had been requested by Denison, and after the MC Project leader had detailed the 'hidden MC agenda' behind the conference, the three explained what it was like to have your 'recent' thoughts visually captured and played back at you!

Their words captured most of the remaining doubters in the audience, but a few dissenting voices could still be heard when the conference ranks prepared for the 'question and answer' session which followed the Braddock visuals. Journalists from the two nations found guilty of treachery at the peace conference spread American conspiracy rumours amongst the collective gathering, but the loudest voices of suspicion came from a small group of Japanese journalists.

Akira Ying Sun was the most dismissive in his tone, and he seemed to represent a powerful self-elected figurehead as far as the 'rejection' totality were concerned. It was Ying Sun who first challenged Denison in the Q and A session and in perfect English, his line of condemnation bit straight into the heart of MC Project operations.

"You will have to try harder Mr Denison, many of us remain unconvinced with regard to the authenticity of what we witnessed. We all know 'America gets what America wants' and many of us are extremely sceptical about your 'all too conclusive' visuals. Where was the invitation for Japan to become involved in MC Project research? It was never given Mr Denison, and now you ask us to believe in your visual constructions with China as your best ally.

"You have inferred yourself that we live in times when visual morphing can create new fictional hyper-realities, and now you ask us to believe in your metamorphosed fairy tales! You quote DNA as a secondary support factor in your research, but with both the CIA and FBI involved in determining this project, isn't it fair to argue that genetic evidence can be easily fabricated? To speak in a language I'm sure you'll understand Mr Denison - can't you do as you damn well please? The Braddock demonstration was just an upgrade of Hollywood wasn't it?"

Denison was tempted to bite back in the hard line style he usually favoured when he felt confronted but on this occasion, he saw the value behind remaining calm. As the journalists briefly debated the merits of Ying Sun's attack, the project leader made up his mind to forego a screening of the exploration performed upon Christopher and give Akira the chance to partake in the 'Braddock option'. He rounded on his quarry keeping his anger firmly under check, with his eyes only registering faint annoyance.

"Well Mr Ying Sun, I'm sorry that you find our work unconvincing. I feel that you are in a minority, but I guess the best way for you to learn the truth will be for you to have your own mindsight read and displayed. I didn't want to have to resort to cheap conjuring tricks Akira, but I guess there will always be those of you who want to keeping the lid on science. If you are willing to have your mindsight read, we can arrange the set-up behind the screens?"

Akira Ying Sun expressed his willingness to be tested, and Denison proceeded to divulge the method of testing. He explained how the individual who underwent mindsight testing would be blindfolded and have their ears covered, so their concentration was of the optimum level. Denison continued to detail how the individual being tested must think of a very powerful series of visual images on a reoccurring basis, and at a point determined by Denison, the individual's mindsight would be read and displayed on the laser screen which Mr Fray controlled. The final instruction that Leif gave to Ying Sun necessitated that the journalist write down brief details of the mental imagery he was going to envisage, and distribute these details to a small sample of fellow journalists at the press conference. Akira Ying Sun could determine which individuals received his visual agenda. As Ying Sun rose in readiness to walk behind the screens, he briefly turned to face both Denison and the press conference totality. His departing line had such a precise tone that it almost seemed rehearsed in its intensity.

"Screen this, America - if you really can climb inside one's mind!"

Vain's team attended to Ying Sun and as the journalist was made ready for the exploration, a silence descended over the venue. Denison was given the signal that the subject was in readiness, and the waiting began. After seven minutes, the laser screen illuminated the images that were destined to 'turn the world round' and act as a new scientifically determined 'dawn' for mankind.

President Delavoy's face was the first image to hit the screen. Ying Sun had framed the man's features in a 'static' capacity, reminiscent of a front-page type of exposure. This image slowly sank into blackness and after a few seconds of suspense, the visuals returned, but this time in a dynamic moving capacity. The initial image in the second batch focused solely on a hand which grabbed an axe with such force that the knuckles were rendered white. The mindsight Memory-Camera then started to retreat to expose the fact that it was Delavoy who brandished the said weapon. The man stood quite still with a malicious look upon his face, and although this was a powerful image in it's own right, the surroundings that housed the President generated great consternation amongst the assembly. The journalists were hardened individuals and they knew that they were witnessing a 'fictional' construct, but that didn't stop some recoiling in horror as they realised that Delavoy was standing with his axe in a maternity ward. Cots on either side flanked the President, with new-born infants being the occupants.

As the world watched events on televised up-links, millions of individuals uttered a collective 'no', but Akira's mindsight couldn't hear the cries for restraint and as the American leader stood poised above the first cot, many had to turn their heads away. The axe came down on the infant's skull, shattering it to a pulp and blood sprayed onto the wall behind. Two of the journalists passed out and several vomited where they sat. Delavoy's rampage continued systematically, and the infant screams reached a shrill pitch as the blade broke more young little bodies. Delavoy was once again 'framed' at this point but now his flesh was scarlet with the blood of the innocent. The blood ran down his face and his tongue licked traces of it from his lips. The portrait closed on a smiling, blood-soaked president. Some of the assembly howled their protest, bidding Fray to shut the screen down, but the project member was so caught up in the evil of what was being witnessed that he had been rendered frozen as far as a shut-down option was concerned.

As more journalists passed out, the carnage continued until the visuals thankfully came to an end with a focus on a tiny coat in a pool of infant blood. The guignol imagery had lasted for a total of just two minutes, twelve seconds, and yet their magnitude had reduced most of the journalistic ranks to tears or convulsions. The presidential guard closed in around their leader, as he looked like his worst nightmare had been played out in front of him and his pallor had diminished to a worrying shade of grey. When Delavoy keeled over, his guards were ready for his fall. The President had passed out after witnessing the fictional evil that Akira had let him star in - the split young bodies had been too much for him to bear. Denison restored order.

"I apologise that you had to witness such a sick mindsight exploration, but I'm sure the doubting Akira would want me to prove that we climbed inside his sick mind, and so I ask the chosen confidants to reveal exactly what Mr Ying Sun had planned to envisage".

One of Akira's trusted Japanese colleagues was the first to read. He stood up and with a nervous half-look at Denison, he read what had been entrusted to him. His use of English was not as flawless as his Japanese compatriot, but the clarity of the mindsight intention was clear for all to understand.

"Delavoy - breaking the children of America".

The other three confidants read out exactly the same words and it became patently obvious that Ying Sun's mindsight had been captured to a perfect degree. As the blindfold and earguard was removed from Ying Sun, he returned from behind the screens and sarcastically asked Denison if project staff had read his mind. Denison grabbed the journalist by the scruff of the neck, partially lifting him off the floor in the process and he screamed his reply straight into the face of his frightened volunteer.

"Oh yes Akira, we've read your filthy stinking scab of a mind, and a few of your colleagues probably want a few fucking choice words with you about what they saw".

Once Denison had reluctantly put his quarry down, he turned to the world's media and summed up the power of what had been witnessed. His closing line had been rehearsed for years - it was Denison's pièce de résistance.

"So we've climbed inside the private corners of the mind, and as far as you're concerned, the world of this morning is a thousand years ago!"

TWELVE

The global exposure of the MC Project and its focus of operation had proved a tremendous success. The press conference had been broadcast live to most countries and the newspapers of the world naturally ensured that the vast majority of their pagination featured coverage of the events in Washington. Akira Ying Sun's doubts had been shared by many individuals who felt, as he did, that the project involved a form of American manipulation, and thus after he had been won over by the witnessing of his mindsight capture, the vast majority of the global population followed suit - becoming 'believers' in the process. When Denison had introduced the focus of MC Project operations he had stressed that the collective personnel involved were American-led, but he did continue to say that project staffing was more cosmopolitan, with Britain being the second most powerful operational presence. Despite this, the overwhelming majority of individuals who witnessed the press conference events, either by a first hand presence or a secondary broadcast capacity, felt that this new scientific breakthrough owed America the biggest debt as far as driving forces were concerned. In many ways this public reaction reflected what Vain and others had been feeling for some time, and those people within the embryo of project confidence knew that this 'superpower' factor determined who was the ultimate project rein handler.

Within a few days of the press conference, repercussions beset France and Germany. Their guilt had been established beyond any doubt now as far as the vast majority of the citizens of the two respective countries were concerned, and pressure was placed on both the political leaders running the said nations.

Gericault resigned due to French public pressure, and Germany organised plans for an election to offer voters a chance to vent their feelings surrounding the exposure of their hidden agenda.

Several nations that traded with the two countries cancelled their commitment forthwith, and thus the Washington events were set to scar the high status of both of these dominant trade players. Gericault longed for a hiatus to slow down the global 'bad press' France had generated, but when he realised that world trust for his nation would take years to recover, he opted for a quicker personal solution.

As his lifeblood ebbed away, his lips offered a half-smile - he hadn't been the first 'French-Gericault' to find release in suicide.

Vain arrived back in Britain to enjoy a short period of project leave. The explorations upon the dead would intensify during this period, but now other front-line teams had been trained to relieve the pressure upon Greg's trio. Diana Fearston headed the support teams and Vain had personally trained her. It was Fearston who would research the gossamer thin membrane between the main MC Vault and the mindsight extension section. Gregory Vain had realised this area of the brain may well hold more answers for neurological science, and he was content to hand over the bulk of the exploration research to a woman of such a capable intellectual pedigree.

When Vain had journeyed through London on his way home, he had seen evidence of reportage surrounding the global press conference which had introduced the MC Project to the world. On newspaper stands, 'Mindreader' headings beckoned attention, and dynamic 'spectacular' display sites had running copy that kept reiterating Denison's power lines. One hoarding read "Who are our MC Heroes?" and for a brief instant, Vain regretted the anonymity that enshrouded his team.

Vain spent two weeks with his family, enjoying his return to the fullest level. His thoughts turned to Levene on occasions, but in many ways she was part of his 'other world' - the closed existence afforded by the MC Project environment. He tended to live a double life with respect to his domestic obligations and his more illicit interactions with Levene. After some initial guilt-determined discomfort, Vain had got used to living as both husband and lover. He felt safe because his two worlds didn't collide, and the secrecy that dominated project operations had effectively hidden his betrayal from those in his domestic world.

When he and Levene had been caught in Alvettis, Vain had been frightened that their security indiscretions may result in severe discipline being imposed on them by the hand of Wheeler, but after the optimum successes surrounding the global press conference, the fear diminished. Before Denison gave his MC Project ranks their leave, he had addressed all personnel. He had been gushing in his praise for each project section and he continued to speak of the 'less restrictive' internal security policies that would be an organisational factor when the MC Project ranks reconvened. Denison had prided himself on waiting for the right moment to globally display MC power, and his caution had been the motivating force behind the restrictions pertaining to internal security. Leif had 'won the day' with regard to global exposure and as far as he was concerned, his staff became the cement that underpinned his victory. He was keen to reward his team, and the reduction of some of the more pedantic 'internal' social policy regulations was part of his new edict. When the MC Project reconvened in England's Designation B, social liaisons between project members would now be permitted and an inquisition wouldn't hang over socially intimate project relationships. Denison's reward ironically seemed to endorse Levene and Vain - a more liberal internal social climate would greet the MC Project staff upon reconvention.

When the project rank and file reassembled at Designation B, the new liberal corporate culture was very much in evidence. The armed guard that lined the driveway to the venue was reduced quite significantly, and a banner proclaiming 'Victory' was hung from the Neo-Gothic pillars in the main entrance. The number of internal security checkpoints were reduced and even Leif Denison seemed less austere, wearing a navy coloured suit as opposed to the black clothing he had previously favoured. The project leader's greeting speech initially concentrated on this form of security relaxation, but then Denison carefully added that the MC Project was still underpinned by the most intense security cover of any Western research group that were currently on 'active' duty.

In the post-Washington ergonomic climate, MC Project staff still had to adhere to Designation curfews for the majority of their 'days in residence', but usually they would have a thirty-six hour weekend leave-facility built into their contractual commitment. When project staff were in attendance at an MC Designation, section heads would organise the hour breakdown with regard to their team's obligation, and Denison would check various section proposals.

Leif could call an intensive work period at any time and all sections would then wait on his instructions alone. The pressurised atmosphere of pre-Washington MC Project operations could subsequently be revisited if Denison felt the need.

Vain's front-line team carried out further mindsight explorations in the first week back at Designation B, and the majority of the volunteers involved Chinese scientists that Denison had invited into the MC Project ranks. These individuals were collectively very sincere with regard to the gratitude they expressed toward Vain's team, and as they 'shadowed' the front-liners a bond built up between the two groups. The good-natured Eastern delegation even seemed to nullify the inherent suspicions Tavini harboured for their countrymen and that represented quite a conversion! The team were more than ready for their thirty-six hour leave period as Friday's working commitment drew to a close, and as Vain packed his travel bag he looked forward to surprising his family with a quick return home.

Denison had introduced the new social freedoms on-site and thus, Vain had not been able to envisage that he would be back home on the first weekend. Usually an MC Project 'tour of duty' lasted a number of unbroken weeks and Tanya had got used to these lengthy separations. Vain felt that she would be pleased to see him despite the fact that they had rowed quite frequently during the recent leave period - Tanya still detested the notion of mindsight-reading even after witnessing the strengths which were evident in the televised global press conference. Vain hadn't had any interactions with Levene during the week, and he had wondered if she had had her 'fix' as far as he was concerned. Vain had only seen Levene from afar during the week and he was surprised that she didn't actively seek his company after Denison's effective endorsement. As Greg's bag was zipped up, he contented himself by envisaging the mental image of his good-looking wife. To Vain, relationships currently seemed to involve a no-lose scenario!

Vain was still mentally trapped in 'social blindness' as he turned towards the door of his quarters and he nearly collided with the figure in the doorway as a result. Leaning against the doorframe stood Levene.

"If that's a family bag you've just packed, I'll understand Greg, but one femme's ready to end the foreplay, if you get my drift!"

"Here?"

"No. I've got a place in mind. You drive, Greg."

The couple didn't exchange any more words before they left the Designation, and as they approached Vain's car, he stole a quick glance at Marcia. She walked with a purposeful stride, her eyes looking ahead with a forthright determination. Vain opened the car door for Levene and as she took her seat, she flashed him a smile that was both elegant and sexual at the same time. Her ivory-white teeth and long black hair proved to be an excellent complement to each other when she wanted to secure a person's attention - Levene's appearance left an indelible impression on the beholder.

Levene directed Vain to proceed toward London's West End, and after an hour, as the car neared her intended destination she added more definition concerning where she and Greg would be spending the night.

"I thought we could go to my 'London Retreat' Greg - a little two bedroom mews house that I bought four years ago. I wanted my own piece of London and when I acquired the house, it was a little dream realised for me.

"I haven't been there since just before the Venison exploration, but I employ a housekeeper - Miss Arnett to come in twice a week and look after the place. She airs the house and makes sure that both the freezer and real fire log pile are well stocked. Miss Arnett never knows when I'll turn up because even I don't know that due to my MC Project commitments! She's nearly seventy but I guess she's what some of you Brits call a 'real diamond'; I wouldn't replace her for the world. The house should be reasonably warm, but I thought that we could throw some logs on the fire because I've found that early May in England involves nights that are a bit chilly usually. Still, we'll probably create enough warmth ourselves won't we, Greg?"

Levene's London hideaway was situated in close proximity to the West End theatres, but the discreet Mews houses had been constructed in cul-de-sacs that enjoyed a quiet serenity which was oppositional to the bright light culture nearby. The houses dated back to the late eighteenth century and although their interiors featured twenty-first century luxury, their exteriors preserved a halcyon London quality from the era of their construction. The facade of Marcia's property was the same as the neighbouring houses with white stone dominance, black wood complement and brass embellishments proving to be three features of structural uniformity. When the couple entered the house, Vain realised immediately that Levene's personality came to the fore with regard to the interior design.

Black wood furniture, similar to the type favoured at Alvettis was used frequently, and on occasions peacock feathers appeared in black glass vases. Some 'Burne-Jones' wall hangings and a tiled 'Morgan' fire place highlighted Levene's affinity with Pre-Raphaelite art, but these expensive art treasures were subdued in their impact when compared to the animal furs splayed out on the white walls. The six furs included pumas and a tiger but the most prominent coat was that of a polar bear, complete with head and paws. Vain asked about the necessity for the collection but Levene's answer challenged his expectations.

"Only two were specifically 'shot to order' for me - the tiger and the polar bear. Fur wall-hangings seem a bit morbid nowadays, but they fulfilled a purpose for me at the time. When I started my collection, I was way down in the CIA ranks, stuck in a department concerned with criminal psychological patterns. I was very young, power-hungry but obviously female. At that time, it was more of a 'man's world' than today, and my struggle to rise was set against a bedrock of misogyny. The furs weren't the centre-piece of my retaliation but they served to make me feel better at the time. You see, as a non-wearer with regard to furs, society expected me to whimper, protest and sob as the fur trade survived - what did it expect of men at the same time? It expected some to be appalled like most women, but it also expected a minority to reap the commercial benefits associated with the fur trade and to actually shoot the fucking animals. With this collection, I was doing my shooting! I was fighting the double standard".

After her explanation, Levene lit the real fire which had been prepared by Miss Arnett and then poured Vain a glass of the red wine that they both favoured. Whilst she undertook these tasks Vain was left to reflect on her reply to his question. His eyes kept returning to the polar bear's head, and a chill ran through him as the words 'shot to order' kept replaying in his mind. When Levene returned to the lounge she handed Vain his drink and then after noticing the apparent unease that the polar bear had instilled in her lover, she placed her jacket over the animal's head. She turned to Vain and in a softer voice she invited the communion that both of them had desired since his initial rebuff on the night of project celebration some months previous.

"I guess the holding back is over now. I've made love with a certain Mr Vain many times in my mind but tonight is going to be our incarnate realisation. I love you Greg, now and for all our tomorrows. Without each other, life is just a skin-deep fixation. Open me up - free me".

When Levene had uttered these words her long fingers dimmed the lights to a degree of illumination that prepared the couple for their release of intimacy. Her fingers loosened Vain's clothing and while her hands were at work, Greg echoed her movements by carefully undoing the buttons, which were the last bridge to their union. Whilst the synchronised loosening took place the couple entwined tongues in the savage style that they had made their own. This time both of them traded a tiny blood bite on the lips of each other, and as the teeth had only made a faint penetration, the blood just coated the lips, remaining within the mouths for the most part; a bitter aperitif that added to the intricacy of the mirrored sexual deliverance. As Levene's clothing dropped to the floor she pulled Vain's head downward to direct his attention toward her breasts, and his tongue proceeded to trace lines around her nipples, fluctuating in pressure, led by her touch as her nails ran down the smooth skin of his back.

The woman's hands proceeded upward to massage Vain's shoulder blades, leaving faint lacerations when his tongue excited the erogenous area around each nipple.

As the couples mutual touch quickened, all garments except their respective briefs were discarded.

The symmetry that choreographed the undressing had remained synchronised to the last. Vain started to massage the silken material of Levene's underwear with his left hand and she arched her back as his fingers gently kneaded the soft flesh below her pubic mound. For a couple of minutes, Marcia broke their symmetry, tilting her head backwards and temporarily ceasing to claw Vain's shoulders. The gusset of her briefs became saturated as she approached orgasm and her hand wildly reached out for Vain's penis just before she came. Levene translated her ecstasy into powerful hand strokes, pulling hard on her lover. She let out a guttural cry when she reached the peak of sensual release and after her delirium subsided, she turned her attention to Greg, crouching down on him, taking his penis deep into her mouth.

Levene's tongue greedily flicked along the sensitive end of Vain's erect penis, whilst her hands rubbed his testicles with a force that was only just short of a painful threshold. Vain looked downwards as his partner became engrossed in her oral stimulation. Her cheekbones were accentuated by the dimmed illumination and as she turned fellatio into an intricate performance, Gregory Vain shut his eyes as he anticipated a powerful ejaculation.

Levene's technique revolved around a heated pressure, which seemed to emanate from within her throat and her teeth were used simultaneously, nipping the thick veins, which ran through to the swollen foreskin.

Vain felt that he was going to cum on numerous occasions but when Levene sensed an approaching climax, she altered the method of oral pressure and intensified the massage that she was directing to her lover's testicles.

The woman teased her partner for a forty-minute spell, before finally conceding to his desperate thrusts. Once Levene stopped restricting intake in her throat, Vain indulged in 'mouth fucking' his partner at breakneck speed and when he had passed the point of 'no return' Levene pulled out his penis, directing his semen across her face and breasts.

It had been the most powerful ejaculation that Vain had experienced, and as his project colleague fastidiously licked his semen from her breasts, he lay down on the floor, reflecting on the sexual excellence that he had just received.

Levene however was in no mood for reflection, and as she ran a comb through her tousled hair, she broke the silence, which the couple had lapsed into.

"Time to return the service, Greg. Lick me like it's the last time!"

After uttering these words, Marcia knelt down and reverse-straddled Vain's face, looking past his legs to the fur hangings on the wall. From his spatial position, Vain saw her perfectly proportioned buttocks drop down toward him and beyond this vision was the smooth skin of Levene's back, complemented by the mane of black hair that he had come to adore.

Vain placed a cushion under his head to enable him to gain a slight elevation that raised his mouth upward towards Levene's vagina. As his tongue started to probe the tight confines of the favoured destination, Vain recognised the distinctive taste that he had experienced second-hand in Alvettis, but this time there was an unlimited supply!

As his tongue reached deeper, Vain's two day old chin stubble made contact with Levene's clitoris and the effect sent the woman into a frenzied state, moaning in a shrill pitch, tightly squeezing her nipples until her nails turned temporarily white.

Vain didn't employ any teasing tactics like Levene had done. He had thought ahead to the ultimate coital union and thus his tongue hammered through at a frenetic pace, bringing his partner to a state of climax in a matter of minutes.

It was now Marcia's turn to shudder into temporary submission, but Vain decided to implement a slight manoeuvre to enable the long awaited copulation. He skilfully pulled his body through the arch afforded by Levene's kneeling legs and gently pushed her onto 'all fours' so that he was kneeling behind her. Taking his freshly erect penis in his hand, he entered the woman from behind with a thrust that was stronger in terms of impact than any previous single stroke performed by the couple. He felt that his entry was deeper than any penetration he had experienced before and Levene used her powerful, compact vaginal muscles to invite every inch of Vain's sizeable penis. When he came, Vain felt as though he was using a 'life supply', and whilst his first ejaculation had been shot in the open, this semen consignment was released 'within' for a duration that seemed to fully savour their completion, holding the moment like a sacred occurrence.

The couple drifted into a contented sleep after their energetic love making, lying sprawled out on the thick-pile burgundy carpet.

* * * * *

Levene awoke Vain the following morning, and the first thing the couple did involved a continuation of the previous night's sexual activity. When the MC Project pair climbed into Vain's car later that day, their collective fatigue couldn't stop them sharing a celebratory French kiss outside Levene's London hideaway.

Levene had asked to drive Vain's car for the return journey to Designation B, and Greg had made no objection concerning her request.

A short distance before the project base, the car's progress was halted by a long tail back. Neither of the project pair suspected anything problematic at this stage, but suddenly a group of individuals started flitting between the halted vehicles and then the couple did start to become suspicious.

Most of the people who snaked through the traffic peered into vehicles, to be met with indignant curses from the infuriated drivers. When Vain noticed that some of the individuals wore press identity badges, he informed Levene and she encoded an emergency call signal on her 'Comm-Lynx'. As two of the figures approached Vain's car, a cold sweat started to form on his brow. Both individuals had tabloid newspaper titles emblazoned on the camera cases that they carried. One of the two seemed to recognise the project pair, and he broke into a run as his rival reporter let out a triumphal shout when he too recognised who the pair were. After this dual recognition, a mad scramble ensued until thirty reporters laid siege to Greg's vehicle.

The pressure of the jostling reporters started to rock the car, and Vain opened his window halfway, to be met by a barrage of questions. He realised that the media avalanche that Denison had expected after the global MC revelation had started. The crowd swelled to over fifty, and scuffles started to break out between angry drivers and loud-mouthed reporters. When Gregory Vain had opened his passenger window he had initially shouted that the reporters had made a mistake and he had been quite adamant in his denial of MC Project involvement. It didn't take long however for the project pair to realise the futility of any further denials and Vain closed his window as howls of protest emanated from the journalistic ranks. When the car started to tilt dangerously, the project pair decided to implement the 'power authorisation' that MC Project affiliation enabled them to call upon in situations like the one they were experiencing and both project members thus reached for their concealed firearms.

After brandishing an Uzi through the car window, Vain intimated that he was going to get out of the vehicle. Upon seeing the weapon, the crowd withdrew a few metres and then Vain got out to read a brief statement that all front-line MC Project personnel carried.

As cameras clicked repeatedly, Vain started to read, whilst his left hand directed the gun toward the crowd.

"As a member of the Memory Camera Exploration Project, I am empowered with the highest authority from both the defence forces of Britain and the United States of America. This authority empowers me to contravene conventional forces of law and order. As a member of the said organisation, I can use a firearm if I have 'reasonable cause' for alarm, with regard to my safety and MC Project security. As a collective force that bars MC Project safe passage, I must warn you that if this form of obstruction remains, I will be forced to use the weapon that I am permitted to carry. You must disperse to enable my access".

After he had read the statement, Vain turned to get back to his car. Questions seemed to come from every direction but one cut through the homogenised verbal chaos, being heard quite easily by Gregory Vain.

"People claim to see a lot, Mr Vain. Christ; the devil; aliens! Are you going to visually determine truth here?"

As Jess Wheeler's security unit arrived to break the crowd up, Vain couldn't resist one sarcastic reply line to the journalist who had been heard above the rest.

"Write me an X-file. Fuck you".

The reason Vain had singled out the one journalist for satirical attack was because she had actually got quite close to areas that Vain wished to explore in future MC Project directions. He didn't want any sensationalist reporter stealing any credit for future exploration areas.

Wheeler's unit created a convoy to guide the project pair back to Designation B and as they entered the building, Denison met them. He was quite jovial in his tone and apparently not angry that the media had again detected the same two MC Project personnel. His words were carefully selected to dispel any fears that Greg and Marcia may have had after this second detection.

"Hey folks, hang those long faces! It was just a matter of time until those bloodhounds sniffed you out. You may have had shit for brains in Washington but things have changed. After the global MC revelation, we knew that media relations would be kinda different. I mean we were fucking lucky before global exposure, you know. Four years back we had to wipe a pack of reporters in Cincinnati, then New York, and of course you know about Lassiter's Washington press unit. Christ, Wheeler's boys must have 'retired' over fifty reporters by now! You handled press detection perfectly - real pros and so long as you keep that up, you've got nothing to fear from me. Go and settle back in. Check out the other front-liners.

They've been working solid on both main vault and mindsight extension explorations".

Vain and Levene parted to go back to their respective rooms. Both Ko-Chai and Tavini were out, and thus Vain was free to envisage the headlines of tomorrow's press on his own. He had settled back into his room when a knock on his door broke his train of thought.

He was pleased to see that it was Diana Fearston who had sought his presence. He had tremendous admiration for this woman and was glad that she was his closest understudy. Fearston had been working solidly during the past week on both individual work and front-line team explorations with Hannah Nichol and Marco Sant. After a courteous greeting she proceeded to tell Vain of a significant finding that she had discovered in the membrane that separated the main visually-determined MC Vault and the 'mindsight' extension.

"I've been working with my team to an intensive level of late Greg, and I have also had the opportunity to further my own neurological research. Our team have undertaken twenty-five mindsight explorations after you guys unlocked Braddock's vault-extension visuals, and one exploration presented me with an enigma that could well upset Leif a bit! I carried out the explorations with Hannah and Marco but I was left to assess the screened results on my own. Braddock heard Levene read a passage from Revelation, but we opted for a fictional piece written by Hannah about a bad LSD trip. It was quite short, describing a series of powerful recurring visuals that envisaged hallucinations in their magnitude. The three key descriptive images concerned the allegorical figure of death in stilettos, a taxidermist devouring entrails from dead animals and blood from an angel's veins lapping around the fires of hell.

"Each subject had the passage read to them three times as with Braddock, but they didn't view their mindsight visuals afterwards. I was the sole reviewer".

Diana Fearston paused for breath and Vain felt that his understudy shook a little as she continued.

"The first twenty-one screenings showed a great deal of commonality Greg, with every subject mentally rendering the three key images in their minds. Personal translations meant that slight variations in depiction occurred, but most imagery was created and stored along very similar visual lines. Subject 22 radically altered my concept of visual storage though, Greg! The mindsight visuals of Subject 22 initially tied in with the previous explorations, with the female volunteer rendering both death and the taxidermist along similar lines to the rest.

"After these two depictions though, there was nothing! You and I both know that 'recent' mindsight visuals mirror storage in the main MC Vault, remaining at the front of the extension close to the dividing membrane for several hours, usually. With this in mind I got my team to undertake a second mindsight probe, deeper toward the core of the extension. As they hadn't witnessed the screening they didn't know what I was looking for, but my team leader prerogative meant that I didn't have to enlarge upon my motivation.

"When I reviewed this secondary exploration, I just encountered images of non-prompted self created thought - there was no angel! I decided to interview Subject 22 in private on my own. I had a theory that the absent imagery may somehow have been transferred to the main visually-determined vault by dropping through a weak section in the dividing membrane.

"In effect my hypothesis pertained that thoughts could permeate the membrane, arriving into the main vault and thus deceiving the recipient in the process - making them believe the 'dropped' thoughts had a concrete reality and were a physical experience like the other images in the main section".

Vain realised that Diana Fearston could well have uncovered an 'Achilles heel' in their project, if thoughts could actually fall through to an area of the brain which housed 'real' sight-determined imagery. After a brief pause for breath, Fearston continued.

"I began my questioning of Subject 22 by asking her what she recalled about her mindsight exploration. Her recollections backed up the absence of any angel imagery, as she only remembered hearing about death and the entrail devouring. That proved that her mindsight vault didn't house the angel anywhere within its parameter. I then decided to test whether my theory pertaining to 'fall-through' had foundation, and asked her questions about imagery she had physically seen. I started by keeping the two themes of previous discussion. I subsequently asked her if she had witnessed any deaths in her lifetime and proceeded to link in horror, asking her about any horrific imagery she had witnessed.

"After she recalled imagery from a road crash she was involved in, I turned the line of inquiry to religious experiences, and after ten minutes, I was able to ask if she had ever seen God or an angel. At first she was quite bemused, saying she wished that she had, and so I prompted further by asking her how she derived her concept of angels. She described books she had read as a child and paintings which she had witnessed in art galleries. Then almost as an afterthought, she added that she thought she had seen some in films. I knew that this was probably my cue and I concentrated on getting her to reveal more about instances where she had seen angels in films. She initially mentioned some light films like *Heaven Can Wait* and *Carousel* but eventually she said that she had some vague recollection of remembering a horror film that involved an angel.

"I decided to ask her if she would be explored one last time, and after some initial reluctance, she eventually agreed.

"I told my team to perform a main vault exploration on Subject 22, and although it was the third exploration, they didn't seem to have any suspicions with regard to my repeated testing of this woman, as occasionally our work had explored both vault sections with regard to the same individual on other occasions.

"Before Subject 22 'went under', I had primed her in private to keep remembering the aforementioned images of angels in film.

"When I reviewed the subsequent visuals in private, I had to initially sit through 'light' viewing but then I got my reward! The bleeding angel and the blood circling the fires of hell were both there, and although the image had a poor visual quality, it made direct links to the read passage. The brain of Subject 22 had encoded the image as film seemingly as a kind of safety device, because if it had been rendered as a product of 'actual experience', you can imagine the psychological damage it could have done to the woman; converting it to a cinema experience was a form of subconscious protection. The image was probably damaged during the journey through the membrane and this would explain the poor visual quality".

Fearston was sweating due to the complexities surrounding what she had revealed to Vain, but he didn't interrupt her because he sensed that she still had more information to divulge. After extending a grateful smile to her front-line mentor, the woman continued.

"This exploration was my déjà-vu research realised and yet extended, Greg. For some years I have believed that thoughts could be conceived as actuality in a person, and the membrane penetration proved this to be correct, but I never anticipated that the main MC Vault section could convert images like I discovered here. The fact that Subject 22 was protected by the dominant vault activating the imagery as a 'distant' eleven-second cinema experience shows just how complex the relationship between the two vault sections is. We now know that the two sections have the capacity to act independently of each other, like a mental duality within one person. There's another issue though Greg, and it's the factor Leif would hate. I have shown that mindsight imagery can break through the membrane into the 'heightened visual' vault of 'experiences', and therefore one could argue that the validity of some of our exploration results could be questioned. I know that we had enough DNA evidence to back up Sandford-Everett's conviction and thus society was certain of his guilt, but not all murderers leave as much genetic information behind. After my Subject 22 findings, people could argue that an individual could envisage their own murder, and yet the guilty party in their mindsight might not perpetrate the killing if it was carried out in actuality. We all envisage people attacking us if our suspicions are aroused, and if some of our mindsight imagery fell through the membrane like in the Subject 22 instance, couldn't our main vaults wrongly implicate a person if the worst befell us?

"We could thus show an innocent person killing us - no problem if we stay alive, but rough justice on somebody if we did get killed. You may think that this scenario is a bit melodramatic Greg, but the point is, I've established that there are potential flaws in MC Project explorations - you see Greg, the Memory-Camera could lie!"

Although Gregory Vain did feel that a wrongful murder conviction was unlikely to result due to mindsight 'fall-through', he had to admit that weak elements in the dividing membrane did present problems. He and Fearston talked into the small hours with regard to whether they should inform Leif Denison of Diana's findings. Fearston felt that they should reveal the information pertaining to Subject 22, but Vain disagreed, feeling that the déjà-vu 'fall-through' discovery could bring Denison down on them, and if revealed to a global audience it could give critics of the MC Project an angle for attack, illuminating the blemish of flawed visual storage. Akira Ying-Sun had been a powerful critic who had been impressively won over at the global MC revelation, but there were others like him who saw the project as an American-led neurological conspiracy, and they would find great ammunition in Fearston's research if the results were exposed to a public audience.

As the senior front-line team leader, Vain could decide on the decision to be taken, but this presented him with a dichotomy, as the key factor involved whether the highest form of project command should be kept in ignorance of the discovery or not. If Denison were not informed, the pair would be in breach of their MC Project duties and this factor had already 'displaced' some of their collective number.

Vain eventually made a decision at just after three in the morning and he chose his words very carefully, so he wouldn't dampen the enthusiasm and commitment of his able understudy.

"We've got to hang fire with your findings for the moment, Diana. If we break your conclusions to Leif now it could definitely go against you. Denison's on the crest of a wave right now. The MC Project has been his baby for years and he has suffered each setback like a personal body blow. Chicago nearly did him in, but he knew that global exposure wasn't far away and this gave him the strength to carry on.

"Subject 22 did highlight a potential project flaw, but in the light of our overwhelming successes, it is not practical to build mindsight 'fall-through' to a level of comparative importance.

"Mishimo Ko-Chai wanted to dwell on the Christopher exploration because it proved we were fallible and couldn't explain everything that we encountered, but Denison pioneered onward rather than arrest the set back. It would be the same if we enlightened him about 'fall-through', but he might move on the attack, as you would have broken his neurological 'Midas touch'! You see, you would represent the harbinger of bad news, an internal threat, temporarily soiling the flood of success. When he goes on the attack things happen, some people get 'wiped', some disappear and others are humiliated in front of the rest of the project ranks. I don't want that to happen to you, Diana. So far there are only two of us that know about a membrane weakness and it's better to keep things hidden right now, with me bearing responsibility for the decision under the auspices of my front-line authority. We might never have to inform him, but we have got to be very careful if we do. I obviously realise how proud you must be with regard to your research findings, you've made brilliant accurate deductions, but a hostile Denison could well say that your work represented personal research at the expense of MC Project gain. I know this isn't the case, but I've crossed swords with Leif before and I felt the unified force of oppression close rank against me when I questioned the handling of the gunfight in Chicago. Anyone who upsets Leif Denison's method of working seems to be cancerous to his dream. You and I should subsequently hold the 'fall-through' secret until any instance occurs where we have to reveal it.

"Remember, I will bear the responsibility for the delay in breaking your findings, and I will worry about any possible reprisal action if the time comes".

Fearston was eventually won over, seeing the sense in waiting before exposing her research findings. She worried for Vain though, after he had decided to bear the responsibility for any late revelation that might have to be divulged. After he and Diana had finished their discussion, she took her leave and Vain drifted into a deep sleep.

The headlines of the morning press were going to surprise Gregory Vain, even though the previous day's media encounter had been temporarily shelved in his mind due to Fearston's enlightening research findings. As the papers were delivered to their points of sale, the front-line leader slept on. Later that day he would have to get used to a new sensationalist identity - 'The Gun-Ho Mindreader'!

THIRTEEN

Vain awoke to find that every newspaper in Britain featured him on the front page, and in the subsequent three weeks that followed, he was placed under curfew in Designation B for his own protection. Denison knew that now the press had detected two key members of the MC Project staff, they would pursue the pair like a pack of hounds if either of them surfaced outside the Designation confines. The security staff looking after Tanya and Vain's children also increased considerably.

The favoured photograph carried by the majority of papers featured Vain brandishing the Uzi at the reporters who were laying siege to his car, and a series of sensationalist headlines supported its usage. 'The Gun-Ho Mindreader' was the headline that television echoed with regard to its coverage of the press exposure, and Vain's career background was illuminated by both media forms with regard to what they could access. Levene was also illuminated and researched, with the majority of the tabloid press elevating her good looks in melodramatic language that remembered film with regard to the use of adjectives. The media interest created a global audience as the UK exposure was exchanged around the globe. Hundreds of reporters camped outside the gates of Designation B, and eventually Mr Fray and Mr Voight activated their security units to physically push the media ranks back in a bloody confrontation that left three reporters dead and injured scores of others. This act generated a media backlash that painted the MC Project in a sinister negative light, and this was maintained when leaked profiles of project members were fed through. Levene was labelled the 'Vampire Ice-Maiden' by the New York tabloids, and Denison was likened to a military dictator in certain parts of the world.

When Denison had softened some of the security repression associated with MC Project involvement upon the return to England, all staff had envisaged a more pleasurable working ethic to be developing. However, when the media interest avalanche showed no signs of abating, the autocratic style of the past returned with regard to certain post-Washington changes that had been implemented. The hard-line restoration involved all staff having to endure the Designation curfews of the past weekend. Project freedom subsequently faded into history. As the world's media continued to uncover and profile more of the MC Project ranks, Denison extended an unusual offer to the staff who were 'exposed'. This offer gave the exposed the chance to radically alter their appearance via plastic surgery, and whilst some 'new' faces did emerge in staff who accepted the offer, the majority turned the offer down, relieved that Denison had let them make the decision, and had not imposed facial change as a mandatory command.

Both Vain and Levene turned the opportunity of a new face down, preferring to take their chance with the world's media when they would next appear out of the Designation confines. Denison had understood their decision, although he strongly advised the pair to stay apart from each other in the public domain.

He didn't implement any specific separation rules for the pair within the confines of the Designation, but he reminded them that their detection had offset the media avalanche, which put pressure on all staff, and subsequently he felt that any witnessed display of affection between the pair might incur the wrath of some of their fellow MC Project colleagues.

As the project ranks started to realise the negative implications that media exposure created, Denison decided to enable his staff to see the outside coverage develop. Television and radio were thus allowed into the Designation environment for the first time, although the Internet was still only made available to the select few. Newspapers had been the one media form that had been allowed on occasions in the past, and now a complete supply were readily made available. The MC Project was naturally bigger in impact than the usual 'nine day wonder' features that the media favoured, and it thus received consistent front-page attention in the global press. A lot of this coverage was motivated by speculation, and as the press became more desperate in their efforts to include new project information, erroneous conclusions abounded. Television also featured some sensationalist programmes, but some of the documentary production on UK TV delivered quality as far as deductions were concerned. During the fourth consecutive week of Designation incarceration, project staff witnessed one such programme and the conclusions that were generated shocked MC Project staff.

The programme was called 'Sinquiry', and it focused upon investigating powerful organisations, by assessing the area of expertise they were involved with and the effect that their line of work could have for the masses. The Sinquiry documentary that assessed the workings of the MC Project typically had a specific line of investigation, and the project's neurological breakthroughs were measured against UK murder statistics in the period after global exposure. The format of the programme involved pre-recorded material initially, and live-studio audience comments made up the last fifteen minutes. Sean Edwards was the reporter who fronted the documentaries and he would set the scene regarding the issue in focus each week. His pre-title words at the start of the 'MC Project Special' were typically aggressive in accent.

"When the world first heard about the Memory-Camera Project, most people envisaged a more crime-free social environment for the years ahead. We had, after all, globally witnessed how one upper-crust murderer met his retribution in just a couple of days, because of the images that the project could access. The public knew that a new kind of visual proof would be available for use in the moral fight against crime on a worldwide level. This factor gave people the sense of security they had been looking for after years of shortcomings surrounding Western World legal practice. The future looked bright, until dramatic new criminal statistics started to emerge.

"Tonight, Sinquiry looks at startling new developments which suggest that MC Project findings may actually be creating killers! We examine the evidence that now suggests the rapist of yesterday may well be turning into the terminal mutilator of today!"

After the dramatic introduction, the title music and credits started to hit the screen. Vain was watching the programme along with Levene in her private quarters, and both had been captivated by the hard-hitting claim in Edward's scene setting.

Edwards began the pre-recorded exposure by highlighting a case study that concerned the violent murder of a nineteen-year-old girl in Reading.

Emma Robertson had been a student at Reading University. She had been popular with her fellow students and the programme profiled her as 'every father's dream-daughter'. Robertson went to a nightclub three days after the global exposure of the MC Project, and as she walked through the University campus on her way back to her hall of residence, she had the misfortune to meet Mark Stevens. This 38-year old man had been sent to prison on two occasions in the past for attempted rape and repetitive stalking. Stevens was an individual who had a low intellect and poor social skills. He was a loner who moved around the South Eastern region of England, undertaking casual menial work. He was quite slight in build and although he had previously been imprisoned for attempted rape, his intended victim had said in court that she didn't feel he would have carried out some of the stronger verbal threats he had made to her. After struggling to pin the victim down, he had lost interest, looking guilty and wandering away from his quarry. He had been arrested without a struggle.

Stevens had been released from prison after serving three years of the custodial sentence that he had received for his attempted rape. His prison report had stated that he had behaved like a model felon and his good behaviour had contributed to the shortening of his sentence. A month after his release, the global MC Project exposure occurred and the divulged neurological information had a profound effect on Stevens.

On the night he killed Emma Robertson, Stevens had packed a range of cutting implements into his workbag. A blunt kitchen knife, a Korean Machete and a large pair of scissors were amongst the contents.

He asphyxiated his victim, but then tried vainly to decapitate the young woman using the blunt knife. Campus security personnel caught him when his workbag spilled its contents after he had panicked due to his futile decapitation attempt. Sinquiry screened a reconstructed portion of the defence testimony from the trial of Mark Stevens.

<u>Defence</u> "Why did you hunt your victim with cutting implements in your possession?"

<u>Stevens</u> "I had to take her head away with me".

<u>Defence</u> "But why?"

<u>Stevens</u> "They can see in dead heads now. That project - they can see everything you know".

<u>Defence</u> "But you didn't use the tools to any great effect did you, Mr Stevens? The scissors weren't touched, and your efforts with the knife were nowhere near achieving decapitation. You had the perfect tool Mark, didn't you - the machete? But you didn't use it. I would like you to tell the jury why you didn't use it"

<u>Stevens</u> (sobbing) "I couldn't, that's sick. The knife made a mess; it made me throw up, but the machete - no that's sick. It would have been too quick, too much blood. Taking the head was too much for me, I couldn't do it. I'm so sorry for her. I just didn't want anyone watching me later. I could have burned just a head but I couldn't do it - I'm so sorry for her".

<u>Defence</u> "But you had killed her, Mark. You had nothing to lose really, did you? One chop, one blow, that's all. You were a killer after strangling Emma, weren't you? You had the bag, you had the tools, but now you say that you didn't have the 'stomach' to decapitate her! Why don't you face up to one fact Mark, you didn't have the guts to be a killer, did you?

Really, you were more comfortable with just being a rapist, weren't you?

"We all know that you did strangle Emma, you did in fact take your victim's life but you only did that to get her head. If you hadn't seen the MC Project findings, decapitation wouldn't have motivated you and you wouldn't have killed - would you Mark?"

Stevens "No I wouldn't - that's right, I wouldn't have killed her".

The trial reconstruction was an excellent simulation, and after the pre-recorded screening, Sean Edwards returned to his 'pulpit' to address the live studio audience. A large contingent of the audience had been alarmed by what they had witnessed, and Edwards had to initially ask for calm so that the programme could proceed. Edwards was notorious for 'loading' his opinions upon his audience and the MC Project Sinquiry once again found him whipping up crowd hysteria. His words of devil's advocate incitement started to cast their spell.

"So what's upset you guys, then? Come off it. We just saw some semi-illiterate loser try to blame his evil actions on man's greatest scientific discovery - didn't we? I mean you didn't buy that pile of excrement, did you? One thing though folks, maybe, just maybe, the actions of the loser illuminated something sinister concerning the discovery our secretive MC Project friends have given us. Tonight, you my friends are going to tell the nation whether you think the MC discovery is backfiring - is it creating killers?"

After Sean Edward's melodramatic audience sparring, some crowd members were invited to give their comments about the MC Project, and reactions ranged from support to suspicion, and castigation was forthcoming from a few individuals. Edward's cut short audience debate to allow for the entrance of the parents of Emma Robertson. In a read statement, Mr

Robertson presented the couple's position.

"The death of our only daughter was our worst nightmare made real. Mark Stevens effectively killed three people the night he ended the life of Emma. My wife Joyce and I have thought of little else since. Some say 'time is a healer', but it is our mutual view that whoever coined that phrase was ignorant of the escalating type of pain that we collectively feel. Things get worse, not better. As our thoughts have returned time and time again to the actual motivation surrounding the murder we both share the same opinion with regard to the attribution of blame. We feel certain now, more than ever, that our daughter would be alive if the MC Project findings hadn't been broken to the world. We realise that the project is foundered in decency, but we also feel that when the world knew how dead minds store heightened visuals, an increase in the more macabre forms of crime would ensue. Unfortunately, it seems as though our daughter was part of this process.

"My wife and I hate Mark Stevens, and we will never forgive him for his vile perpetration, but we both feel that Emma met her death because of her killer's fear regarding detection. It was fear that made him kill, fear that made him attempt to mutilate her body and fear that changed him from a rapist to a killer. The MC Project effectively killed our daughter".

Mr and Mrs Robertson withdrew from the Sinquiry studio, and the assembled audience applauded their gallantry in light of their loss. The applause was encouraged by Edwards to a level approaching fanaticism, although some of the people who witnessed his efforts felt that clapping hands should stay in the realms of quiz shows and not be utilised for hard hitting docu-dramas like Sinquiry. Whilst

Vain felt slightly perturbed by the applause, Levene remained unaffected.

Despite this difference, both project members were very surprised by Sinquiry's next live studio appearance. As the Robertson's left, in walked Mr Fray to take a position in one of the interviewee chairs. Edwards gave the high-ranking project figure another one of his melodramatic cued-up introductions.

"Well guys, thanks for that big hand, and keep the applause coming for Mr Vance Fray. Mr Fray is a key security figure within the MC Project. Now hold on guys, I know what you're thinking - isn't that the project division that keeps killing our journalists and blocking off our highways? Well, put that aside, and let Mr Fray persuade us otherwise - if he can! Let's see if he can make us feel secure about MC Project security".

As Mr Fray sat uncomfortably in his chair, the audience became uniformly silent. Mr Fray didn't like the interview style of Edwards but there was no going back now. The ordeal began.

"Mr Fray, we're all very grateful to you for appearing on Sinquiry tonight, and we'd like to extend our congratulations to the whole MC Project team for taking the fiction out of mindreading".

"Thank you".

"Vance, if I can call you that…"

Fray interrupted

"No".

"Oh, very well, I'll keep things formal. Do you feel Mr Fray, that your explorations have been worthwhile on scientific and moral levels?"

"Without a doubt, as far as furthering scientific advancement is concerned. I am a key figure in MC Project security as you said, so I feel that I am an inappropriate source to answer any ethics based questions.

"Therefore, I can't answer the second part of your question".

"But, Mr Fray, some innocent people are starting to hit the sidewalk - journalists, photographers, inter..."

A second cessation occurred.

"You call them innocent, do you? If they get in our way, they are gonna have to suffer the consequences you know. That usually just means moving groups of media people on, but occasionally we have to deal with things in a slightly firmer fashion".

"Oh, like the thirty-eight journalists that are believed to have been 'wiped' in this country by your organisation in the last five years".

"I deal in reality, not melodramatic speculation, Mr Edwards".

"Oh come on Mr Fray, loss of life, murder - that's reality. Are you saying that your organisation hasn't had a hand in any deaths in this country?"

"I can see your loaded intentions here, Edwards. No comment".

"Fair enough Mr Fray, let's examine some statistics that show a heavy relevance for your project then".

"I can't wait, Mr Edwards".

"Sinquiry have gathered in evidence that shows an alarming increase in macabre crime. Crime involving the act of decapitation that Mark Stevens couldn't quite perpetrate. Since global MC Project exposure, decapitated corpses have been discovered all over the UK. It seems other people are, like Stevens, terrified of having their crime 'replayed' from their victim's mind and subsequently many are 'taking the head'. As Stevens intimated at his trial, a head is easy to dispose of in comparison to a whole body.

"Since exposure, the British Police forces have located ninety-two decapitated corpses, and thirteen other corpses showed signs that murderers had 'tried' to decapitate their victims. Of the ninety-two missing heads, the police retrieval score was just four!

"Some of the victims looked like gangland killings, some died after rape and a few were murdered for small change. The bottom line, Mr Fray, as far as Sinquiry is concerned, argues that the global exposure of MC Project operations has offset a desperate 'new' type of criminal.

"Prior to MC exposure, decapitation in Britain was hardly practised, but now it is relatively commonplace!

"Sinquiry believes that the MC Project are guilty of introducing a new vicious trend into the criminal culture of the UK. Since your exposure, things are worse, not better - how do you answer that charge?"

Two hundred studio audience members and millions of television viewers awaited Fray's response.

"With two words Mr Edwards - fuck you!"

Edwards had riled Fray from the outset. He hated the way that the interviewer tried to paint the MC Project as a guilty party as far as escalating criminal practice was concerned, and he felt that Edwards was representative of the narrow-mindedness that could slow his beloved project down. After his expletive based utterance, Fray stood up and ripped off his neck-mic. He barged past Edwards and exited the Sinquiry studio.

Sinquiry had been scheduled to include fifteen minutes of 'questions and answers' involving the studio audience and Mr Fray, but his departure meant a gap needed filling. Edwards took this opportunity to further incite the crowd.

"Well people, that was a representative of the way things are now! Mr Fray obviously didn't feel that you folks were worth listening to, did he? You can bet your bottom dollar that his kids haven't been 'sliced up', and he probably feels his conscience is clear when his unit wipe our reporters out. I think he's wrong though. I think that the MC Project has become too unaccountable, and I think that we ought to let them know that we aren't going to suffer the implications of their decisions any longer! I know that many people are heading to Trafalgar Square folks. It's time we protested, loud and proud - 'cos many of us are fed up with having our future mind-read. See you there!"

As Sean Edwards left the Sinquiry studio, he kicked over the MC Project display placards that had been installed to tie in with Fray's appearance. The audience took this as a cue to start vandalising the studio, and the chair that Fray had sat in was ripped apart by the incited throng in a matter of seconds. As glass partitions were kicked in and seats ripped out, the studio cameras initially kept shooting and the television viewers were fed the violent outrage for over five minutes. Eventually, security staff restored order and the programme was terminated, being replaced with a repeated drama production for the duration.

Whilst Edwards didn't go on to lead a revolution in Trafalgar Square, Sinquiry had acted as a catalyst for many MC sceptical viewers, and several thousand people did assemble in the heart of central London. Conventional security forces took over seven hours to quell the rioting that ensued after a selection of orators had echoed the type of hysteria that Edwards had put in place.

Central London wasn't the only place to feel the chaos which mass anger generated.

Violence and rioting took place throughout the nation, and the pivotal Designation B became the prime target for many. The venue exterior had been highlighted by the media to a high level of frequency and subsequently the enraged demonstrators had a clear target to aim for in addition to Trafalgar Square.

As over twenty thousand MC Project doubters made their way toward the Designation, dispirited conventional security ranks started to buckle, and Leif Denison made his second evacuation order. Fire had prompted his first decision in Chicago, but now it was mass hysteria that moulded his edict. Four 'splinter' convoys left the Designation and rocket launchers had to fire shells into the crowd to create a safe passage for escape. The MC Project would be re-housed in a rural Designation south of Oxford, but the organisational venue secrecy of previous years now looked a very remote restoration option. Vain and Levene left with the last splinter convoy and as their group left, petrol bombs rained down on Designation B. The future of London-region Designations looked very doubtful as hundreds of protesters ran unchecked in the grounds of the 'favoured' Neo-Gothic venue. As Designation B burned out of control, the place where Julia Venison's mind was unlocked became a charred symbol of safer days.

The flames licked throughout the building, and yet in the Lower Chamber, a chance meeting took place. Both men had their own reasons for seeing life out this way.

"I thought I'd be alone here. A fry up is hardly a crowd-pleaser is it?"

"Well I guess I'm sick of seeing the four horsemen. They didn't tell me that the imagery would magnify over time!"

"Fair enough. Unlucky you, first of firsts!"

"So how come your present, then? I thought you'd be counting the dead ones in until the final round!"

"It all began here really, didn't it? In a way it seems fitting that it should end here".

"Yeah, there's a lot in that my friend. Too many know now anyway. Until the next day!"

"Yes until that day - goodbye".

FOURTEEN

Designation B had represented more than just a building to most project members. The Neo-Gothic majesty evident in the architectural design had given the residence a presence beyond mere bricks and mortar. When fire raised this structure to a state of ruin, most MC Project members felt the collective loss and morale was very low when the four splinter convoys arrived in the substitute Designation. The fire which engulfed Designation B seemed worse than the Chicago blaze to many, because 'mass' public anger had generated the flames, and not the kind of 'cabin fever' which had been the probable cause in America. Thus, the flames in England had been supported by many, and weren't an outcome of an individual rogue protest.

Conventional security forces had given way without much resistance, and it seemed likely that some of these law enforcers had actually been 'with the people', contributing to the rampage that saw the end of the Designation. Several project staff claimed to have seen British Riot Police turning their batons into demolition tools and not preventative devices to repel the crowd. This riot had been brewing for some time and Sinquiry had been the last straw for those who were fearful of the lawless power that the MC Project seemed to possess. Mr Fray's TV anger had obviously been one contributory factor behind the violence, but many signs of public unrest had come to light before the project security chief's TV appearance. Even the Church of England had attacked MC Project methods, commenting that the organisation "tampered with the soul!"

After the devastation at Designation B, Leif Denison looked forward to the day when his beloved project would be permanently sited in his home nation. He was getting rather tired of the seemingly universal protest Britain was levelling against 'his' scientists and he was particularly angered by the Anti-project stance of the conventional security forces of Britain. When the riot was taking place, Jess Wheeler had implored him to use a fatal nerve gas upon both the rioting crowd and one section of apathetic riot police officers. Denison had told him that he was being far too headstrong, but mentally he was 'right in line' with the request of the would-be executioner. Denison knew that if the project had to metaphorically 'return underground' and sever media relations, he could count on men like Wheeler to violently repress any attempt to gain project information. In the past he had always kept Jess under control and rarely let him really express his obsessive protective urges. As far as he was concerned, it was now time to let Jess Wheeler off his leash. He would be promoted as the new Anglo-American 'Active' Security Chief.

Before the Designation 'B' evacuation, mindsight explorations had been the order of the day as far as MC Project work was concerned, but now Denison was going to temporarily suspend all front-line work. He had several issues to raise with his project staff, and all the personnel who were resident in the new Designation were summoned to attend a collective audience with the MC Project controller the afternoon after the late-night arrival.

Denison was an individual who thrived on this type of verbal address, but on this day his usual buoyant swagger was non-evident, with his preferred ostentation giving way to an almost world-worn sobriety as he began his speech.

"As I stand here in front of you, I have to admit that I made a mistake. To think that we could 'go public' and not suffer the consequences was an error of judgement that I must bear on my conscience to the optimum level, due to my pivotal project status. I apologise for believing that we could undertake a duality of roles - leading edge scientific researchers and media 'house-hold names'. I realise now that the two identities are oppositional and no such coexistence is possible. The days of project concealment will thus return from this day onwards.

"I can hear some sighs out there, some discontented mutterings, but I wasn't the only one who made a mistake, was I? I didn't blow the script on national UK TV, I didn't brandish an Uzi at reporters after my sexual shenanigans offset my media detection, and I didn't leak high security MC Project info to the world's gutter press. I could go on, and indeed I will.

"It wasn't me who tried to create a snuff market from archived MC Project explorations and I didn't ignite the Chicago flames. You see my friends, the bottom line points an ugly finger in your direction. Not all of you for sure, but jeez some of you have been disloyal across a range of indiscretions. Agreed, there is one helluva difference between careless actions brought about by an overcharged libido, and the sleazy calculated activity associated with a media informant.

"We've 'wiped' the latter scum category as far as we know, but now all public indiscretions have got to be history, and the following steps aim to return us to our former 'safer-day' sanctuary".

The collective MC Project audience waited in trepidation as Denison drank from a glass of water before continuing.

"The initial protection step involves an immediate scaling down of our work in England. This country has seen a greater level of project treachery, and the public have proved hostile towards us, to say the least. In the States we seem heroes to many, but over here most people seem to have a Dark Age fucking mentality when it comes to our brilliant scientific discoveries! The aforementioned snuff-trading attempt took place when most of us were in Chicago, and so today is the first you will have heard surrounding that crime of project treachery. You can draw your own conclusions as to who was the guilty party in question there, but my reason for dwelling on that particularly despicable act further emphasises my point surrounding the bad fortune England holds for our project. We dealt with that problem to the required level of severity and as I reiterate, that will be our course of action for the slightest offences from now on.

"Mr Wheeler has been promoted accordingly, and he is now subsequently the head of all holistic security departments. Jess is a man who gets things done. He will rid us of the internal cancer that has beset our ranks. He will have total right of passage to visit any areas of the MC Project and he will answer solely to myself. Mr Wheeler's promotion thus means that he now has the second highest level of project authority. Jess is going to help me to turn the clock back and re-secure the future of our beloved MC Project".

Denison broke for a few seconds so that the MC Project cohort could digest the implications surrounding the new appointment. The adjustment obviously meant demotion for Vance Fray and he looked ashen-faced as he heard Denison's words. Mr Voight also appeared to be slightly disturbed by the words of his leader, not because of Wheeler's promotion, but because of the scaling down of MC Project operations in England. Denison referenced this point for the last time when he started to speak again.

"Our work in England won't totally cease, and this country will keep a skeleton staff to undertake some of our archiving work, but all active front-line exploration work will take place in America. We will break for a forced one month period of leave in three days time and when we reconvene, our new permanent working base will be situated in Washington DC - the city of our greatest achievements thus far.

"Our Designation will be a new construction. It is another underground venue and all our future workstations will be similarly hidden. The curfews will also return through necessity, and when staff are in working residence no outside excursion will be granted. Outside Designations promoted a laxity amongst us that made our collective number too off guard and we were ripe for intrusive targeting from external sources - the events at Designation 'B' proved this".

Dwight Richards, an MC Project member prone to claustrophobia, sunk his head in his hands when he heard the latest edict from his leader. Denison seemed oblivious to the displeasure he had offset amongst most of his project staff and he directed his next words directly at the MC Project staff who resided in Britain.

"Our British MC Project contingent will notice some radical domicile changes when they meet their families again in a few days time. You don't live where you did and your children all attend the same school in Guildford. It is an institution specifically set up for the dependants of MC Project members. We had to take this hard line after Sinquiry made us public enemy number one in this country, and the reallocations are taking place as I speak. The bottom line holds that your families could end up as bait for lynch mobs if they stayed where they were, and we've already witnessed the ineffective nature of conventional security forces in this country. We safeguard your dependants, they sure as hell wouldn't. The British based MC Project members will be taken to their new domicile, when we break in three days time. Don't worry, we've had these reallocation contingency plans in readiness for over four years now, and so your new homes bear the hallmarks of quality that characterised your previous estate. So far you have heard me relate some significant changes to protect the leading edge nature of the MC Project. I tell you to contemplate these alterations with a collective determination that helps obliterate any further obstacles, rather than a weak will that keeps recalling your brief 'freedom'. My next decision will fully test your resolve".

Denison paused momentarily, probably in deliberation, stalling his crowd and playing his power rein to the fullest capacity.

"In five weeks time all of us, I repeat all of us, are going to receive a new face - literally".

Uproar broke out amongst the project rank. Some people just shook their heads as his words stung them to the core, some shouted abuse in Denison's direction and others pleaded for calm so that they could hear more specifics pertaining to their leader's maverick command.

Vain felt his sharp cheekbones and Levene nervously tweaked the ends of her raven black hair. Narcissus became an invited guest.

When order was eventually restored, Denison elaborated.

"A bedlam befitting a child when their favourite toy lies broken in the nursery! Get a grip on yourselves my friends, and listen. I know some of you feel harshly done by. You've never been recognised by the media, you've never occupied front-line status, and your job is insignificant when compared to some of the leading MC players. Stop those thoughts. You see, we don't know how many of our number are known to the media, and all positions represent a threat in that context, because as soon as one of us is located, their scent leads the media pack back to the rest of us. I'm not talking broken jaws to alter facial structure and crows feet to weather a young face. I'm not talking 'devil's-venom' to alter your skin colourisation or a two-month hospital lay up to hold you from your work. I'm talking the 'Rochaux Treatment'. No scars, no breaking, just plastic modifications over an eight-day period. Before you ask, I can hear your collective question - will you look very different? Of course you will. What would be the point of the treatment if you didn't appear 'altered' to a level of significant difference? Our old face is a mask of the old days - a cancer that will block our return to closed-door security.

"We will select the appropriate alterations, because if self determination shaped a 'new' face, two likely weaknesses would emerge. Firstly, human nature is such that the modifications would be too slight due to the fears surrounding facial changes, and secondly, people would subconsciously be drawn towards replicating facial traits evident in some of the icons that inspire them. We'd have film star dimples and catwalk beauty spots!

"Some of you had your interests shredded by the global media and if they received a plastic-surgery tip-off, they would start looking for evidence of any possible 'wannabe' influences.

"We aren't going to paint you ugly folks and give you the last mask in the joke shop! I won't reveal all the details of the Rochaux method yet, because you have already had to cope with several changes and a descriptive account of the intricacies surrounding the Rochaux method would be a form of information overload".

Diana Fearston interrupted her project leader.

"Mr Denison. Isn't the Rochaux treatment the one that involves dye injections through the iris to change eye colour permanently, and didn't some individuals go blind as a result?"

"Yes, seven years ago some prototype problems were encountered, but the treatment has been made flawless since. Some of you may feel that you could use coloured contact lenses instead, but you know as well as I that lenses would be lost and the old eye hues would return in time. As I stated, I didn't want to divulge any further details pertaining to the Rochaux method just yet, but I guess Ms Fearston has forced my hand a little with regard to eye colour change. You see, most of you will have this alteration because eyes are one part of the face that firmly indicates identity. Changing eye colour will be a definite alteration for most of our project entourage but for now the Rochaux Treatment is a closed subject".

The sinister prospect of a person's new face being chosen by the French surgeons hardly appealed to the

MC Project members, even though the Rochaux unit had been woven into the project ranks three years hence, and the possibility of plastic surgery had therefore already been anticipated by some of the assembled staff members. Vain had been relatively unenlightened, and had thought the recruitment bizarre until Denison's edict. He could now see how Denison's mind had prefigured their current crisis situation. The MC Project leader showed no signs of leaving his speaker's podium and after inter-unit discussions had abated, he continued with his address.

"From now on, main MC Vault explorations will largely be a thing of the past. On occasions we will get a front-line team to access images from dead minds when we are ushering in new project recruits, but our mindsight vault-extension work is going to take a heavy precedence. Seeing into the living thinking mind is obviously our route forward, and our primary function will involve us detecting potentially dangerous intentions before they result in lawless actions. Mindsight scanning will therefore enable us to penetrate evil minds before their sick intentions have been incarnated. A testing program has already been set up with potential felons in mind. We have started to catalogue deviants who represent a threat to moral society and wider Western security".

Fearston and Vain had caught each other's eyes when Denison had revealed that mindsight testing was to be increased. They were both thinking of the membrane-penetration factor that Fearston had discovered, but neither of them felt it was worth risking Denison's wrath by explaining the fall-through discovery in front of such a large project audience. Their leader would almost certainly condemn them for undertaking 'hidden-agenda' type work, and his attack would be strengthened by the fact that Fearston's work illuminated cracks in his beloved project. Leif Denison was nearing the end of his verbal address, but he wanted to close by paying his respect to the Designation 'B' casualties.

"I know that facial changes and going back underground have hardly pleased you folks, but at least you are still alive. Six of your colleagues weren't so fortunate in the fire that condemned Designation B. In a moment, we will observe two minutes of silence for all six collectively, but two of the dead were well known to all of you and they deserve a brief verbal testimony from their leader at this massed gathering. We have lost the skills of Mr Mason. His charred remains were found in the Lower Chamber of Designation B and we will miss his pathological expertise greatly. He hardly took a day of his leave entitlement and his tenacious commitment to our cause will be fondly remembered. Mr Mason was an MC Project member from day one.

"A second corpse was discovered close to Mason's remains, that of Matthew Braddock. This man had the kind of guts that set him apart from most people. He volunteered to be our first full-scale mindsight test subject, being willing to allow his mind to have a real deep reading. This man didn't flinch from the responsibility he had chosen, and he maintained his cheerful disposition up until the day he died. Jeez, I bet Matt Braddock went to his grave smiling!

"Food for thought, you guys - two fellas who had no qualms about personal sacrifices. If your eyes change from brown to blue in a few weeks time, is that anywhere near the same kind of sacrifice? Hell, no!

"Let us remember our dead".

After Denison's words, the two minutes of silence were observed and then the assembly made their way back to their respective sectionalised areas.

Vain and Levene left the hall together and each of them surveyed the other, with a gaze that envisaged the possible physical changes that might soon beset their lover. Marcia usually rode above repressive directives with a shrug of her shoulders, but the facial change edict had left her visibly shaken and she shook slightly, taking Vain's arm as they moved through the Designation corridors. When the pair entered the room that they were temporarily sharing, the woman spoke in a clinical icy tone.

"Christ Greg, they can have my soul, but they can stick their scalpels up their fucking arses! I don't want some Rochaux bastard throwing an ugly sister spell in my direction. I am what I am, and I fucking love it. Unless they make any changes to my prerogative, they can kiss goodbye to Marcia Levene. If I don't look like the Marcia I moulded, I don't want to play ball anymore. Do you get that, Greg?"

"Yeah, I can follow your drift, but you're no wrist slitter and if you were, Denison is in the sort of mood that would bury you not barter with you.

"He sure as hell wouldn't crumble if you approached him, and don't you think that we've used up all our cards anyway. A fair bit of his address was coming smack-bang in our direction you know. Perhaps it is time to play it their way for a while, I've got others to look out for you know".

"Yeah I know, Mr Family Man, I noticed your family loyalty bond back in my London residence. I bet my housekeeper is still wiping your semen from the carpet now!"

Levene turned away angry at Vain's line of referencing. After a short silence she spoke again in softer tones, looking deeply at her lover, playing him with her new modified style of speech.

"Look Mr Vain, I think we're both locked in egocentric confines right now, don't you? Me with my face, you with your family. Part of Marcia Levene really kicks the dark lust Greg Vain inspires in her, part of her wants more, and maybe part of her needs to shed his presence on a physical level. Right now she's trying out a third-person type of reflection and maybe you should do the same".

Levene left their room with that line, and the ensuing three days became a kind of mutual separation for the pair. This was agony for Vain though, as his state of mind had started to become more and more dominated by thoughts of his project lover. He knew in his heart that his family should be the dominant ingredient in his thoughts but he had become entranced with Levene to a significant level. At times he felt that physical lust was the sole reason the two enjoyed each other's company, but this reasoning was always broken down by a realisation that a deeper bond existed between them. Vain was in need of time to 'escape' to his family, and he hoped he would re-discover the ultimate love he had once reserved solely for them. Greg really needed to do exactly what Levene recommended but surely following her advice was another part of her spell!

When Greg was placed on the convoy to rejoin MC Project loved ones, he was still in a state of flux, a confused individual with his heartstrings and sexual urges pulling for two women.

The convoy pulled out of the Designation in darkness and Gregory Vain's thoughts turned to the family that had been denied him for the last couple of months. He had missed Gary's eighth birthday and Rachel's tenth birthday during his absence - two more key dates that the MC Project had stolen from him.

In six days Tanya would turn thirty-three, and he looked forward to sharing her birthday to the fullest level, especially as his lengthy absences had rendered her a 'virtual' wife for the best part of the last six years. He tried to envisage their new project-sectioned domicile, and he wondered how Tan had coped with the pressure of his recent media status. She would have seen images of him brandishing the Uzi at reporters, and the papers had profiled his university years in licentious accounts that thrived on his womanising. A fair amount of lies and fiction had made up the bulk of the reports, but he felt sure that Tanya would have dismissed the trash amidst the truisms. Sinquiry would have terrified his wife, of that he was certain, but he was content in the knowledge that his family would have been protected before the lynch mobs traced their address - surely that would have been the case!

Vain fell into a light sleep whilst contemplating the last three days without Levene. Somehow their parting had seemed more than reactionary bickering, and maybe her last hint was the direction the pair should follow.

The jarring motion of the MC Project vehicle woke Vain and he saw Mr Voight individually conversing with each project member, speaking in hushed tones. In time he reached Vain's seat. The air felt rather chilly for a mid-English summer and the countryside looked alien to that of the greenbelt type Vain had expected - too green, too beautiful. Voight spoke.

"Welcome to Scotland, Gregory".

"What? I thought that the Guildford region was going to be our new project corral!"

"Merely a bluff, Gregory. Mr Denison played it that way in case any wayward project member felt impelled to fuel the press with details of our whereabouts. Sure, there is a decoy educational institution set up around Guildford, but it's just a charade. Plenty of coaches going in, but no actual project children on board them. You see, some of those who got leaks out did so despite our heavy security cordon, and so Leif chose to throw all of us in the wrong geographical direction. In two hours we'll reach our real base, a highland locale - our first project village!

"A masterstroke, don't you think? Our convoy will split soon, so we reach our destination in small batches that won't excite any untoward media attention. Now enjoy the glens, my friend, through your one-way window. You will soon see your loved ones again in the village".

After a duration that was closer to three hours rather than the stated two, the vehicle carrying the MC Project contingent which included Vain, entered a tunnel that bore into a verdant hillside. After a few minutes of travelling through the dimly lit tunnel, the transportation vehicle slowed to a halt. The reason for the stop involved a roadblock that was manned by a heavy MC security cohort.

All project members had their papers checked by two of the guards who had boarded their vehicle, and after Voight had verbally reiterated all the names of the personnel aboard once more, the cohort were granted passage. This form of document checking was repeated when the vehicle reached the last stage of the tunnel. When daylight was finally encountered, a breathtaking sight met MC Project eyes.

The tunnel road dropped down into a heather-dominated landscape, and dotted amongst the greenery were a collection of imposing white stone villas. The design of these villas added a surreal dimension to the typical highland panorama that held their foundations.

The MC Project personnel alighted outside one of the white stone buildings and Vain started to scan the wider terrain.

On three sides, sheer granite rock faces towered upwards to a height of several hundred metres, and lower mountain slopes accounted for the remaining valley side. This most distant side involved a fern clad hillside, which initially rose up in a more leisurely climb. After a distance of three or four kilometres, this gradual climb started to develop into a steep rise, echoing the sheer faces that accounted for the other valley sides. The fourth side eventually rose to a height that dwarfed the other flanks, culminating in a mountain peak of over two thousand metres. Vain thought that this craggy 'lock-in' represented one of the most beautiful landscape visions that he had ever encountered.

A posse of jet fighters roared overhead, breaking Greg's concentration for a moment. The grey planes were reflected in the river that meandered through the settlement, and as the fighters split to patrol different valley sides, Vain was dragged back into his less aesthetic reality. Voight placed his hand on Vain's shoulder and ushered him toward a white villa close by. As the two walked, he added more details pertaining to their surroundings.

"Call it what you want Gregory, a village, a settlement, even a refuge! Either way, it's now home to over two hundred MC Project members. In addition to the houses, we've installed a school, some food stores and a doctor's surgery. Right now things may be a bit spartan outside the residences, but the houses themselves are upmarket luxury. The only thing that they really lack is 'live' media - for obvious reasons".

Voight hadn't lied. The entrance hall had a black and white marble-tiled floor and mahogany-panelling rose from the floor to the ceiling. Black wood trappings added an embellished degree of finish, and the downstairs was split into open-plan glass partitioned sections.

A spiral staircase was located centrally in the hall, and the overall effect seemed compromised somewhere between retro-Bauhaus and deconstructionalist minimalism.

After ascending the staircase, Vain entered the sleeping quarters. All four bedrooms were empty and he started to feel uneasy - first the silence, now the absence. The sound of juvenile laughter broke his pessimistic train of thought. The sound came from above him and as he progressed back onto the landing he located a second staircase, this time straight in form. He proceeded to climb the stairs and was rewarded this time by finding all his family together, watching a *Laurel and Hardy* video on a laser screen. They hadn't heard his quiet footfall, and so Greg had the rare privilege of being the first to speak.

"Has this breakfast club got room for another bum gang?"

"Daddy" chorused the children and Vain was swamped by the hugs of his children.

After Gary and Rachel had greeted their father, Tanya Vain took her husband in her arms and loved him with her eyes, saying nothing initially. With the video forgotten, the family filled in the key domestic details that had taken place in Greg's absence. Although all the family members now had some idea of Greg's nature of work, the conversation stayed on birthdays and juvenile milestones. All the Vain family had experienced what life had been like as a 'public enemy', but this first precious reunion day was spent walking along the margins of the valley river and fun-wrestling in their heather clad surroundings. The day had subsequently been a celebration for Greg and Tanya's children and the 'expected' conversation didn't ensue until late in the evening when the adults were in their bedroom. With the children asleep in their adjoining rooms, Tanya spoke to her husband in colder tones than the daylight hours had witnessed.

"Do you think your project buddies ever played 'happy families', Greg?"

"You what?"

"Well if they did, they've got one fucking obscure definition of happiness, you know. If you could have seen the tears on our kid's faces when the lynch-mob stormed our old house, you would have wept yourself - Christ I did! You see all we had was the Sinquiry prompt, that was our only expectation level.

"What the hell would have happened if Rachel and I hadn't seen that programme, what if we'd been out in central London? Don't answer that one, Greg, because you know that we would have been wiped out - the public were like a rabid fucking animal!"

"Come off it Tan, you're speaking as though I had expected that type of public reaction and as though I could have got word to you. I thought I'd..."

Tanya cut her husband short.

"Let me finish, Gregory. You have got to understand how things were for us - one minute you were a media hero, but the next you were the reason our lives were in jeopardy! I mean, look at us now, Greg, is this a Scottish haven like they tell us, or is it a prison in disguise? We can't leave you know, we can't even buy a loaf of bread without our every move being scanned by guards and cameras. I bet that even if we made love tonight, some of your colleagues would video scan my orgasms!"

"What do you mean 'even if we made love?'"

"Still a one track mind then, Greg. Oh yeah I

forget, you haven't seen the Greg Vain media profile we've all witnessed have you? You'd better refresh your memory then love, because the British TV cameras weren't quite as naive as you obviously think I was. Why the hell were you and Marcia Levene going back to the project Designation together? The fucking media said that you had received new project freedoms! What the hell did that mean to you, Greg - the freedom to fuck someone else!

"When your lot briefly tried to play things media-friendly, the tabloids had a field day. What was I supposed to think, Greg, I mean she's not exactly ugly is she, but screw her - you probably have - there is still one area you've got to clear up with me, mister. Did you have any opportunity to warn me and the kids of the hell that would confront us?"

"No I bloody didn't, Tan! God, you three are everything to me. She's nothing. When the cameras shot us in the same car, I'd been on project business - jeez I'd pulled the Uzi because I had confidential project info in the car! Remember, sometimes telly is a twisted reality. Look, you've given me chances in the past, more than an angel, but she's work and all the routine that goes with it".

"Fuck her Greg, you've still side-tracked my main question - could you have pre-warned us?"

"No, no, a fucking thousand times, no! Do you think I'd let you and the kids suffer if I could do anything about it, love?"

The pair continued talking into the small hours. Tanya became convinced that Vain still loved her and their children like he always had, although she still doubted her husband's account of his feelings towards Levene. Despite her doubts she saw that area as secondary to their family bond, especially after the devastation that had affected them all in recent days.

As the conversation turned less heated, Tanya took Vain through their London evacuation in detail and then filled him in on their journey to the highlands. The pair drifted into a more uneasy sleep than on previous reunions - they didn't make love that night.

Tanya was pleased when she realised that Greg and the family would be together for just over a month, and as the summer days rolled by, the Vains enjoyed some of their happiest times as a unified family. Greg and Gary went fishing in the small tributaries that left the river, whilst Tanya and Rachel prepared them campfire food close by. All four of them climbed the lower slopes of the furthest valley reaches and their only reminder of the MC Project were the fighter fly-overs every seven or eight minutes. Tanya feared that these times were 'too good to last', as Greg and her seemed to be as close as they ever had been by the end of the first week. Their love making had reflected this with a regained tenderness replacing the suspicion of their first reunion night.

Greg also felt like he had never been away, never strayed, never lusted or loved another. He had adored the natural love his family had showered him and hadn't felt the need to ruin this ambience with revelations to Tanya about the plastic alterations he would shortly fall victim to.

At dawn, on day seventeen their tranquillity was shattered, and Tanya's fears proved to be foundered. The couple were rudely awakened on that morning by the harsh penetrating signal of Gregory Vain's Comm-Lynx device. Mr Voight substituted the speaker's role that Mason previously used to enjoy. His first on-line call to Vain was the most important message carried by this device thus far!

"Gather your things together Gregory, Mishimo Ko-Chai... is... DEAD!".

Vain was shocked to the core - his best project

friend was dead! It took him several seconds to build a reply.

"But how Mr Voight? He was all project, he will be irreplaceable".

"A heart attack, a massive one. He worked himself to death, he couldn't stop, you know. He will never die in terms of spirit, and like you say he was all project. We are going to send him out with full military honours in Washington in three days time. The man is an American hero and all MC Project staff will be in attendance following his funeral cortege. It will mark the last time that the world will see us on a public level - the Rochaux treatment has been brought forward accordingly, following a week after the funeral. Now get your things together, we are out of here in twenty minutes time".

As Vain flung clothes into a travel bag and other essentials into a suitcase, he turned to his long-suffering wife.

"Tan, I love ya more than ever you know.

"If I could rewind the clock, I wouldn't have put y..."

Tanya took his words away.

"Don't say it, love. I followed you then and I'll wait again, you know".

"Even if I come back with a different fucking face, love? They're going to give us plastic to mask our old identities. We don't have any say in the matter. Jeez, I feel fucking guilty going on about my fucking face, love - my best project buddy is gone and all I can do is go on about my fucking face".

For the first time since childhood, Vain cried. Tanya finished her husband's packing and briefly cradled Greg in her arms. She had the last line before he departed, one of the most beautiful that Greg had ever heard.

"If every part of your face is rendered plastic, Greg, I'll still kiss your tears and taste your mouth, I'll still love you for thousands of yesterdays and seventeen days of highland paradise. Plastic doesn't change the man. I love you, Vain".

FIFTEEN

Vain's hand released the moist soil, and it fell across the lid of Mishimo Ko-Chai's coffin. America had honoured their naturalised brother, and the faint drizzle hadn't deterred the two million citizens who had flanked the funeral cortege route. After a seventeen cannon salute in the Arlington National Cemetery, Ko-Chai's hearse had been ceremonially driven through the streets of Washington DC, and following the vehicle containing the body of Ko-Chai, President Delavoy's limousine had escorted the funeral cars in their slow progression. The President had personally requested this duty, and Denison had granted favour with the elegance that America had expected of him. In addition to his skilled organisational expertise, Leif was blessed with a solemnity of purpose that endeared him to the bastions of protocol and reserve. Some saw the MC Project leader as a man possessed with the kind of mettle that might some day see him succeed Delavoy in a presidential role.

The crowds had watched the funeral procession in a dignified silence that was quite uncanny when compared to the usual level of noise associated with DC on a Wednesday morning. The fact that Delavoy was in attendance did provide a reason for a proportion of the interest, but Ko-Chai's death had brought the calm and quiet atmosphere.

America had always saluted the MC Project members, and Ko-Chai had been a figure who had experienced frequent media profiling, as he had turned from his home country in favour of residing in the 'land of the free'. The average American thus behaved in a converse fashion to their British equivalents, celebrating rather than chastising MC Project personnel. Ko-Chai's funeral subsequently became a metaphor for unified American emotion, and the tears on Twenty First Street encapsulated Ko-Chai's latent magnitude to a level of great testimony.

After the funeral service was over, the MC Project cohort were briefly given time to pass on their condolences to Mishimo's wife before they would have to board transportation vehicles to take them back to Designation Y - their permanent Washington base.

Vain was glad that he would finally meet Mrs Ko-Chai, and he was also pleased that his friend had been laid to rest in a private service that didn't allow for any intrusive crowds. He took the woman's hands in his and found the words to fully express his grief.

"Alice, I bet Mishimo's smiling down on us right now, you know. I've never met a man with a better sense of honour, and a tenderness that left the rest of us morally trailing in his wake. He was my best friend, and my heart goes out to you".

"Thank you Gregory, he loved you like a son. I know you through the descriptions he gave to me; you were his best friend likewise. Now part of me feels that this may be our first and last meeting - so please give your wife or daughter this".

As the pair embraced in friendship, Alice Ko-Chai pushed a small amethyst broach into Vain's hand. Ko-Chai would stay with the Vain family.

Vain looked around him, and as he headed towards the MC Project transportation vehicle.

He saw Tavini looking rather brash in a black power suit, with Marco Sant and Hannah Nichol walking at his side. Denison was locked in conversation with Jess Wheeler, and Fray was an isolated figure, looking quite disconsolate. Vain wondered how long it would be before the ex-security head would prove additional to project requirements. A chill ran through him.

Designation Y was the most sumptuous underground Designation yet, being a far cry from the claustrophobic horrors of Chicago's hellhole. The sleeping quarters were quite luxurious, and when Vain returned from Ko-Chai's funeral he relaxed, splaying his frame across the soft cover sheets of his double bed. Denison had stated that MC Project work didn't resume until Friday, and he looked forward to tracking Diana Fearston down later in the day. After Ko-Chai's death, Fearston represented Vain's closest professional friendship within the ranks of the MC Project, and he felt that both of them shared a bond concerning their mutual working prerogatives. His mind didn't turn to Levene. After his family bond had been rejuvenated in Scotland, Marcia's hold on him had weakened to a significant level. Vain was envisaging the workload that lay ahead of him, when a recorded message from Dwight Richards came down his Comm-Lynx.

"Hi, Greg. Your presence is requested for an audience with David Tavini at 17:00 in Room 18 Level 4".

Vain shook his head. He felt that whatever the context, Tavini was walking on the grave of his friend by appointing a meeting only a few hours after the funeral service. He initially thought about showing his disgust by observing a policy of non-attendance, but he knew that his maverick attitude had led him into disrepute before.

Although he technically still had a higher project rank than Tavini, he felt that the opinions of the MC Project chain of command seemed to favour his American front-line colleague. He decided that common sense should prevail ahead of moral-bound valour. He would go.

When he entered the designated meeting room at 16:55, he was reasonably surprised to find the entire top ranking MC Project cohort in attendance. Vain caught the eye of Levene. She smiled, but when his gaze contacted Jess Wheeler's eyes, the security number one looked through him. At the appointed hour, Dwight Richards spoke to the assembly, echoing the unusual level of formality that hung over the venue.

"This audience has been requested by Mr David Marius Tavini. Mr Tavini holds the most senior position with regard to our digital conversion work, and he believes that our future practical direction should involve a new third prerogative. In addition to our primary work and our more recent 'mindsight' focus, Mr Tavini wishes to concentrate on some physical sections of brain structure during developmental stages. Mr Denison has witnessed the efforts of David and his research team with regard to this third prerogative, and he gave his full consent for this audience to take place. Mr Tavini will now relate the details surrounding our third prerogative".

As Richards had spoken, Vain had felt both anger and fear run through him. He was highly suspicious of Tavini's private research team, but he guessed that Marco Sant and Hannah Nicol would be part of it. He was also suspicious of the 'third prerogative', as it seemed to lie in his neurological domain, and yet this was the first he had heard of a possible new direction. The late-arriving Diana Fearston stopped Vain's reflections.

She sat next to Greg, smiling her greetings. Tavini moved toward the front of the room after he had vacated his seat. His seating position had been right next to Wheeler, and Vain hoped that this wasn't indicative of a closer power alliance between the two. Tavini spoke.

"Yo, guys. Thanks Dwight for the formality. Look - this is gonna be a brand new subject area for most of you, so I'm going to break things to you in my own language, my own style. Leif thinks that will be better and so do I. When my enthusiasm kicks in, my language sounds like a Seattle pile-driver and as this new prerogative has a 'white hot' interest factor for me, you can expect a few words will be used that may differ somewhat from some of my more well spoken colleagues! If any of you need to ask me questions, try and wait for a convenient pause, but if you can't find one hurl them out my way. Right, here goes".

After talking at the pace of a speed addict, Tavini drew a very audible breath before launching into his audience.

"We have been working back to front folks, back to fucking front! We've been working from corpses to villains. Yeah, our primary research area did bang up some undesirables - for sure, but let's face it people, we're dealing with a 'tip of the iceberg' success ratio here. As criminals wisen up, more systemised decapitation and brain destruction will feature on a more professional level. Our criminal impetus was our MC showcase - nothing more".

As if awaiting an argument, Tavini paused. Some of the assembly wondered whether to engage with Tavini after his primary stage write-off, but all present were curious to know more, and thus silence was preserved. He began again with a sweat already forming on his brow.

"Our mindsight work was one helluva stage two guys, but the third prerogative humbles this secondary research area in terms of power and control!"

"Control?" Queried Fearston.

"Here me out" was the reply before the continuation.

"You see everyone, Greg held the cards for the perfect third-prerogative all the time, he started the research way back, but he left without any completion. Before Gregory Vain became an MC Project member he had pioneered and then discarded neurological research into sections of the brain that he had christened the Auto-Vendetta Vaults. His discovery had located parts of the brain which dealt with negative behavioural responses - anger, revenge, aggression and sorrow. You may feel that to have sorrow is a positive reaction, but in the context of the other three, a negative drive can often be the dominant outcome. You shouldn't have stopped your research, Greg".

On this occasion Tavini's pause for breath was deliberate, beckoning a response from Vain, and Greg took up the metaphorical gauntlet.

"Yeah, I located the Auto-Vendetta vault, like you say Dave, but the deeper my research went the more sceptical I became about delving too deep".

Tavini bit back asking why, and so Vain elaborated.

"I was reasonably sure that the auto-vendetta sections did indeed contain answers surrounding negative behavioural responses, but I didn't commit myself to practical research because my theoretical deductions presented what I felt were sinister implications for mankind. You see, I became seventy-five percent certain that these sections could be altered, controlled, even obliterated".

"The power to obliterate aggression! Why is that such a bad thing, Greg?"

"Society needs the whole neuro-package, David. Aggression is a pivotal ingredient of our survival mechanism, and man also 'needs' badness to establish goodness in his system of converse-determined logic. Purity only seems white when it's surrounded by pollution".

"Losing talk Gregory - nice parallels drawn, but if people have the power to remove these 'heavy negs' from society, they should act. It is their duty, their moral role to play. You shut your research down, but left seeds for others to carry it on, and I think you are gonna wish we could have involved you with our third-prerogative. I want you to meet someone, Greg".

Tavini left his speaker's position and sat back down. Then two medical staff entered the speaker's area, emerging from a screened out section of the assembly hall. They carried a large dolls house and proceeded to place the toy on the small stage just in front of the project audience. A third member of medical personnel followed, gently leading a little girl into the spotlight. The child was smiling sweetly, appearing demure and totally unfazed by the ranks of people that scanned her entrance. As her white blonde hair shone in the fluorescent lighting, she was led toward the dolls house. Her smile seemed to register even more pleasure when she recognised the nature of the toy on the stage in front of her. Tavini walked back to his previous front-line position, making ready to speak again. As the child started to play, he extended a warm glance in her direction and then introduced the juvenile presence who had warmed the hearts of most of those present.

"Meet Belinda, guys. She's an example of our Prerogative Three, born to our project, born through a new mould. Belinda has blessed us with her presence for over four years now. That dolls house has been her favourite toy since we gave it to her on her second birth date. Smash it to pieces, Greg!"

Vain swallowed hard, not being able to understand how such an evil-natured command could be uttered, let alone condoned by a person. He spat back a reply which Fearston felt paralleled the savagery of the moment.

"You sick, twisted bastard, Tavini. You need help, you fucking pervert".

Tavini didn't even flinch at Vain's words. He turned instead to the MC security cohort that were resident in the room.

"Do the honours, Jess".

Without a moment's hesitation, Wheeler reached the stage in five strides.

His fist splintered the roof and his boots kicked the structure into a state of total ruin. After ten seconds, he was finished, smiling at Tavini, who appeared to be gratified by his demolition job.

Belinda was still smiling - at Tavini, at Wheeler, at anyone who caught her gaze! She seemed to be totally oblivious to the destruction that had taken place, and she actually began to chuckle to herself as she started to reassemble the broken pieces of her doll's house. Her eyes still sparkled. To her life seemed beautiful, unblemished and perfect! To Vain, life had turned irrevocably sour. He stood up and walked toward Tavini, polemically announcing his new found hatred.

"So this is our Prerogative Three is it, fucker? How long has she been conditioned like this?"

"Life's been her smile - it's all she's ever known, Greg".

"What! Are you saying that she was born into this state of complete passive surrender?"

"Yes, we modified her mind when she was a foetus, Greg. You had laid the ground rules with your initial research programme; we had the guts to put your theories into practice. We actually chose the eradication option as far as the auto-vendetta sections were concerned. You see, all she knows is bliss, she lives in an Arcadia... when you compare her world with ours. Her mother didn't realise that her scan number three in week thirty changed her daughter's future. How many pregnant mothers ask any real specifics concerning the gadgetry that scans their developing foetus? All they want to see is the thumb sucking and all they want to hear is the affirmative 'everything's okay' line from their doctor. In Belinda's case, her mother cried with happiness, while our laser took out her daughter's Auto-Vendetta sections. She had no knowledge of the neurological research that was being incarnated in her womb! Look Greg, you may have bottled out of the program that you set up but you didn't have a divine seal on its completion".

"Robotics, Tavini - that's what you should have fuckin' majored in, after all that's what you've created here, isn't it? You have stolen Belinda's will to survive and replaced it with an overdose of positive responses. Would you have done this to your own kid, fucker?"

The two men moved closer to each other.

"You'll go too far here if you're not careful, Vain. I don't stand around to be insulted on my own, let alone in front of a congregation! What's your fucking problem? We're aiming to create a better world here, and Belinda is our first rung. We are just in our test phase, for Christ's sake. People would think that we'd brainwashed legions, the way you're burning at me!"

"You said it yourself Tavini - brainwashed".

"Jeez, someone take this creep away from me, will ya? We've created a child without a concept of violence for god's sake, and this guy wants her to suffer in the same shit that the rest of us live in! If we all thought like Belinda, in a hundred years time, there wouldn't be any human violence - got that Vain?"

"Well allow me to exercise my violence privilege while I've still got one, then"

Vain snapped. The altercation had been building for some months.

Tavini may have warmed to the verbal sparring Gregory Vain had put in place, but he hadn't envisaged that his much smaller project colleague would deliver the first blow! Vain launched himself at Tavini releasing a head butt that broke the latter's Romanesque nose in two places. This element of surprise gave Vain an initial advantage, and he hammered home a series of body blows that his distant years of amateur boxing had taught him. The American countered with a volley of punches that smashed into Greg's left cheekbone, and after a few seconds of mayhem, the MC security cohort leapt into the action.

Wheeler took out Vain with a butt that shattered the side of his face that Tavini had severely bruised. This attack proved a catalyst for others to join the fracas, and four of the Chinese recruits from the peace conference days pitched in to aid the floored front-line leader. Vain had rightly been promoted as a leading project figure in the media-friendly post-conference days, and the Chinese delegation had seen his work as a motivating force for their entry into the holistic MC Project. They saw Vain as the incarnation of all that was decent in the project and they wouldn't see 'their' hero lying broken on the ground, with a security posse reigning blows down upon him.

Several of the Chinese contingents had brought some martial arts expertise with them, and Wheeler's men started to hit the floor like dominoes.

The Chinese recruits weren't the only people to join the fracas on Vain's side, and Fearston had decided to 'lend a hand' as soon as Wheeler had floored her front-line mentor. She hadn't any fighting experience but she rushed in to pull Greg out of the melee when unconscious bodies started to drop around him.

Denison had been surveying the scene from his seat, inwardly smiling because he had recognised an almost 'slapstick' quality to the brawl in front of him. This perception altered when he saw one of Wheeler's crew reaching for his firearm. Leif beat him to the draw, firing a blast of his own weapon upward toward the ornate encrusted ceiling. The shots rendered the warring factions into a 'freeze-frame' posture, and only Belinda resumed a mode of previous behaviour - laughing at those around her.

The MC Project leader chastised his wayward personnel.

"Don't spoil the Rochaux party, folks! Look at you! In a few days some of us are going to get a different face - why start now?

"You may have noticed that I now say some not all, but I have revised my initial edict - it's my prerogative after all! If a person has caused a big wave in the past, they kinda deserve a new face, but those who have towed the line and remained hidden are due a break. It looks like Greg's started his own modification work - well fair enough, he is in line for 'visage numéro deux' anyway, so if he wants to start now I guess he isn't changing anything major".

Belinda chose that moment to walk amongst the assembled MC Project members, and her steps seemed to cast a spell of uncanny silence on the project ranks for an instant. There was something fragile about the steps, almost like the infant had just left her embryo. As the girl continued to flit through the project ranks, Denison carried on speaking.

"I know that some of you have been rocked spiritually by what you have seen tonight, but David is actually correct - Belinda is just a test phase. The ideal is beautiful - no one could dispute that, could they, but I agree with Mr Vain too. We judge things by what we know, and right now that means retaining Auto-Vendetta negatives to ensure our survival. David is possibly a bit optimistic in referencing a century to build change, but Greg is too 'head in the sand' if he feels that our Prerogative Three shouldn't embrace the idea of a violence-modified society. Science has to direct us, my friends and our collective duty is to serve science, for the generations ahead of us. Clean up our wounded you medics, thank you".

Denison's last remark had been a bit of an understatement. Vain and Tavini both had broken facial bones and the pair would be confined in the MC Medical Ward until their Rochaux treatment in a few days time. The project brawl may have been a relatively short altercation, but most of the project members who had entered the fracas had scars to evidence their involvement. Wheeler was an exception. The MC Project honcho had hardly broken sweat in the fight, and although he had encountered a lot of direct physical engagement after he had put Vain down, not one significant retaliation blow had dented his guard. Wheeler was essentially in a different league as far as physical combat was concerned.

As Vain's stretcher was wheeled out of the room, Diana Fearston attempted to follow her front-line mentor, but Marcia Levene intercepted this route of loyalty. Levene had the advantage of surprise and her initial words were uttered in a soft tone that was alien to her usual form of sharp verbal delivery.

"Let them go, Diana. The medics will look after him. We love him for all that he has done for our project, we love him for his scientific brilliance, and some of us love him for his naiveté - Christ I should know! Leif and David were right though, if we arrest progress, we let 'yesterday' blight our tomorrows. Nice to see you in the 'action' girl, he needs that".

The sensitivity displayed by Levene halted Fearston in her tracks, and whilst she didn't fully trust the woman whose specific project role always seemed shrouded in grey, she had detected genuine care in the words, despite Levene's predominant sense of duty.

Gregory Vain had been oblivious to the inter-unit fighting that had taken place after he had attacked Tavini. His rage had made him blank out the American's 'return-fire' but he was totally unprepared for Wheeler's onslaught, and the butt in question rendered him unconscious for several minutes.

The MC Project medical unit tended Vain with great care in the ensuing four days. His shattered cheekbone was reset through a wire mould, despite the fact that surgeons would modify Greg's face in a matter of days. The MC Medics liked the front-line leader, and yet they felt sure that he was going to be a project individual that would have the full Rochaux treatment performed upon him. By wiring up Greg's face, they hoped to preserve his angular features - it was a small mercy they felt he deserved.

When Vain was led to the Rochaux wing four days later, his thoughts weren't true to his name. As far as he was concerned, a new face would be an adventure, something that was beyond his control.

When his eyes started to close after his anaesthetising injection two issues dominated his thoughts - the robotic reliance of Belinda and the egocentric idealism of Tavini. As Vain started to sink into a medicinal netherworld he voiced a phrase that epitomised his disillusionment.

"She'll laugh at your fire.., burn in your fire..., die in your fire..."

SIXTEEN

Vain saw the door handle turn. At last he could see his new face! He had been in a state of bondage for the initial seventeen days since his consciousness had returned, being denied a mirror or a verbal description concerning the facial changes that had been performed upon him. His surgeon had promised him that day eighteen was to be his visual revelation. The Rochaux surgeon was going to be true to his word, as Vain could see that an assistant medical officer carried the mirror that Gregory had awaited for, for what seemed like a lifetime. Before Vain was given the mirror, the surgeon Monsieur Garron had some choice words for him to digest. He proceeded in perfect English.

"Mr Vain, you have endured quite a change. Since my team first started modification work thirty-seven days ago, your face has undergone a series of Rochaux adjustments which were responding to a seventy-percent alteration brief requested by your superiors. They didn't specify beyond the percentage. We were the decision-makers behind your effective remould. Our work has involved tissue adjustment, bone reshaping and colourised iris modification. We have cut in part, we have tucked to a minor degree and we have utilised a series of plastic toning stratagems to render the finished product. The reshaping was speeded up through our most advanced fixing agents and in short, your new face arrived nine days ahead of our predicted delivery date. We will leave you alone to survey our work".

The Rochaux surgeon handed Vain the mirror, and the pair left Vain to contemplate his reflection. Greg had turned the mirror on its face whilst the pair remained in the room, but when they departed he turned it back to meet it face-on.

A pair of dull yellow eyes stared back at Vain. The selected colour hue had a deep lustre which intensified the blackness of the pupils. The 'favoured' bottom lip had been retained, but the top lip had been tightened, cut through to half the previous volume. The cheekbones had been altered after Jess Wheeler's deliverance, and the Rochaux team had echoed his demolition with contours of gauntness that remembered the suffering and yet retained a haggard attraction. Vain's dark hair had been kept in spirit, but a jet-black colour modification added a sharper dimension. The hair had altered in terms of texture, feeling coarse now, dropping out of symmetrical adherence. The most noticeable alteration feature save the eyes, involved the colour of Vain's skin. Before modification, Vain had retained a tanned complexion that survived the seasons, but the surgeons had chosen a very pallid alteration. Vain's skin was now closer to a Scandinavian-white in comparison.

Vain reflected on his new image. He knew that the changes made to his face were permanent. The yellow iris dye was a 'living' pigment that would reproduce itself over time and he also knew that the black hair was fixed as his roots had been tethered by another Rochaux longevity chemical. All Rochaux alterations had been devised to last, and Greg knew that his old appearance would never return.

Later that evening Vain was allowed to leave his medical unit, and then he surveyed his facial changes in relation to his whole body. He carelessly shed his hospital robe and confronted himself naked in front of a full-length mirror. Whilst the Rochaux surgeons primarily specialised in facial changes, the toned pigmentation changed the neck and chest regions. In Vain's case this meant that the ashen white facial skin was modified by reduction from his neck downwards. Because of the sliding pigmentation scale the changes weren't blatant as far as tonal comparison was concerned. Vain only noticed radical hue difference if he compared his face to the skin colour below his naval region. His surgeon had told him that within six months his tonal skin colour would all be consistent with his face. The new living pigmentation would in time permeate downwards to colour his whole frame.

Greg was relatively impressed with his avant-garde metamorphosis. He was pleased with his new eyes because he had only met two people with a similar colour in his life thus far, and he subsequently felt that the alteration added a rarefied quality to his countenance. The other changes added a gothic dimension to his character, and although the sum total made him appear a product of malnutrition he felt that a 'wasted' rock-star type status had washed over him!

All MC Project staff in the Washington Designation were set to meet the following morning and the occasion would evidence the Rochaux work in its entirety. Vain had been provided with a lapel badge bearing his name and his new divisional identity. He and Tavini had obviously now been separated, and he and Fearston were going to be aligned to a unit that Vance Fray had been entrusted

253

with. This was an obvious demotion for Fray, and Greg wondered how it would alter the former security figurehead.

Greg was still reflecting on his new appearance and unit placement when he tried to sleep later that evening. Tanya and Levene also crept into his thoughts. He wondered if his wife could possibly get used to his new face and he tried to envisage the Rochaux changes that would have consumed Marcia. Sleep eventually claimed him.

When he entered the meeting room the following morning he was initially surprised at how few altered faces were in evidence. MC Project staff had been encouraged to stand and mingle in an informal fashion. All wore the lapel name badges, but there was no need for the vast majority of those in attendance. Vain saw Voight unchanged, Carson unchanged and Leif Denison - unchanged! Eventually he decided to move away from the doorway and walk amongst his colleagues. This prompted a uniform silence to come over those who witnessed his new countenance, and he walked around for a full two minutes before anyone actually spoke to him. In effect he was regarded as an artistic display, a living sculpture!

Vain felt like a leper, and just when he was about to exit the arena of embarrassment, a friendly, familiar voice from behind him changed his mind. He turned expecting to see Diana Fearston, but he hadn't bargained for the alterations which had been performed upon his understudy.

"The price for knowing me I suppose - the bastards!"

"Not your usual charm, Greg!"

"Sorry Diana, I didn't mean it to sound like that, you know".

"I know Greg. It's okay, really it is.

"I mean we all knew a few 'cave-ins' might occur didn't we? You look wild though, I wouldn't have recognised you without the badge!"

Vain was horrified. Some of the early Rochaux treatments had cruelly been branded as 'cave-ins' by the American press, because the victim suffered a reaction, which involved skin tissue rejection and brittle bone formation. Unfortunately Fearston had suffered both side-effects with her skin turning a sickly jaundiced yellow, and some of her facial bones had collapsed, ageing her a good ten years. She had retained her noble demeanour despite her ill fortune and Vain placed his arm around her, hugging her to him, expressing how glad he was that the two of them would retain their working relationship.

Whilst the pair conversed, Mr Fray entered the room, and it didn't take the onlookers long to realise that the Rochaux treatment that this individual had received was a revenge-edict for his Sinquiry outburst. The MC Project lost public face in Britain during that instance, and now Fray was paying for it in private, losing his own 'established' face.

The changes performed upon the former main-player bore out the visual hallmarks of Denison's directive vendetta. Fray had been metaphorically 'tarred and feathered!' The sleek white hair of old was now totally absent, shaved out of existence and never to reappear - Rochaux's follicle-blocking agents would ensure that.

Fray's piercing eyes had been radically altered, with the iris injections draining the vivid blue lustre and replacing it with a dull-grey colour that had a lifeless tonality in comparison. Vance Fray's facial skin had been 'tucked' very tightly to his cheekbone contours, and the man winced in pain if his mouth registered any expression that deviated from poker-faced neutrality. Already new pain-derived wrinkle lines cut tracks across the mouth region and a smile or laugh would invite the highest pain threshold. The selected pigmentation involved blotches of the white hue which cast Vain's face and more dominant outcrops of tissue colour that had a more ruddy complexion. Fray's face looked blemished and unnatural.

He said little to the assembled ranks, preferring to stay close to the back wall. After a few words with Denison, Fray exited the room. He was a twisted shadow of his former self, looking out of place in the company of the high ranks that he had once been part of. The unaltered face of Jess Wheeler sneered as he watched the broken man depart.

After witnessing the radical alterations to Fearston and Fray, Gregory Vain temporarily forgot to look out for Levene, but shortly after Fray's departure she entered the room - a typical late entrance. Levene knew that she looked good, different but still beautiful. The long hair was now cut short in a wrap-around bob. The raven black colour of old had been altered significantly to a uniform dark burgundy and the pert nose was now pierced with a small diamond stud. Levene's eyes had been changed to a dark green colour hue, but her ashen pallor had been kept. There was little evidence of any cuts or tucks. Marcia purred her greetings, fixing Greg's yellow eyes with a stare of sensual intensity.

"Nice show Greg, off the wall, but cool in a rebel way! I guess there's a cyber-punk spirit running through some of the Rochaux guys. Your eyes and my nose kinda bear that out, don't they? Are you pleased with your changes?"

"The alterations are reasonable, but others weren't so lucky, were they? Have you seen Diana and Fray?"

"I've seen them, but they're not me or you are they, Greg?

"I mean, I'm not going to lose sleep over them. I was so damned pleased that I could live with my own changes. You haven't said anything yet Greg, what do you think of the new me?"

"You mean the 'book cover'. Oh you're still beautiful, Marcia".

"You're pretty true to your surname yourself, Mr Vain. You can skip the false humility!"

Greg's book cover line had annoyed Levene, making her feel that he was implying that she let a superficiality mould her character. The spiky exchange would probably have developed further but David Tavini cut in. Neither Levene nor Vain had seen the Prerogative Three controllers watching them, but that gave Tavini the chance to mentally rehearse his chosen words to Vain.

"Well I know that those yellow eyes weren't chosen to signify a cowardly streak, Greg! You pack quite a butt, Mr Vain - helluva rumble my friend, wasn't it?"

Vain accepted Tavini's handshake, but he couldn't forget the robotic form of mind control which had accounted for Belinda. The pair continued to talk for a while, but Vain made an excuse to leave when Levene addressed Tavini's further on Prerogative Three. She had congratulated Tavini for being made honcho of the said MC unit, but Vain couldn't verbally engage in that subject and he took his leave. Tavini turned his attention to Marcia.

"See him back into the fold, Marcia. He hasn't got many cards left, you know. He's too fucking moral for his own good, but I still kinda like the guy".

"I'll try David, but I'm starting to wonder if Mr Vain has gone as far as he can. Some might say that he's treading water right now but others may counter, saying that he's scared of our future, wanting to stop the clock and not advance further".

The new face exposure had been an example of gross discrimination as far as Vain was concerned. Denison had initially told the MC Project ranks that the Rochaux surgeons would facially alter all staff. He had then modified his original decision, and what had transpired in actuality strongly suggested that a retribution-determined 'branding' had taken place. Vain knew that he had displayed too many 'loose cannon' behavioural traits to escape his own branding, but he felt it was unjust that Wheeler's face remained unaltered. His new divisional boss bore the deepest scars of Denison's retribution.

Fray's mindsight unit undertook random MC Vault explorations intensively for the next two weeks. Vain and Fearston worked in tandem, being assisted by two project newcomers. Leanne Jackson, a neurosurgeon prodigy from Chicago, handled digital conversion.

At twenty-three she was one of the youngest MC Project specialists. The laser extraction work was performed by one of the Chinese recruits taken on after the Washington peace conference. his preferred name was 'Silo' and he was a staunch Vainite as far as allegiance was concerned. Silo had been one of the 'right-hand' supporters who had fought with Vain after the Tavini altercation. The team of four had great communal respect for each other and this counted for a lot, as eighteen-hour working days became the norm. Vain's team undertook between seven and ten mindsight-explorations each day, upon living subjects brought to them by the Security division. Wheeler, Voight or Dwight Richards would deliver the test-subjects, but no names or circumstances were ever given concerning whom exactly was having their mind read. On occasions Vain's crew had to read to a subject, and record their subsequent mindsight, but usually the team were told to break directly into the vault-extension without any prompted stimuli.

Fear was a common denominator in the eyes of the subjects, and Vain felt that 'victims' was a better collective name for them. It had been rumoured for some time that Denison may 'hit the streets' to find new test subjects, and Vain deduced that his team were probably bearing front-line testimony to this recruitment method. None of the four could be certain that Denison was using press-gang tactics though, because the team were always denied visual access to the generated material. After each exploration, the subject would be taken away, along with the recorded laser proofs and another subject was led in, passing the previous test-individual on their way. The MC Project was entering 'mass production'!

Fray only surveyed his division's work on rare occasions. He was privy to handling the laser recordings, and his Rochaux wounds seemed to worsen on each successive day. The one important announcement that he did make to Vain's team was uttered on operational day eleven. His message was short, being encoded with safety as his main prerogative.

"Press on, my team. Your work is progressing better than all expectations by all accounts, and a rest period is penned in after day seventeen. I have been permitted to tell you that your work will soon be activated throughout internal project divisions. Random mindsight readings will be performed upon individuals as they go about their MC business, with activation instances being selected by Leif.

"In short, an individual will wear the sonic vault-splicer for a period of some hours, possibly a day. Mr Denison will scan-activate on occasions during this period of monitoring. Press on, my team".

The last utterance was said almost as a sigh and Vain felt sorrow for his new superior. He didn't have time to share comments with his colleagues though, as the excessive workload was turning each team member into a temporary work-eat-sleep creature. Day fifteen involved a nineteen-hour working day, and only five-sleep hours were penned in before the next shift. Vain slumped asleep in the recess room that adjoined the exploration venue. A rough shake woke him, with a new urgency sounding in Fray's voice.

"Get up, Vain. You've got an exploration to undertake. The whole team, right now! This one's my order. Denison's conveyor belt will start in less than three hours, so we've gotta move it!"

Vain stood up and turned on Fray, angry at being forced awake after another day of project-overload.

"Sorry Vance. This sounds 'Hidden A' stuff. I've probably used up my chances with Leif you know, try another exploration crew".

The gun cut into Vain's temple.

"This isn't a fucking option, Vain! Here's the low-down. Some of my security guys have stayed loyal and they've brought us a present next door! We've got a subject strapped in the mindsight chair. Strapped because he's reputed to be possessed! Catholicism had him booked for an exorcism yesterday but my guys intercepted him. Can you see the possibilities here?"

"No".

"Franco Molvetti had been housebound for thirty days. He recently rampaged through the streets asking for deliverance from Satan!

"Up until a month ago he was a veritable pillar of the community, working for the homeless and under-privileged in Washington. That was before the violence, the self-mutilation and the seizure type contortions. The phlegm was a trickle at first, but now it's a torrent! His language became as foetid as his breath and his skin has welts breaking the surface. Molvetti either has some fucking serious illness or the devil that he claims to see is for real, Greg! Religion undertakes thousands of exorcisms each year, one MC Project interception is hardly greedy Greg, it's *our* divine fucking right!"

Fray was charging through his words at an excitable pace, and Vain was still struggling to understand exactly how Molvetti's condition held special interest for the ranks of the MC Project. Greg voiced his confusion and after a sigh of exasperation, Fray slowed down, measuring his words with more precision.

"Smell the coffee, Vain! The guy says that he sees the devil. If we explore both of his MC Vaults, we'll have our answer, one of man's eternal questions answered!

"If the vault-extension delivers a mindsight devil, we'll know that Molvetti is 'imagining' his own Lucifer, but if we find satanic imagery in his main vault we'll know that he has physically witnessed the devil. If the result is the latter, then heaven help us! But we'll never know until we try!"

Vain knew that membrane fall-through could still distort visual truth, after Fearston's revelations, but his understudy had only encountered one example of this image-source aberration. Adrenaline started to pulse through his body as his mind took on board the enormity of the exploration that awaited him.

He said nothing to Fray about membrane fall-through, keeping Fearston's research secret. He then followed Fray into the exploration arena, with his own mind still undecided - should they track and unlock Satan, or was this exploration tempting fate?

Franco Molvetti had been heavily sedated and as Silo set up his laser extraction equipment the subject remained still, with laboured breathing. Residue of a phlegm-based substance dribbled from Molvetti's mouth and fresh knuckle bite marks dripped blood on to the exploration chair. Greg placed the sonic vault-splicer around the head of the subject. Still no awakening resulted. Fray gesticulated to Fearston to activate the viewing screen. He made a vehement utterance to accompany the said activation.

"Unlike you Denison, unlike you Wheeler, I show my team their explorations. Your private screening prerogative can get fucked!"

The room lights were dimmed as Vain probed amongst Molvetti's main MC Vault. The screen rendered a uniform silver colour hue, and then Vance Fray's luck ran out. The arena door was smashed open and Jess Wheeler's voice boomed an entrance.

"On the deck, fuckers. Take those still standing, guys".

Vain's unit instinctively hit the floor, but Fray's men briefly countered with some useless resistance. Dwight Richards took out one of Fray's 'loyalists' with a volley of shots, whilst Voight accounted for the other with a single shot to the head. Wheeler shot Fray's gun from his hands and the security head then felled the man with a deft roundhouse kick. As blood poured from Fray's fingerless right hand, Wheeler spoke and shock waves resounded throughout the exploration arena.

"Voight, Richards, check them for weapons. It looks like a Fray wild card though. None of the others should have any guns down here, so if you find any, then shoot the fuckers. Not Fray though, I've got something special in mind!"

As Wheeler's security ranks strip-searched Vain's team, Greg managed to ask one question to Wheeler.

"What about Molvetti. What's going to happen to him?"

"Same as we do with all the fodder, Vain".

Wheeler walked behind Molvetti's chair and wrenched the subject's head back toward him. He forced a pistol into the mouth of the bleary-eyed subject, delivering one of his bespoke execution lines. Molvetti had recovered consciousness - just in time to register his own death!

"Chew on this, paleface. Here's your fucking exorcism!"

The trigger was pulled, and pieces of Molvetti's brain slid down the far wall. His teeth and jawbone were blasted in all directions. The 'possessed' head had only been preserved to a twenty percent ratio! Wheeler then turned on the whimpering Fray, bringing his boots down on the man's rib cage. A vicious kick to the testicles rendered the man unconscious. Wheeler again spoke out to everyone, standing amidst the bloodfest that lay on all sides.

"Richards, take four guys and escort these four back to their sleeping zones. Leave them naked though, a lesson, or some kinda bull like that. Voight, you're coming with me. We're taking a crew of eight. We're gonna use the Kingstonhill Wharf. I want cameras and some fucking petroleum. Oh, and bring some cord, we'll use some metal shit for a tight hold".

The van raced away from the Designation and Fray awoke, vomiting due to the fumes of the petrol that soaked his whole body. He had been stripped naked and severely beaten around his chest and waist regions. The petrol stung into his cuts and it burned to a level of excruciating pain where digits used to be on his right hand. Fray knew that he was going to die. *How* was the only unanswered question.

The vehicle screeched to a halt at the gates of the industrial junkyard that represented Kingstonhill Wharf. The security entourage dragged Fray toward the submarine graveyard. A variety of transport forms lay in states of decay, but Wheeler had his mind set on using one of the derelict conning-towers for illumination purposes. When they located a suitable rusting hulk, Wheeler spoke.

"Strap him up with the cord guys, upside-down, in an X-shape, across the tower. He's gonna be our saint Peter!"

Some of Wheeler's men did as their leader had instructed, and as the man was secured, other security staff arranged a pile of planks and loose wood directly below the 'staked' Vance Fray. Many litres of additional combustible fuel were dowsed on Fray and the woodpile. Jess Wheeler started to bark further orders when the stake was ready.

"Hamilton, Mace, get ready with those cameras. Set me a long trail, Easton. I want to be out of range when he fires up!"

Then Wheeler approached Fray, who had again started to slump into unconsciousness. Even when Fray was so close to death, Jess couldn't resist a mocking gesture.

"Now stay awake, pretty-boy. You've got a nice bonfire coming your way and I don't want you to miss a second of it".

After slapping Fray around a bit more, Wheeler walked over to the start of the fuel trail that would ignite the man who had once been his front-line boss. Fortune had changed for both of them! Voight approached his former security-equal, with a more humane inclination in his mind.

"What goes around comes around, doesn't it, Vance? Perhaps you enjoyed your Chicago slayings too much. Still, this should help, bite on it. Farewell".

Voight had managed to insert the suicide pill into Fray's mouth without the others seeing his action. He descended the conning-tower and rejoined Wheeler. The trail was lit and Fray's eyes rolled shut for the last time, just before his body was claimed in the mass of flames.

"Shoot, fellas". Wheeler cried to his cameramen, and stark against the night-sky, a terrifying image of MC Project retribution was captured - a flame-branded cross with a pyre beneath.

SEVENTEEN

The MC Project ranks awoke to a nightmarish image the next morning. Hanging from the ceiling and stuck to the walls of the Designation were vivid colour posters of Fray's charred body amidst the flames. To comply with Wheeler's directives, Fray had been strung up in an X formation - upside down! His charred black frame could be seen with the flames devouring the form. The night sky 'framed' the image to good effect and written across the midnight blue on the posters was a chilling warning...

> **...THE PRICE FOR HIDDEN AGENDAS. FROM THIS DAY FORWARD - DON'T CRUCIFY OUR PROJECT FOR YOUR OWN PREROGATIVE.**

The posters had been in production within an hour of Fray's execution. Vance had been engulfed by flames just after 01:00, and yet by 07:00 that same morning, several hundred prints decorated the Washington venue.

Both the image and the warning scared Diana Fearston to a level that forced a cold sweat to break out on her brow. She knew that her fall-through discovery could easily be construed as a hidden agenda, and she had heard that some MC staff would shortly have their own mindsight read.

Evidence of her discovery would be almost certainly locked in both her MC Vaults and this caused the fear to grow within her. She decided that her only survival option involved her seeking a personal audience with Leif Denison - immediately!

The woman had to wait for a couple of hours as Denison was being briefed by Wheeler following Fray's execution. The security head had acted rashly, without obeying the 'green-light' edict that the MC Project controller usually had to authorise for summary executions. Despite this disregard for protocol, Denison favoured both the killing and the poster bombardment. After initially castigating Wheeler to a level that left Jess temporarily fearing for the 'gun hand', Leif proceeded to congratulate his wayward security head for the climate of fear that he had intensified in the Designation. As far as Denison was concerned, fear aligned his workforce, breeding passive conformity and ostracising maverick tendencies. As Wheeler made to leave Denison's control-room, the project leader summarised his message with a near perfect hookline.

"You're our security king at twenty-nine, Jess - tow my line but don't dull your razor!"

Fearston eventually received her desired audience with Denison, and she launched straight into her membrane fall-through confession. Like Wheeler before her, she was fearful of the retribution outcomes that may get fired in her direction. She shook with trepidation.

Denison surveyed her intently, as she blurted out her story. When she had finished her account of the fall-through discovery, the project leader made her sweat for a minute of 'pregnant' silence before commencing his inquisition.

"Subject 22 was the only person who exhibited fall-through symptoms in your research sample?"

"Yes sir".

"Are you quite sure about that?"

"Yes Mr Denison, all my other explorations went to form".

"Good, so why tell me now, Miss Fearston?"

"I was petrified that you would see evidence of my research in my MC Vaults, sir. I believe that we are going to be explored via neurological probing, as we have explored others in the past".

"You won't be in the first test-phase, if at all. We don't see you as a main-line threat. A few blemishes have occurred, but essentially we admire your loyalty".

"Why was I on the Rochaux list then, sir?"

"Greg's a good man but too many people were catching his fire. You, as his understudy naturally caught his flame".

Denison's words had so far calmed Fearston to a level, but his line of inquiry persisted nonetheless.

"You and who else carried out the fall-through research?"

"No one, Mr Denison. The work was a continuation of the déjà vu project that I commenced at the Sorbonne".

"So no one else knows about your findings, then?"

"Just Gregory sir, but he has kept silent. I trust him totally and have the utmost respect for him".

A wry smile crept across Leif Denison's face before he continued.

"Oh yes. Gregory has kept your silence, hasn't he?"

"He's a good man sir. You said so yourself. He was only trying to protect me".

Denison went silent again and after gaining more confidence, Fearston took the verbal lead.

"Is Greg amongst the first MC Project test batch?

Can you tell me when it commences?"

"Getting braver. That's good, it shows spirit, Diana. Affirmative with regard to your first question and 'tomorrow' with regard to your secondary line of enquiry. Six MC Project staff will wear the mobile exploration headgear. We will activate from these quarters. Mr Sant has already undertaken some of these 'fly on the wall' type explorations upon non-project individuals. He will be our 'main-man' with regard to the control of our workforce exploration sampling. Now, head up woman. Every great invention has a margin of error. Subject 22 never happened. Do you understand me?"

"Yes sir".

"Good. Encode it as a bad dream. If anyone else hears, we know what could happen, don't we?"

"Yes".

"I bid you good day, Miss Fearston. Enjoy your work".

Fearston left Denison's quarters with his choice words ringing in her ears. She knew that a 'low-profile' now beckoned her and with that in mind, she resisted any temptation to confide in Vain. Fray's old division were going to be amalgamated with other exploration teams under the auspices of Dwight Richards, but that would not take place until after the week-long leave period that most project members would enjoy in three days time. Diana Fearston retired to her sleeping quarters, to escape into the classical music that always rejuvenated her spirit.

Greg heard about the unit transfer and impending leave-period on his Comm-Lynx. He as yet knew nothing of the mobile MC scanning that would await him in the morning. Vain looked forward to being reunited with Tanya and his children. The highland project-village was an enticing prospect and he would be back to share early September with his wife, to share a slice of autumn, their favourite season.

He wondered what Tanya would make of his 'new face', but he also knew that the 'face-value' had never been one of her highest concerns and so old 'yellow-eyes' wouldn't be turned away! Greg turned his thoughts to the project. He hated what MC directives now seemed to represent. He hated Prerogative Three, he hated Wheeler's gun-determined control and he hated most of those who were key players in the new MC directions. As far as Vain was concerned, a form of dictatorial project control had replaced the ethics that had cemented the initial active exploration work. He envisaged a global culture would ensue where MC Project initiatives would wean society from the womb to the coffin and he was sure that if this transpired, resistance would be quelled by the bullet. Greg understood that the first metaphorical dominoes in this chain had already fallen and he felt that humility, innocence and autonomy had fifty years at best. The 'Tavini hundred' had already been halved in his mind.

Greg tried to contact Diana Fearston several times that day, but when her door remained shut after his third attempt, he assumed that his understudy was still exhausted after Fray's execution. He had seen the warning posters but he hadn't been surprised by their presence. This kind of fear on display was, to him, just another symptom of the immoral crevice that his once beloved project had fallen into. He saw no one that day.

Greg found sleep difficult to obtain that night, and only three hours had been acquired when Dwight Richards and Marco Sant awoke him. The latter detailed the purpose of the visit.

"Morning, Greg. You're one of the chosen few! You and five other project staff are going to be in our first wave of personnel vault surveillance. We felt you deserved to be amongst the honoured six.

"After all, no one has contributed more to our cause than you did in your pioneering research period".

As Sant and Richards fitted the tracking equipment onto Vain's head, Greg inwardly laughed at the black satire behind Sant's complimentary words. He said nothing in reply, but winced a bit as the contraption was anchored across his temple region. The headgear contained the conversion and extraction parts that were featured in the arena explorations that he had undertaken, but he essentially wore a prototype - a machine that could explore him as he moved about the Designation. Vain knew an 'activation centre' existed somewhere in the building, but he wasn't scared any longer. He knew that he had no way of removing the hate and anger in his mind. He also knew that he had wished Wheeler, Tavini and even Denison dead many times, and he was certain that each 'mindsight slaying' would paint a vivid visual picture - one of non-compliance, of revolutionary thinking. Dwight Richards ironically seemed to read his mind.

"Don't worry, Greg. You know yourself that we all think things that we would never incarnate into action. Mr Denison has been quite insistent with myself and Mr Sant, that we point this factor out to all the first phase subjects. He wants to allay fears, he wants you to think freely. Now, do have any questions before we commence your twenty-four hour surveillance period?"

"Just one, gentlemen. Have you ever seen a triceratops on a skateboard?"

Vain collapsed into a fit of laughter as the pair left. Their faces were masks of sobriety.

The wisecrack had temporarily brought Gregory Vain out of his melancholia and he decided that he would socialise amongst his peers, rather than sink into the hatred he now felt for the project. Greg made straight for the breakfast cafeterias, and his appearance made for a surreal portrait amidst the well-dressed ranks of the project assemblage. When people saw that Vain was one of those in the first surveillance phase, many rallied around him, giving him their support and shaking his hand. Most MC Project staff had received news of the commencement of surveillance early that morning through either their Comm-Lynx or word of mouth. Greg was a popular figure as far as the vast majority of the project cohort were concerned, and as the personnel were enjoying a three-day 'wind down' before the leave period, a gregarious collective attitude ensued. People knew that Vain would fare better if numbers surrounded him and if he entered non-project topics of discussion. Silo and Blyth Carson were instrumental in cracking open vintage red wines in what turned out to be an almost unheard of 'project drinking session'! When Greg slipped into his thoughts, a Vainite around him would take his mind off project parameters. Greg was deeply touched by the loyalty of such a collective gesture, but he, like his friends around him, knew that potentially damaging visual material lay in the recesses of both of his MC Vaults. In many ways his was the party as the boat was sinking.

Carson and one of the original 'forty' from the Venison exploration eventually carried Greg back to his quarters. He hadn't been rendered paralytic through drink, he had just sunk quietly into a sleep, worn down by the rare tide of so much good emotion within a Designation. Fearston and Levene hadn't been in attendance at the impromptu social gathering, but he had hardly registered their absence due to the sustained 'bonhomie'.

Vain awoke, and laughed to himself as he felt mock party streamers around his surveillance headgear. Alone in the darkness of his room he started to realise that a sound from just inside the doorway had woken him.

"Who the fuck's there?"

"Long time no see, Mr Vain."

Levene came and sat on Vain's bed. He could discern her more clearly as his eyes became accustomed to the faint illumination generated by the corridor lighting that stole in from the base of his door.

"Yeah it's a long time, Marcia.

"I thought you were in Tavini's pocket".

"No just his bed, Gregory."

Vain fought the anger that was mounting inside him.

"So why the visit then?"

The fingers clawed inside the sheets, kneading the foreskin of his semi-hard penis.

"I thought maybe a last time, Greg. I'd like to take you whilst you're wearing your surveillance scanner. It's a device that entraps you, it excites my libido. You must know that. I mean, they won't be activating it right now, will they Greg?"

Vain's penis stiffened as Levene's long hands set to work. The red wine profusion had made him less sharp than usual, but slowly the woman's masturbation started to weave its spell. Vain allowed Levene to continue, if only to pay Tavini back in some carnal point score. Marcia Levene continued to speak in an imploring tone.

"You've got to make up with David you know.

He's a big part of our future - the only future. Prerogative Three is a bliss-ticket really, Greg. Yeah sure, I see your point about needing hate but..."

Levene's voice dropped to a very low pitch that made meaning impossible, and her fingers simultaneously quickened to prepare Vain for a powerful climax.

The audible tone returned.

"...I mean Belinda probably had more bliss in her four years than we will register in seventy".

Vain broke free from the woman's hold.

"Hold on Levene, that line was too final, too past tense. What the hell has happened to her?"

"A tragic accident Greg, really tragic".

Vain lost control and shook the woman violently.

"What the fuck happened to her?"

"Electrocuted, Greg. To her tiny hands plug sockets were a game. Life was a game, a beautiful game".

Gregory Vain realised that he was falling into Levene's trap and he responded accordingly.

"Fuck you. Get out, bitch. You twisted sick bitch. You want me to activate a 'hate performance' in my head don't you? You fool, it's all locked in me anyway. More pure hatred than you could ever contemplate, wall-to-wall project hatred. There you go, I've fucking said it bitch, there's your fucking performance! Go and press yourself on Tavini, you and he share the same scent. The stench of foetid copulation!"

Levene left, and maybe she had lost for the first time - maybe.

Greg had the exploration headgear removed the next day.

He knew that surveillance of his vaults would have taken place, but he was now tired of the fight. As he was conveyed back to Scotland a few days later, he thought long and hard about his project future.

He felt reasonably confident that Denison wouldn't let him be put to the torch like Fray, but he wasn't so sure that he would let him leave. Vain waited to be the first, he wanted to retire from the MC Project.

EIGHTEEN

Tanya saw Vain before he noticed her and Rachel. She would recognise his loping gait anywhere. For once she got the first words in.

"Rock star makes it home! Nice eyes, shame about the hair, though!"

The three Vains shared an embrace that was foundered on deep affection and long absence. Gary was fishing in the valley river. He would share the welcome home later. The first day home always revolved around the children until the adults could converse more openly in the late evening, when the juveniles had gone to bed. Several areas needed to be addressed on the first night on this occasion - a metaphorical cross-roads beckoned the whole family. Greg launched into the conversation in the lower reaches of the villa gardens - the pair didn't assume that their residence would be devoid of any project bugging devices, so the garden represented their sanctuary. Vain whispered his initial polemic line of delivery, expelling the overpowering hatred he now felt for most things that were connected with the MC Project. He divulged the prerogative three conditioning and detailed the brawl that split project ranks. He then proceeded to take Tanya through the events surrounding Fray's satanic probing and his eventual demise in flames on a corroding submarine conning tower. Tanya listened entranced and only when Vain detailed Levene's evil incitement when he was under surveillance, did she interrupt.

"You've stopped fucking her then, Greg?"

Vain initially played the straight card.

"Yes, some time ago, love. I guess I caught Levene's poison for a while. I was hooked in her stagnation!"

"You can cut the bull there, Mr Vain. Confessions through flowery metaphors are never quite as honest as real heartfelt words, are they?
Just give me events straight as they were. Don't just blame her. I mean she didn't have possession rights on your penis did she?"

Vain realised that his words were indeed entrenched in excuses and hand over blame allocation. He launched into profiling Levene from start to finish. His words had truth moulded into them this time around. The speech wouldn't be a total catharsis as he would always carry a level of guilt with him, but they finally killed the spell that Marcia Levene represented.

"At first I resisted her, curious and enchanted by her looks, but I managed to preserve a distance that was anchored by my love for you. As time progressed the project exacted more and more out of me. The workloads became more arduous and my time with you was severely restricted. In the Designations, Levene started to become an outlet, a release from the claustrophobia that force-fed all project members. In Chicago we nearly died and I guess that experience brought us closer. In hindsight, she was different then, more tender. Perhaps I even started to love her. In Washington during the days of the peace conference we were caught in a wine bar, sexually preoccupied. The affair wasn't consummated then, and we came within an inch of summary execution for breaking the project protocol surrounding the no-contact edict that **MC Project** were meant to observe. We were like wayward kids getting caught in our first heavy-petting session. She was the directive partner at this point, a woman with a dark edge that somehow drew me in rather than repelled me. Back in London we eventually did engage in sex. I feel as guilty as hell now, but at the time I was caught by her. Ironically it was Tavini who helped me break her hold. His foetal conditioning work represented a kind of hell on earth to me, and by supporting his prerogative three direction, her attraction waned in my eyes. I was effectively set free from her, but my rebel status magnified as a result of my opposition to Tavini's work. After breaking her hold on me I learnt to hate Marcia Levene. This culminated in the 'twisted sick bitch' line I threw at her when I was under surveillance. I'm sorry, Tan. I guess I was attracted to her. There was deep feeling between us, but now there is nothing but hate. My feeling for Levene, Wheeler, Tavini and others is equal - a uniform *hatred* that makes me repulsed by their collective presence".

"Thanks for the truth, Greg. I'm glad she was just a passing phase. Your eyes had told me about Levene months ago anyway".

Gregory Vain knew that his wife had been hurt by his words, but he felt like a weight had been lifted from his shoulders with his confession. He wanted to express his love for his wife straight away, but Tan pressed him to bring her up to date with his current project standing. Vain told her that he was going to ask Denison in person if he could be the first **MC Project** resignation. He was about to divulge his intended approach when Tanya halted him in his tracks.

"If you go back to Washington you know you're a dead man Greg, and they aren't going to keep the rest of us alive as a mark of respect, are they?

"We've got to leave tomorrow night, I know a way".

Vain was amazed. He thought that his wife had taken leave of her senses.

"No one escapes, Tan. You must be mad to contemplate the idea! Leif wouldn't wipe me. I'm like a second project son to him. A formal release would benefit everyone, it would sow a good seed and relax the bad feelings that are blowing through project ranks".

Tanya clasped Vain's face with both hands. A gesture, which had been utilised once before by other hands in a far off place. She hooked his full attention.

"I've had months to think. Greg. I've anticipated your current situation countless times. Not the specifics, but the baseline has never been far from my thoughts. The project doesn't need you anymore. You've been pushed to the periphery more and more. To them you're a bad seed now! Sure you're popular, but not with those who drive things. You're so fucking naive - staring into the barrel of a gun and yet still hoping for a 'job well done' pay off! Get real Greg, you'll be the next Fray".

Vain knew that she was right. On occasions even now, he would try to run away from the reality of a situation. He had shot his mouth off too often in project circles, and his actions had made him a potentially dangerous incarnate maverick spirit. He asked a question to Tanya, as he felt that she might harbour the survival plan that was essentially out of his grasp.

"What is your way out of here then, Tan?"

"At last it listens! Mark Davies is one of the security patrol guys here. I recognised him six weeks back. We were at Art College when I was in my teens.

We were very good friends then and we've envisaged a similar situation to this arising for some time now.

"We've talked about a way out many times. There's a 'blind spot' pick up point behind our residence, where all four of us could be concealed - smuggled out in his security vehicle. Mark leaves the confines of the project village at eleven each evening. He enjoys a high status and his vehicle isn't scanned thoroughly like most of the others that leave the village. I know, I've been through with him twice before, to survey escape possibilities for myself".

Vain broke in with senses of excitement and jealousy conspiring together.

"What's in it for this guy? I mean, was your friendship a between the sheets affair in your college days or what?"

Tanya was momentarily indignant.

"Hypocrite. I almost wish it had been! Rest assured 'oh-so-worthy' husband, Mark's gay. Always has been. Some people still do decent things, you know. You've been too long in the confines of your fucking project. Society is still blessed with those who don't seek an alterior motive".

As Vain contemplated his wife's words, one of the surveillance fighter planes flew overhead. Tanya continued after the noise subsided.

"Look, our villas have a security inspection every second day. They'll give us the once over tomorrow, sometime in the morning. If we go tomorrow night, we'll have around thirty-six hours to escape and seek a place of refuge. I've already got a journey in mind, involving a safe haven where we can lay low before eventually losing ourselves in Europe, when our scent has been hidden for some time".

"You've got it all figured out love, haven't you?"

"Yeah. How much cash have you got? Obviously we're going to use pseudonyms, so hard cash will be our only source to enable transactions".

"Only about six or seven grand".

"Luckily I've got a fair bit more. I've seen this day coming for some time like I said, so I've been making preparations. We should survive for a year or so on what we've got between us".

The pair talked for a while longer before going back into the villa. After making love, they fell asleep, sprawled out naked on the living-room floor.

In the morning Voight came round to undertake the aforementioned security checks. He was surprisingly gushing in his warmth, proffering a smile to all the Vains and conducting his inspection with an informal air that went with his good-natured demeanour. Greg and Tanya both knew that they were witnessing a beguiling falsehood in the man. They knew that if Vain did return to Washington, Voight would probably be at the forefront of the trigger-pullers.

As night dawned, Mark Davies was true to his word. When Tanya had contacted him in the grounds of the project village earlier that day, he had been more than pleased to comply with the escape plan. After all, he and Tanya had prepared its execution as an envisaged real-life scenario and not a supposition.

Hiding the Vains in the confines of Mark's security vehicle went without a hitch, and the children were very mature as Greg concealed them. Rachel and Gary had both detected the seriousness of their escape from the fraught worry-lines hanging over the faces of their parents, and they were determined to support their mum and dad with impeccable behaviour. Davies drove his security vehicle through the tunnel and no searches apprehended their progress. The Vains had broken out without breaking sweat.

An old friendship had effectively extended a middle-digit farewell to the 'total-control' prerogatives of the MC Project.

The world hadn't fully changed yet.

Davies dropped the family outside the main Edinburgh railway station, Vain with a baseball cap and Tanya with a 'last resort' haircut administered by her own hands. They briefly whispered their gratitude to Davies, hugging him close to their family unit. After his departure, their journey continued. The Vains now running under Peterson as a pseudonym if anyone asked, boarded the 06:07 train to Poole in Dorset and when this destination was reached, a further eastern bound rail journey to Portsmouth Harbour was taken. A taxi was then the chosen method of transport, conveying the family to a ferry terminal that dealt with Channel Island crossings. The Vains boarded a ferry and alighted in Guernsey. Tanya's flawless escape route was nearly over.

After the family had enjoyed a small breakfast at a hotel called 'Auberge des Isles', one further sailing awaited the group - a twenty-minute crossing to Herm, the smallest of the Channel Islands. This was Tanya's envisaged retreat. None of the Vains had been there before, but Tanya had read about the beautiful Island and when she realised that Greg could fall out of project-favour, it seemed the perfect place to hide. All the Vains were booking into the winter-let accommodation on Herm some four hours before the project listed them as 'missing'.

NINETEEN

After three weeks on Herm, the Vains felt as though they were locked in paradise. They were acclimatising to being known as the Petersons with ease, as only a handful of families forged an existence on the island in the winter months, and most days were spent free from any searching conversation from others. Only a white stone hotel and a clutch of shops reminded the family of the outside world, and subsequently a uniform blanket of privacy hid their existence. Gary and Greg went fishing off the wilder side of the island, whilst Rachel and Tanya made their own keepsake jewellery from the shells that they collected on the beaches. The weather had remained mild during their settling-in period and the family often remained close to the shoreline until night started to fall. Even then, magenta shreds of colour refused to die in the fading sky, until the stars were apparent for some considerable duration.

The whole family acquired favourite areas on Herm, but a common-denominator for all of them existed in Belvoir Bay. This beautiful area of the coastline featured a small cove with ivory-white sand. The azure-blue sea that enclosed the bay seemed more akin to foreign climes, and the temperature echoed this continental feel. On September 26 the whole family travelled to their favourite collective haunt once again.

Greg had brought the small mobile barbecue, for what would probably be their last opportunity before winter would *rape* the autumnal warmth that hung over Herm. The obligatory football had also been taken with them. A solitary speedboat weaved through the waves close to the beach itself. Like the Vains, it seemed to be playing out summer.

Greg was about to turn his attention to setting up the barbecue when Tanya and Gary playfully knocked him over, kicking the football in front of them.

Vain joined in the shenanigans, punting the ball with some force. It disappeared behind an outcrop of rocks and Rachel was overjoyed to play her part at last.

"I'll get it, Daddy!"

The boat turned to the shore, with a strong revving of its engines. A man in a half-mast wetsuit got out. His feet contacted the white sand. He was twenty metres from the family when Vain saw the gun in his right hand. Time seemed to freeze as the figure drew nearer. Gary stood open-mouthed looking straight at the man. As the man placed both hands on his machine-gun, Vain drew Tanya and Gary to him. His voice was hoarse.

"I love you. Love you".

The gun reports rocked the tranquillity of Belvoir Bay. Twenty-five rounds and then an empty magazine. The blood of the Vains entwined, flowing as one towards the surf.

The man halted and then spoke to the dead in front of him.

"I'll leave your 'Tsar's privilege'".

He turned to walk back into the waves. His feet didn't touch the blood of the Vains.

EPILOGUE

The little girl had nearly reached the football, when loud engine noises distracted her.

From her vantage point, she saw a man walking towards her family. She saw the gun in his hands, but the scream that she longed to release never came.

She heard her Daddy say something, but she wasn't quite able to detect his specific word choices due to the whispered nature of the utterance.

Then she saw her family die and heard the killer mutter something afterwards - exactly what, she couldn't decipher.

Rachel sat down as the man got back into his boat and departed.

After staying motionless for some time, she felt inside her dress pocket. She carefully took out the small amethyst broach. Daddy had given her it - he would stay with her.

ABOUT THE AUTHOR

Visit: www.steve-h-kaye.co.uk

Find *Steve Hammond Kaye* **and** *Thirty Four Minutes Dead* **on** facebook | *Tweet* with: **#TFMD**

I started writing **Thirty Four Minutes Dead** in 1990 and concluded the said novel in 1998. I deliberately chose to write the book in a style that is intricate, expansive and visually aware. I wanted the book to engage with the reader in a similar fashion to film on occasions and thus my plot arteries were often determined by a heightened visual perspective.

Upon completion of TFMD my chosen test readers conveyed favourable responses and from the collective number, I chose two gentlemen to undertake agent-type rolls for my novel.

Initially the two gentlemen worked cohesively together to promote my novel in the literary world, but then they fell out. This split actually helped my book's market awareness as the two gentlemen battled against each other to get the best deal for me.

A Representative of a well-known Perfume Company and a Television Thespian were two people who wanted to throw money at new business ventures but I mistrusted the motives of the first contact and with this in mind, I declined further involvement from these two sources.

I also had offers from more main-stream publishers, but despite the lucrative possibilities, I declined all offers that entailed *dumbing down* the novel.

In 2001 a friend of mine (Ms Hannah Cundall) suggested that I looked at the possibilities surrounding online publishing. She got in touch with Nospine.com who were based in Milton Keynes.

On the 25th April 2001 TFMD was available online with the said company.

Two years later I completed my sequel (*The Scream of Feyer*) and this book was also placed online via the same outlet, I liked the honesty of Nospine.com and enjoyed a good working relationship with this online provider until the company ended online work in 2008.

My books performed well through Nospine.com with TFMD achieving a rank position of number 19 (out of 694 online authors).

For the next four years I let my novel rest in cobwebs - a great waste of my literarily potential. I then responded to a phone call from Mr Steve Mullins of Standard Cut Media, who advised me of the possibilities of publishing on various platforms such as Amazon, and to finally see a paperback version sold worldwide. I agreed, as this enabled me to reach out to a wider global audience that platforms such as Amazon provide.

Companies such as Amazon value the integrity of authors and they don't seek to put manipulative handcuffs on an authors artistic creativity.

STEVE HAMMOND KAYE

ACKNOWLEDGEMENTS

MS. H. CUNDALL

MS. C. LANZON

MR. M. MARCHAM

MR. H. SLIDELL

MRS. A. M. KAYE

MRS. A. C. KAYE

MR. S. MULLINS

MS. S. SWAYBE-BARRETT

a macabre journey into the mind

Published by

www.standardcut.co.uk | publishing@standardcut.co.uk

THE
SCREAM OF **FEVER**

hitching a ride with a suicide bomber

The Sequel to **Thirty Four Minutes Dead**
By **Steve Hammond Kaye**

F●UR

The form writhed in the icy depths and darkness enveloped its frame. Splinters of blue ice tore into *Klue's* lungs, but as the surface drew nearer the creature's savage rejuvenation began. The eyes bore through the blackness as the strength of the predator grew. Moonlight started to penetrate down through the Lofoten waters and this furthered the dark inspiration that pushed the creature upwards. Klue sensed the imminence of the second arrival and fetid excretions were expelled from the form as the moment approached.

With only seconds left. The propulsion turned the creature momentarily on its side, but a vertical entry position was regained by wild thrashing strokes from the hind - quarters. The beast tore into the world for a second time, amidst a cloak of Phosphorescence and Klue was catapulted a few metres above the surface – due to the cumulative pressure behind the upward journey.

As it trod water, saliva was brushed from the mouth: like a man in motion but essentially a creature through the frame. It sensed land and moved towards the indistinct mass close by. It sensed prey but wanted to tame the misery of hunger - lock it in place with cruel desires that allowed play before the kill. Klue trembled as a hunter's anticipation coursed through cold veins. It had been too long, so he was going to savour the first slaying – starve himself just that bit longer until they arrived on the scene. He expected them, the unwitting servants of his black desires – the sacrifice to usher in his rebirth.

As his form contacted land, he drew himself up to his full height. Klue was a man when he needed that shape, but a beast when he revealed his true nature.

Both forms entwined as he surveyed the Maelstrom. He waited for them, his glinting eyes forcing a cold marriage with the dark waters. They would come.

*   *   *   *   *

Klue slept on a hard rock until the light of dawn awakened him. His eyes instantly returned to the sea and a small fishing vessel could be seen navigating the channel. The Maelstrom was Klue's playground and the four fishermen were about to receive his blessing for the first and last time.

The beast climbed higher up the outcrop and hatefully stared at his liquid domain. A faint smile creased his face as the first ripples of his presence spread across the water. Klue flexed his lean frame and let his malevolence incite the Maelstrom. As the waves increased in height the fishermen looked upwards to the darkening sky. The skipper feared the vortex that had claimed the lives of so many that had tried to navigate these harsh waters. He gave the order to return to port, but then Klue started to spin the currents, forcing the vessel into the circular movement that signified an impending whirlpool. A white sea mist blew across the channel and the waves rose to an awesome sight. The vessel had now been sucked into the eye of the Maelstrom and Klue directed the impending tragedy from his dark pulpit.

As the waves increased in force a howling wind could be heard, but the screams of those on the boat still managed to penetrate the chaos. Klue smiled as he heard them suffer. He enjoyed prolonging the torture of his victims and when the waves looked like they would suck the vessel under, he would relax his hold just a little, let the boat spin out to a calmer area and raise the hopes of the four men on board. After the bluff the creature would pull the vessel back into the whirlpool and the screams would rise again. Klue tired of playing after his sixth mock – release and he sank the boat with a savage fell swoop. As the boat was pulled deeper down it split apart and the four occupants drowned before their lungs exploded with the pressure. Their dead faces told the story of Klue's torture, but none would see the portraits of suffering because both the wreckage and corpses sank into the oblivion of the darkest fathoms.

After his work was done, Klue lay outstretched on the stark rock outcrop. His chameleon form melted into his surroundings. He had enjoyed his play, but he looked forward to the impending days when his enemy would seek him out.

A journey would call him soon, but on that morning he was savouring his rebirth. This was his lair and his Lofoten outpost had a fitting name to carry his presence. The Lofoten people knew his temporary home by a memorable name – Hell!

THE SCREAM OF FEYER

hitching a ride with a suicide bomber

Available in Paperback and eBook formats from:

Amazon

Printed in Great Britain
by Amazon